D0476933

THE SOLDIER AND
THE GENTLEWOMAN

Hilda Vaughan is the author of *Here are Lovers* and *Iron and Gold*, both available from Honno, and the novella *A Thing of Nought*, which appears in the Honno Classic *A View Across the Valley*. Other titles by Hilda Vaughan: *The Battle to the Weak*, *The Invader, Her Father's House, The Curtain Rises, Harvest Home, Pardon and Peace* and *The Candle and the Light*.

THE SOLDIER AND THE GENTLEWOMAN

by

HILDA VAUGHAN

With an introduction by
Lucy Thomas

WELSH WOMEN'S CLASSICS

Published by Honno
'Ailsa Craig', Heol y Cawl, Dinas Powys,
South Glamorgan, Wales, CF64 4AH

1 2 3 4 5 6 7 8 9 10

First published in Great Britain by Victor Gollancz, 1932
First published by Honno in 2014

© Introduction Lucy Thomas 2014

British Library Cataloguing in Publication Data
A catalogue record for this book is available from the British Library.

Print ISBN: 978-1-909983-11-3
Ebook ISBN: 978-1-909983-18-2

All rights reserved. No part of this book may be reproduced, stored in
a retrieval system, or transmitted in any form, or by any means,
electronic, mechanical, photocopying, recording or otherwise without
the prior permission of the publishers.

Published with the financial support of the Welsh Books Council.

Cover image: Taken from the US edition, published by Charles
Scribner's Sons, 1932. Image scan courtesy of Babylon Revisited
Rare Books, East Woodstock, CT, USA. Honno has made every effort
to trace the copyright holder of this image without success. If you have
any information regarding this, please contact Honno.

Text design: Elaine Sharples
Printed by

To
SIR CHARLES MORGAN

Will you, whom my children know as the best of grandfathers, and I as the best of Victorians, please accept this book, for, though it be not a tale after your own heart, it comes to you with the affection of mine.

H.V.

CONTENTS

Introduction

LUCY THOMAS

It is a characteristic moment of marital discord between the central protagonists of *The Soldier and the Gentlewoman*: at 'two o' clock on a black morning', tired and irritable, Gwenllian Einon-Thomas hears her husband, Dick, return to her family's ancestral home following a night at the Country Club, where he has been squandering the money she has saved by her prudence and industry. As they walk towards one another, the pair bicker in stilted exchanges. They suppress their more extreme urges, and at first glance it seems little more than a commonplace squabble. But a far more suggestive scene is played out behind them, seen only by the reader, where '[g]iant shadows of a man and a woman rushed towards each other and fled away, in a fierce dance across the armoury on the walls.' In their shadowy forms, projected onto the wall behind them like figures from a silent film, Gwenllian and Dick take on more epic proportions, their struggles becoming emblematic. In the darkest and most disturbing of Hilda Vaughan's novels, we often find a gap between appearance and reality; the action takes place unseen, in thoughts and subtle words, hidden manoeuvres and deeds left undone.

Though it is a fleeting moment in the book, this is a subtle image from the assured hand of an author at the height of her writing career. *The Soldier and the Gentlewoman* was published in 1932, the fifth of the ten novels, one novella and several short stories and autobiographical essays by Vaughan that appeared during her lifetime. Her previous work had been met with enthusiasm by the press, bringing international attention. *The Soldier and the Gentlewoman* was no exception. The *Evening News* declared that it was 'undoubtedly the best book Miss Vaughan has written'.[1] The *Book Society News* announced it as the 'selected Book for May'.[2] Only three months before, her husband Charles Morgan's novel, *The Fountain,* had received the same plaudit. The couple had met ten years previously, when Vaughan left her native Builth Wells for London, to enrol on a writing course at Bedford College for Women. Morgan was then the up-and-coming drama critic for *The Times* and he would go on to become a highly renowned author and playwright, enjoying a worldwide reputation that it is hard for us to imagine today, since his work has been largely forgotten. The pair became a formidable partnership and moved in elite literary circles. While Morgan's letters attest to his admiration for his wife's narrative abilities and despite her successes in her own right, there is a suggestion that Vaughan was somewhat in her husband's shadow.[3] Tellingly, in a speech she delivered at the *Sunday Times* Book Exhibition in 1934, she described her husband as an artist and herself as merely a novelist.[4] There was a great deal of press interest in the couple and a number of articles promoting *The Soldier and the Gentlewoman* also provide an insight into the pair's domestic life, describing with admiration their house in Campden Hill Square in London, where they lived with their children Shirley and Roger, and recounting the couple's advice on childcare alongside their thoughts on writing practices.[5] Though its positive critical reception did not quite match the rapturous reviews of Vaughan's first novel, *The Battle to the Weak* (1925) or those elicited by her haunting novella, *A Thing of Nought* (1934), in many respects *The Soldier and the Gentlewoman* could be seen as one of Vaughan's most successful works. It was translated into French and German, adapted for the stage by Dorothy Massingham in 1933 and broadcast on television by the BBC in January 1957.

The novel is one of five of Vaughan's works to depict war or its aftermath. It opens with the return of a soldier. During the four long years of the First World War, Captain Dick Einon-Thomas has 'hoped daily for nothing better than to escape death'. On his return from Mesopotamia the young Englishman learns that he has inherited Plâs Einon (sic), a country estate in Wales, following the death of two of his male cousins in combat. Dick rejoices in his inheritance: 'Property, this miracle, made everything easy. Already it had freed him of the Army, and now – he could have pretty well what he chose.' For others, however, it is a period of loss. The estate is entailed upon the nearest male heir and in order for him to take possession of Plâs Einon it must be vacated by its female inhabitants. He prepares to meet his cousins, Mrs Cecily Einon-Thomas, widow of the eldest son of the estate, Gwenllian the eldest daughter of the family and her younger sister, Frances, who has married a naval officer and lives in England. As Dick pays this awkward call, he feels sorry for the women. 'That little glow of chivalry towards the disinherited gave him pleasure. Such feelings, he knew, became a soldier.' The widowed Mrs Einon-Thomas leaves for the South of France with an air of polite resignation. Instead, it is her spinster sister-in-law, Gwenllian Einon-Thomas who most keenly feels the pain of the dispossessed. Determined and capable, more so than any of her male relatives, Gwenllian has managed the estate singlehandedly during the war. As one villager comments, 'she'd have made a first rate man o' business. Pity indeed she were born the wrong shape!'

Gwenllian's increased responsibilities reflect the experience of many women across the UK during the First World War. In March 1915 females between the ages of sixteen and sixty-five were called upon to register at labour exchanges and, for some of them, this meant taking up roles that had previously been inaccessible to them. At the outbreak of war, Hilda Vaughan was twenty-two years old and she, too, became immersed in the war effort, serving first as a cook in a Red Cross hospital, where, due to her unfamiliarity with domestic tasks, she hid a cookery book under her apron. She went on to become Organising Secretary for the Women's Land Army in Breconshire and Radnorshire. It was in this position that she particularly excelled, and at a recruitment meeting in Newtown, she gave a speech that impressed the novelist Berta Ruck to such an extent that Ruck portrayed the young Vaughan as a character in one of her books, recreating her stirring speech almost verbatim.[6] Letters dated to this time refer to Vaughan's efforts in helping to secure work for mothers of illegitimate children and coping with the elopement of her Land Girls. This role also brought her into close contact with the women who lived on the farms, and her experiences during this period played a formative part in the work she would go on to write, in particular, her notably sympathetic portrayal of working women.

In *The Soldier and the Gentlewoman*, the end of the war heralds not only the homecoming of the soldiers but also the expected return of its protagonists to traditional gender roles.

Having been forced to relinquish her management of the estate, Gwenllian, Dick supposes, will now 'take up something… Poultry, or breeding pet dogs.' His assumption that the old order will resume is undermined by the text, however, which alludes to the destabilising effect upon gender roles that has been introduced as a result of the war. Textual descriptions of Gwenllian become increasingly masculine, and Dick is often perturbed by her characteristically male behaviour. By the end of the novel, having committed an act more terrible than any of the deeds perpetrated by her brutish male relatives, she looks up at her father's portrait, realising 'she had transcended him. Would you, a man, have dared as much? she asked silently.'

The end of the war did indeed bring some degree of change to the position of women in British society. It was partly in recognition of the contribution they had made to the war effort that the Representation of the People Act 1918 was passed, which provided the vote to women over 30 who met stipulated criteria, a fact that Dick refers to in the novel. While Gwenllian has proven her strength during wartime, Dick returns from active service physically weakened. His heart has been damaged, he has lost his nerve and, rather crucially when considering the future of his inherited estate, we are told that his life is now uninsurable. Descriptions of Dick constantly undermine his masculinity. His features are girlish and as Frances remarks, he is 'so like a nice little pink fledgling, you can't call him a man.' As late at the 1930s, 639,000 British ex-servicemen were still drawing disability pensions as a result of physical injuries and mental illness brought about by war. The image of the damaged, war-enfeebled soldier is, unsurprisingly, a motif found in many novels written during the decades that followed the Great War. Virginia Woolf's *Mrs Dalloway* (1925) notably portrays how the failure of maimed masculinity to be reincorporated into society has tragic consequences, and injured soldiers feature in prominent texts from *The Return of the Soldier* (1918) by Rebecca West to D. H. Lawrence's *Lady Chatterley's Lover* (1928).

While Vaughan's novel can be seen as part of this literary engagement with war and its aftermath, it offers a specifically Welsh perspective. As Dick pays his first call on his female cousins, he attempts to make polite conversation about 'the weather, the state of the roads'. This leads to a discussion that is rather more political than he had anticipated. The widowed Mrs Einon-Thomas tells him that the roads 'are terribly cut up … So much timber-hauling during the war, you know'. She describes how the Welsh countryside has been exploited for the British war effort, with the valleys deforested for 'the supply of pit-props to the collieries of South Wales'. Her remarks make reference to the fact that the British fleet during World War One was powered primarily by Welsh coal and Wales was mined and deforested to meet the huge demand during this period. Gwenllian laments the effect this has had on the landscape: '"It's ruined," she said. "There's almost nothing left"'. Gwenllian's comments lead Dick to question, '[w]as she thinking of men as well as of trees?' The destruction of the countryside is linked with the slaughter of Gwenllian's brothers and it is suggested that Welsh life and landscape have both been sacrificed for the greater demand of the British state.

For Dick, however, the Welsh landscape represents the safety he has longed for during the terrifying years of battle:

'…he drew a long breath. The air was newly washed by
rain. It held the saltness of the sea, and the sweetness of
rising sap. The pungency of wet leaf mould and moss
was in it, rank woodland scents, stealing up from the
dingle below and blending with the tonic breeze that
swept the hilltops. Cool, he thought, clean, restful, safe!
He shut his eyes and smiled. *Safe*, he repeated to
himself and then – *home*. He was poignantly happy. He
wanted to cry.'

The 'tonic breeze' inhaled by Dick is suggestive of the
perceived restorative powers of the Welsh pastoral landscape.
It recalls another of Vaughan's novels, *Pardon and Peace*
(1945) in which the English soldier, Mark, returns from war
to revisit a former Welsh holiday destination, in order 'to be
made whole again.' There are early signs, however, that Dick's
presence in his new home is not to be as peaceful as he had
foreseen. Not only does his inheritance of Plâs Einon displace
its female inhabitants but it also removes the land from Welsh
ownership. The tension this creates is insinuated as Dick's
relationship with his new surroundings is presented in terms
that employ the imagery of imperialism. A villager shows
Dick his estate from a distant vantage point, describing the
vista as 'unrolled like a map just for you to read'. As Dick
surveys the landscape we are told that 'he took off his felt hat
with a delicious sensation of challenge, as though it had been
a topee.' This reference to a topee, a Hindi pith helmet, worn
by the English in tropical countries in the-mid nineteenth
century, is ideologically suggestive, and subtly implies that
Dick's possession of the estate can be read as an act of
appropriation.

Dick's enthusiasm for this rural Welsh idyll is somewhat tempered as he begins to notice the cultural differences between himself and the inhabitants of his new surroundings. Though he acknowledges that his cousins Gwenllian and Frances are undoubtedly beautiful, his first impression is that they appear uncomfortably alien. They are 'too foreign, too much what you expected of the Welsh… those Italian features with so little flesh upon them, suggested bad temper, or worse, fanaticism. He shouldn't wonder if they were rabid teetotallers, or religious, or something of the kind.' Despite his initial efforts to ingratiate himself, he is even more disconcerted by his tenants:

> 'He failed to understand half they said, and was at times unsure whether they were addressing him in English, or in the Welsh language which they used amongst themselves. When the good news had reached him that he had inherited an estate at home, he had not bargained for its being inhabited by a lot of jabbering foreigners.'

Early in her writing career, Vaughan had been made keenly aware of the difficulties faced by a Welsh writer depicting her country for a readership situated upon both sides of Offa's Dyke. A letter from an editor, rejecting an early version of *The Battle to the Weak* informs her that years ago he 'made great efforts to find a Welsh writer of idyll who would do for Wales what has been done for Scotland. I tried at least half a dozen. They found their severest critics among the Welsh themselves.'[7] In this context, the effect that his encounter with cultural difference has upon Dick is interesting. The narrative reflects Dick's point of view and the reader encounters Wales and the Welsh alongside him. This position becomes less stable, however, as Dick begins to 'wonder whether the studied monotony of his own speech might seem as comic to them as the chanting cadence of theirs was to him strange and irritating. Well, not comic perhaps. They would know of course that his way of speaking was correct. But he was ill at ease among them.' As Dick attempts to reassert the superiority of his own culture, this is delicately undermined by the author.

The politics of ownership and inheritance are explored most intently, however, in relation to Gwenllian herself. She has forfeited love, youth and happiness out of a sense of duty. For Gwenlllian preserving the estate for future generations takes precedence over any other obligations. As she tells Dick, 'I managed to fight moss and plantains even during the war, when one felt it wasn't right to put men on a job like that. I did everything else we were supposed to do, but I wasn't going to have the beauty of Plâs Einon spoiled.' She holds an unwavering reverence for traditions and customs and she is fiercely proud of her ancestry. Throughout the book the Einon-Thomas family are referred to as a 'race' in a manner that invites a reading of the familial line as representative of Welsh identity in a broader sense. Gwenllian declares, 'English people with French names who are proud of having "come over with the Conqueror" can't show a pedigree that compares with ours. We fought the Romans, and the Saxons after them, and held on to our own.' With the estate entailed upon her English cousin, it is now falls upon Gwenllian to hold onto her own. For the Welsh woman, lacking the power or weaponry at the disposal of her forefathers, this means enticing Dick into matrimony and producing an heir.

Gwenllian's name has particularly evocative cultural connotations, recalling two iconic heroines of Welsh history. Gwenllian Ferch Gruffydd (1097-1136), Princess Consort of Deheubarth, led an army during the Great Revolt of 1136 in which the Welsh endeavoured to recapture lands lost to the Marcher Lords. A later namesake, Gwenllian Ferch Llywelyn (1282-1337) was the only child of Llywelyn ap Gruffudd, the last native Prince of Wales. She was captured by the English and held in a convent until her death in order to prevent the noble Welsh bloodline from continuing. Vaughan's characterisation draws on both the need to protect her land and produce an heir and viewed in this context, Gwenllian takes on emblematic qualities. Despite being a member of the squirearchy, a social class that was widely viewed as anglicised, Gwenllian speaks Welsh with the tenants and villagers, her voice becoming 'more resonant and flexible when she spoke the language of her race.' While the use of the Welsh language is referred to in several of Vaughan's novels, it is interesting that the author chose to locate this particular book that so explicitly examines the politics of identity, in Carmarthenshire, one of the Welsh-speaking heartlands. This is one of only a few notable geographical departures for Vaughan. Her work was largely set in or around her native Builth Wells on the Breconshire and Radnorshire border, a propensity that led the *New York Times* to suggest that she had made Radnorshire 'as much hers as the Brontes did their moors.'[8]

The novel presents two opposing approaches towards inheritance; not only in terms of monetised land and property but also in its cultural, ideological and emotive aspects. Sisters Gwenllian and Frances have both been brought up in Plâs

Einon. While Gwenllian has stayed at home and devoted herself entirely to the estate, Frances has taken flight as a young woman, giving up the comfort and security of a woman of her social class and finding 'glorious freedom', first at a post in the secretariat of a suffrage organisation in London and then as the happy wife of a naval officer, 'without means or prospects', and as a mother of three children. As nomadic as Gwenllian is rooted, Frances and her family move from one naval port to another. During her occasional visits to Plâs Einon, Frances shocks Dick with her liberal political views and exasperates Gwenllian with her apparent lack of regard for tradition. Frances muses the she and Gwenllian are:

> '...more alike than many sisters, alike in our appearance, alike in our streak of fanaticism. But all Gwen's fanaticism has dragged her inward and inward on to the property; she's given up everything for that. And mine has forced me outward, away from this property and all property. I want my life to be an adventure, full of love. I've flung away everything else – even things beautiful in themselves – things I do love and prize...for fear they'd become more precious than human affections – growth – change of ideas. She wants her life to be set, like a frozen stream. There must be no warmth in it, for then the stream would melt, and begin to flow, and carry her away.'

Interestingly, following the death of all the male members of the immediate family, Gwenllian and Frances take on roles that would traditionally have been ascribed to the eldest and the second sons. In their opposing relationship with their home and inheritance, two choices are presented in the construction of identity; a choice between an identification with a particular place and a people and a wider affinity with all humanity.

The themes of inheritance and identity explored here rework many of the chief concerns of Vaughan's novel *Her Father's House* (1930), the title that had immediately preceded *The Soldier and the Gentlewoman*. In many ways one is a photo-negative of the other, with the earlier book favourably presenting its heroine's commitment to upholding tradition and identity and the latter providing a depiction that is infinitely darker. Nell in *Her Father's House* walks from London to Wales while heavily pregnant in order to ensure that her child is born in her ancestral home. The novel concludes with her having successfully reinvigorated her family's crumbling estate and it is suggested that her newborn child betokens hope for the future. Conversely, Gwenllian's firstborn child, loved so little for his own sake, is viewed primarily as 'this gift of hers to the race she worshipped' and the novel ends with the estate referred to as a place of death, decay and destruction. It would be all too easy to read the later novel as a rejection of patriotism or even nationalist principles, however. In an explanation of her fervour, Gwenllian describes the agonising emotional burden of her role as a guardian of her family's lands: 'It seems to me so base to be the weak link in a long chain – the first poor soft thing to let it break.' In so doing, a more complex picture emerges as she voices a sentiment that resonates with the work of Welsh-language poets such as Gwenallt, a key voice in twentieth-century Welsh-language literature and an early member of Plaid Cymru. His poem 'Cymru', published three years after *The Soldier and the*

Gentlewoman, articulates the painful and relentless sense of duty in striving to protect a language and culture under threat. It asks of Wales, '[w]hy have you given us this misery, / The pain like leaden weights on flesh and blood? / Your language on our shoulders like a load, / And your traditions shackles round our feet.' (*Paham y rhoddaist inni'r tristwch hwn, / A'r boen fel pwysau plwm ar gnawd a gwaed? / Dy iaith ar ein hysgwyddau megis pwn, / A'th draddodiadau hual am ein traed?*)[9]

Gwenllian's gender adds yet further nuance to her position as a cultural custodian. Her battle with Dick to gain control over the estate is so fiercely waged because it is the last of a series of acts of dispossession, all of which have previously been committed against her by Welsh men, suggesting that the Welsh woman is doubly disenfranchised by both her gender and her nationality. Despite her superior skill, bravery and intelligence she has had to take a secondary role to her brothers, whose 'invasion of her home' she resentfully endured as a child. She has strived to gain the respect of a father who refused to see his daughter as of equal worth as his sons, and the culmination of this has left her feeling bitterly disempowered. Men are according to Gwenllian, 'in possession, hour by hour and generation by generation, of all that she desired to possess; they invaded her integrity, usurped the inheritance of her soul. Without them, how little evil there would be in her...' Her final act to win control of the estate is, in fact, not really an *act* at all but a form of neglecting to do what is expected of her as a caring wife. It is significant that in Vaughan's novel the disenfranchised Welsh woman can only gain power by rejecting the gendered roles demanded of her as a nurturing wife and loving mother.

As the title of the novel makes clear, Gwenllian is not simply a woman but a 'gentlewoman'. The mismatched pairing of the daughter of a squire and the son of a governess provoked a critic in *The Times* to write that 'the final tragedy, impressively staged though it is, fails of its effect because the conflict turns on a difference of breeding and social usage rather than on the clash of character.'[10] It is indeed suggested that Dick's middle-class upbringing leaves him ill-equipped to run the Plâs Einon Estate. He eventually acknowledges that, 'though he scarcely liked to admit it to himself, he was envious of the city clerks who lived in comfortable obscurity among their own class.' Similarly, the *Liverpool Post* objected to the book's reliance upon the country house which, it asserted, 'harbours a society whose point of view is very remote from that of the average Welsh man or woman.'[11] Though Vaughan skilfully portrays the lives of the working class Welsh in many of her novels, she hailed from a rather different background. The author was the daughter of a country solicitor, Henry Vaughan, Clerk of the Peace and Under Sheriff of Radnorshire. She recounts her relatively privileged upbringing in her autobiographical essays 'A Country Childhood' (1934) and 'Far Away: Not Long Ago' (1935). Vaughan's social class was one reason cited for the critical neglect of her work in the latter part of the twentieth century. In an act of literary dispossession, she was not included in the influential study of Welsh writing in English *The Dragon Has Two Tongues* by Glyn Jones on the grounds that she writes 'about the squirearchy and its anglicised apers.'[12]

The contemporary mainstream press in Wales, however, was enthusiastic in its approval of Vaughan's writing. She was seen to inhabit the 'truthful' ground between the 'pretty stories' of Allen Raine and the 'scabrous piffle' of Caradoc Evans, whose fictional portrayal of the rural nonconformist communities of Ceredigion had provoked a national scandal.[13] In a review of *The Soldier and the Gentlewoman* the *Western Mail* decreed that if 'Hilda Vaughan were to devote herself entirely to her native heath as the background for her stories her countrymen would no longer have reason to complain of misrepresentation in the field of fiction.'[14] Such an assertion is somewhat surprising, however, given the dark portrayal of its Welsh (anti-)heroine. Just as the chapel elders in Caradoc Evans' *My People* (1915) commit acts of abuse and violence that go unpunished by the community so long as they contribute to the chapel's coffers, Gwenllian's crimes are concealed under a veneer of pious respectability, with the neighbourhood 'beginning to speak of her as of a saint.' This is thrown into sharp relief when the local vicar pays a call moments after Gwenllian has created a poppet or voodoo-style doll of her husband. She donates the brooch used to stick a pin through the wax doll's heart to the sale of work in aid of the Church Lads' Brigade.

As the latter image suggests, the novel owes much to the Gothic tradition of writing and can be seen as inhabiting a specifically Welsh strand of that genre, only recently considered in its own right by Jane Aaron in *Welsh Gothic* (2013). At first glance, Plâs Einon represents culture and civilization. It is the very image of the British country house with its paintings by Romney on the walls, the Nantgarw and Crown Derby in the china cabinet and the Chelsea and Bow figures on the mantelshelves. Amongst the waterfalls, artificial ponds and picturesque follies, however, there are clues that it holds a more primitive and specifically Welsh past. At the edge of the drive there stands a ring of yew trees that 'were never planted in the Age of Reason. They seemed, rather to be survivals, like very ancient witches, of a time of faith and fear, when the land was still haunted by ghosts and demons.' It is here that, early on in the novel, Gwenllian comes to hatch her plan to regain control of the estate. From time to time we gain occasional glimpses of the more Gothic elements of Welsh folklore. From the servants' talk of death portents, to Gwenllian's assertion that a stormy night heralds the coming of the Cŵn Annwn, 'the pack of fiends, hunting for the souls of the wicked.' It is during a moment of extreme frustration with her husband's lack of regard for the future of the estate, that Gwenllian forms a wax effigy of him. She recalls being taught how to bring about the death of a man by an old 'wise'oman', who is believed to have been a distant relative. This is one of the few direct examples of the passing on of traditions found in the novel and it is significant that it manifests itself in the most sinister of forms.

The novel ends with the sense of Gothic menace in which it began. Having realised the full horror of the acts committed by her sister to ensure the future of the estate, Frances stands on the ancient burial chamber, the vantage point from which Dick first viewed his inheritance. She takes a final glimpse of 'beautiful, devouring Plâs Einon' before fleeing for England, never to return. The description seems to suggest that the characters have been figures in a sinister landscape that has itself been a powerful agent in bringing about this terrible conclusion. The novel provides a brutal and unblinking exploration of what it means to be Welsh, but above all, what it means to be a Welsh woman. At its close we witness the full implications of the choices made by the two sisters. Though Gwenllian now has sole possession of the estate 'as if she were an only son', her triumph has come at the price of her goodness. The narrative presents Frances' decision to flee for England as the more rational and humane choice. This is not in itself an indictment of tradition, patriotism, or nationalism but instead it issues a warning against extremism in any of its forms, without consideration of the human cost. Vaughan herself was keen to lovingly preserve in her writing a rural way of life in Wales that she felt was rapidly changing. We see this in her novels but also in her autobiographical essay, 'Far Away: Not Long Ago' which makes explicit the author's intention to record the past for future generations. Vaughan's portrayal of rural Wales was not as an idyll, however, and she was ready to examine the more negative aspects of her land and its traditions, nowhere more incisively, perhaps, than in the dark tale of *The Soldier and the Gentlewoman*. As the sisters, Gwenllian and Frances, occupy opposing positions in their relationship with their homeland, perhaps it is Vaughan's work itself, in its implicit call for moderation, which succeeds in negotiating a path between the two stances.

Notes

[1] *Evening News*, 5 May 1932.

[2] *The Book Society News*, May 1932.

[3] See Eiluned Lewis, ed. *Selected Letters of Charles Morgan*, London and Melbourne: Macmillan, 1967, p.17.

[4] Hilda Vaughan in an unpublished speech entitled, 'Why authors are cads', given at the *Sunday Times* Book Exhibition at Grosvenor House, London on 20 November 1934. I am indebted to Mr Roger Morgan for this reference.

[5] See for example, *The New Era*, April 1933 and *Launceston Post*, 30 April 1932.

[6] Hilda Vaughan quoted in Deirdre Beddoe, *Out of the Shadows: A History of Women in Twentieth-Century Wales*, Cardiff: University of Wales Press, 2000, p. 67. Vaughan's speech appears in almost exact replica, spoken by a recruiting officer for the Land Army in Berta Ruck, *The Land Girl's Love Story*, London: Hodder and Stoughton, 1919, p. 24.

[7] Unpublished letter from W. Robertson Nicoll to Hilda Vaughan, dated 1 February 1921. Reproduced by kind permission of Mr Roger Morgan.

[8] *New York Times*, 7 September 1930.

[9] Gwenallt, 'Cymru', *Ysgubau'r Awen*, Aberystwyth: Gwasg Aberystwyth, 1935, p. 84; trans. J. P. Clancy, 'Wales', in Menna Elfyn and John Rowlands (eds), *The Bloodaxe Book of Modern Welsh Poetry: Twentieth-century Welsh-language Poetry in Translation*, Tarset: Bloodaxe Books, 2003, p. 12.

[10] *The Times*, 6 May 1932.

[11] *Liverpool Post*, 19 December 1932.

[12] Glyn Jones, *The Dragon Has Two Tongues: Essays on Anglo-Welsh Writers and Writing*, London: Dent, 1986, p.42.

[13] Dr. J. Gwenogvryn Evans in the *Western Mail*, 25 September 1926.

[14] *Western Mail*, 5 May 1932.

Further Reading

Aaron, Jane, ed. *A View Across the Valley: Short Stories by Women from Wales* (Dinas Powys: Honno, 1999)

Aaron, Jane, *Welsh Gothic* (Cardiff: University of Wales Press, 2013)

Gramich, Katie, *Twentieth-Century Women's Writing in Wales: Land, Gender, Belonging* (Cardiff: University of Wales Press, 2007)

Newman, Christopher, *Hilda Vaughan*, Writers of Wales series (Cardiff: University of Wales Press, 1981)

Thomas, Lucy, 'The Fiction of Hilda Vaughan (1892-1985):

Negotiating the Boundaries of Welsh Identity', unpublished PhD thesis, Cardiff University, 2008

Vaughan, Hilda, *Her Father's House* (London: William Heinemann Ltd., 1930)

Vaughan, Hilda, 'A Country Childhood', [1934] *Radnorshire Society Transactions*, 1982, 9-18

Vaughan, Hilda, 'Far Away: Not Long Ago', [1935] *Radnorshire Society Transactions*, 1982, 19-26

Wallace, Diana, '"Mixed Marriages": three Welsh historical novels in English by women writers', *Moment of Earth: Poems and Essays in Honour of Jeremy Hooker*, ed. Christopher Meredith (Aberystwyth: Celtic Studies Publications, 2007), pp. 171-184

Williams, Jeni, 'The Intertexts of Literary History: "Gender" and Welsh Writing', *European Intertexts: Women's Writing in English in a European Context*, eds. Patsy Stoneman and Ana María Sánchez-Arce with Angela Leighton (Oxford: Peter Lang, 2005), pp. 156-176

BOOK I

Chapter I

HE LOOKS ON HIS INHERITANCE

"There you are, Captain," said the man who had insisted upon shewing him the way. "There's your estate, sir."

"Where?"

The sharp breath on which the word was spoken betrayed Dick's excitement, and his cheeks flushed. He wished that he could be less obviously eager, but already he had put on the brakes with clumsy haste and the car was groaning under them.

The countryman in the seat beside him grinned. "We're four fields off it yet, sir, " he said.

Dick glanced at him with resentment. The man was a small, assertive fellow with a facetious manner; every word he spoke was like a nudge in the ribs. He sat up in the car with a straight back and his head cocked like a sparrow's. Dick had seen his wink at the crowd that had watched their departure from the Green Dragon at Llanon and had been ruffled by it. Though he had been in the village but one night, he was, he knew, the object of everyone's curiosity, and he had thought more than once with sympathy of the Prince of Wales. To be followed, smiled at and saluted by strangers made him shy, but until Jones had exchanged winks with the crowd there had been compensations in flattery. You couldn't tell what thought was moving behind those dark, keen eyes. You couldn't be sure why the man winked.

"Tell me when to stop, then," Dick said with pretended indifference, and drove on.

Ten minutes straining of his new car on bottom gear had brought them up out of Llanon on to a high plateau. For six or seven miles they had driven across it, with a hazy sea far below on their left, and mountains, faint as clouds, on their right. Around them a wide tableland was divided into fields by hedges and by stone walls that had a grey and ancient look. To Dick, whose weak blue eyes had not long ago been blinking at the arid glare of Mesopotamia, the colours of this landscape—the rich brown of peat bogs, the bronze of last year's bracken, the mauve cloud shadows and pale cobalt of ocean and sky, the gay sprouting green of the foreground—were magically soft. He liked the little white farmhouses with their folds awash with liquid mud. He was amused by the ducks quacking and splashing on stream and pond, and by the lambs at frolic in the fields. Gorse in flower beside the wilder stretches of the road brought agreeably to his mind the proverb about kissing. There were golden kingcups, too, like a spendthrift's scatter of sovereigns, wherever water ran; and the whole country sparkled with running water. Never had he seen any land so wet and soft and harmless. You could fall off your horse anywhere and not be hurt. This sun had no sting in it; it wouldn't raise a freckle on a girl; and he took off his felt hat with a delicious sensation of challenge, as though it had been a topee. Jones's quizzical glance brought him back to his habitual self-consciousness.

"Are you seeing that there small little tump?" "That *what*?" said Dick.

"There, sir, on the brow o' the high land, straight ahead o' us,"

"Oh yes," Dick answered. "A tumulus, isn't it?"

"That I couldn't say, but an ancient old burial place some do reckon it. There's not many as will pass near him after dark," the man continued with his offensive wink. "That do make him a grand safe place to go courting on, so long as you're careful not to show against the skyline. But you 'on't need to seek such cover as that, sir," he added with a chuckle. "There's summer-houses in your grounds and all."

"Where am I to stop?" Dick asked with impatience.

"Stop you at this gate, sir," said the man, "and we'll be going through Cross-eyed Owen's clover field, and climbing up on top o' the old tump. You'll be able to see your property from there, unrolled like a map just for you to read."

"No objection to my leaving the car here on the high road?" Dick enquired, as he jumped out.

"If the Constable should happen to pass by, and to be so foolish as to say something, you tell 'en, sir, as you'll soon be on the Bench."

Jones pushed open a gate and led Dick across country, climbing several hedges without any regard for their preservation. Dick was uneasy, but thought it wiser not to protest. The custom of this country might be different from that prevailing near London, in the neat fields, crossed by footpaths, where, before the war, he had taken girls to picnic on fine Sundays. He saw no notices here threatening trespassers or offering milk for sale, and scarcely a dwelling was visible. But when he had panted after his guide up to the top of the prehistoric burial mound, he saw below him the chimneys of a large country house.

"That looks a fine place, " he said. "Whose is it? " The Welshman slapped his knee and cackled like a hen whose egg is newly laid. "Well indeed now! That's rich! That's champion! That do beat all!

Fancy you asking me—" and he mimicked Dick's drawl— "whose is it? 'Tis *yours,* Captain, 'tis your own."

Dick turned his back on him and wished him at the devil. He wanted to be left alone—alone with his property. Digging his stick into the earth, he leaned back upon it. The grass was too wet for him to sit on, even though he wore a Burberry, but that did not deter the native from squatting down close to his feet. There was no shaking him off; and he would talk and talk.

"This great big beech wood running all the length o' the dingle is yours, sir, and the open park land over on the far side yonder with them clumps o' trees in him here and there. Them fine farms as you can count high up above the park on the ridge is yours too. And the home farm, as they do call it, close behind the mansion, see? There's another tidy-sized farm higher up, near the top o' the dingle, look. You can't see the house for them old spruces all blowed one way by the wind. The grazing rights on the open hill above is going with it up to the skyline. And over the top, sir, there's two-three bye-tacks and small holdings like, and a rare bit o' grouse shooting with 'em. They do say there's as many pheasant as leaves down in the coverts in the valley; and there be a plenty o' partridge, too, up on the brow o' either slope. And as to trout, sir, there's three miles and more o' the tidiest fishing in the county. The Lord Lieutenant couldn't wish for better."

I know. I know, Dick longed to cry out. It's a miracle. But do, for God's sake, shut up, and let me get used to it all! He remained silent, and the Welshman talked on.

"Are you seeing the smoke from the keeper's cottage, in

among the woods? There's half a dozen grand cottages, besides the head gardener's close to the walled garden there, water laid on inside, and all. You're not coming into an estate crumbling to pieces like stale bread same as what most o' them be these days. No indeed. Miss Gwenllian, she've seen to that. Everything is done up as smart and ready to be looked into as a bride's underwear. Now if you'll follow the line o' my finger, sir, you'll ketch sight o' yet another nice farm—the biggest in the parish—down where the valley is opening out beyond the lodge and the drive gates yonder. Your land is stretching on that side almost into Cwmnant village. And then there's a couple more farms as we can't see from here. They do go along o' the dower house, where they did use to put away the widows. 'Tis let off now to an old lady—no relation. They do say Miss Gwenllian was raising the rent on her on account o' the air raids. She knowed she couldn't be safer nor she was here. So she's paying a hundred and twenty pounds a year for a place as never brought the estate in a pennypiece before. That's the talk, whatever. Miss Gwenllian she'd have made a first rate man o' business. Pity indeed she were bom the wrong shape! "

Dick could think of no reply to make. He had never been able, like Flash Frank and other officers in the regiment, to crack jokes with his inferiors and, at the same time, keep them in their place. He had always hated the uncertain ground of N.C.O.s' dances, finding that the social game was easiest when it was played by a strict rule and he was left in no doubt of what it was correct for him to do and say. Now he shifted his feet and was silent.

"Pity indeed!" Jones continued. "'Twas Miss Gwenllian had the notion o' making a bit o' money by the dower house, since they hadn't a widow handy at the time o' the old Squire's death. He buried his missus ten years afore. Ah, he was a fine handsome gentleman, with a neck on him like a prize bull! And a voice as 'ould carry very near as far as a ship's foghorn at sea. He'd have lived to put any number o' wives underground if he hadn't followed the bottle, as he followed hounds, without ever drawing rein. Miss Gwennie's father, I'm speaking of, sir. And the talk is that her brother's widow won't be needin' the dower-house neither as she do intend going back into foreign parts. England's where she was coming from—a stranger to us. But you'll be knowing best about that, sir?"

Blast you, exclaimed Dick inwardly, I wish to heaven you'd keep quiet and just let me look!… "Oh yes," he said aloud, "she wrote to tell me something about it."

The countryman's bright eyes were fixed upon him, making him as uncomfortable as though two sharp pieces of jet had been thrust against his face. "And might I be so bold, Captain, as to ask where Miss Gwenllian is going?"

"Who? Oh, the unmarried sister?"

"Yes, Captain, sister to them two poor gentlemen as the Huns was killing. Ah," the little man added with venom, "and some do reckon Government be going to let that there Kayzer off scot free! You don't think that could ever be now, do you, sir? David Lloyd George, he'll see justice done, if he has to hang 'en with his own hands."

Dick grinned. "Well, I don't know, " he said. "I'm a soldier, not a politician. I've had enough slaughter for a bit." And he returned to complacent survey of his property.

"May I take the liberty o' asking what Miss Gwenllian is going to do?"

"Oh, take up something, I expect. Poultry, or breeding pet dogs."

"She 'on't shift far from Plâs Einon, sir, I'll swear. Her couldn't thrive off of the old Squire's land. She'd never fatten on no other."

"Oh," said Dick, without interest in this middle-aged cousin whom he had never seen.

The Welshman chattered on; but receiving no encouragement, rose at last.

"I'll be getting along now, Captain. I'm much obliged to you for the lift," he said, still lingering with an expression of hope upon his sharp features.

Dick hastily gave him half-a-crown, and bade him good-day. He could afford to tip well now; that was another of the many comfortable prospects before him.

When he was alone, he drew a long breath. The air was newly washed by rain. It held the saltness of the sea, and the sweetness of rising sap. The pungency of wet leaf mould and of moss was in it, rank woodland scents, stealing up from the dingle below and blending with the tonic breeze that swept the hilltops. Cool, he thought, clean, restful, safe! He shut his eyes and smiled. *Safe,* he repeated to himself, and then— *home.* He was poignantly happy. He wanted to cry.

After a while he opened his eyes again. They were round, slightly prominent, and had the anxious pucker of brow above them to be seen on the face of a puppy that has been cuffed. But now the pucker was almost gone. His face was as smooth as a contented baby's. He let his gaze travel round the circle of the horizon. Nearly all that he saw was his. It was unbelievable. During four years he had hoped daily for nothing better than to escape death. Suddenly, with the news of peace, this had come to him, the inheritance of two other soldiers, now dead.

Long valley and winding river, open mountains on either hand, neat white farms, a park stately with oak, enclosed fields spread out like a patch-work quilt, and, to crown all, the great house built in the grey stone of the district, with its terraces and wide flights of steps, that seemed to have been hewn out of the hillside—these, and more, were his.

He gave a choky little laugh and lit a cigarette. His hand shook. He burnt his fingers.

He had never dreamed of being other than poor. With what misgivings had his mother allowed him to go into the Army! "I'm afraid you will feel your position, dear, when you cannot spend as freely as the others," she had said, while he argued that the Service was more gentlemanly than a bank. Her fears had been justified in the years before the war. But since 1914, nothing had mattered as much as thirst and lice and the terror of being proved a coward—forms of misery which, because they were shared by officers who had despised him, had affected him less deeply than a lack of cash. Little enough had he got out of the war—no distinctions of any kind, the common ration of medals, no more —but he was alive. He drew in the air and let it stroke the wet roof of his mouth so that he might feel that he was alive and not thirsty. The doctors said his heart was bad—well, he'd take it easy now. Towards the end his nerve had gone; it would come back. And I've been drinking too much, he thought. That will have to stop.…It would be easy now.

Property, this miracle, made everything easy. Already it had freed him of the Army, and now—he could have pretty well what he chose. Twenty-eight; not like the poor devils of forty odd; time enough to forget and start again. Thank God, he'd escaped a bachelor from the entanglements of calf-love. Now he could take his pick. Not just a pretty girl or a good mover, but more—someone who would see that, though he might be shy, he wasn't a fool, and draw him out and be fond of him and not say sharp things that made him curl into himself. Someone kind; there were women like that—even young and pretty ones; besides, he'd be master, the property would be his, not hers. But he'd be cautious. No man knew as well as he how to make use of wealth and freedom, for none had ever wanted them more. How he meant to enjoy them! By God, how he did!

So excited and jubilant was he, that he clapped his hands together like a child. This, unfortunately, made him aware of his wrist-watch and of the time. He had forgotten the awkward call he must pay on the ladies whom he was turning out of their home.

Come on Dickie, old boy, he exhorted himself, better get it over and done with. You'll only have to see 'em this once to be civil, and that will be the end of it.

He marched back to the car of which he was still newly proud and gazed at it.

"Poor women," he thought cheerfully. "I'm sorry for 'em. Must be decent about it. Must do the right thing."

That little glow of chivalry towards the disinherited gave him pleasure. Such feelings, he knew, became a soldier.

Chapter II

HE MEETS HIS COUSIN

"Captain Einon-Thomas," the parlour-maid announced, opening the door in front of Dick. She wore a grey alpaca uniform with a tight fitting bodice. Nice, old-fashioned servant, he thought, and then: Mother used to dress in grey. He remembered shrinking behind her skirts at children's parties, ashamed of his suit, afraid lest some big boy in an Eton jacket might ask him if he rode a pony. There had been a great house, belonging to a friend of his father's, to which he had been invited when he was a child—a house as chill and marbled as a town hall. The journey to it from Streatham had been full of terrors. For a week before their going, his mother had been nervously critical of his manners, and in the train her searching eye had keyed him to his ordeal. When he went to school at Dulwich, the yearly invitation to Carlton House Terrace had ceased. He would have been glad, but that his mother was sorry. "I wonder," she used to sigh, "if you did anything to give offence."

At these recollections, his hand went up to his tie. Was it straight and correct? He jerked his hand down and tugged at a button of his waistcoat. To hell with this nonsense, he thought. Couldn't he be done with it now? Wasn't he Einon-Thomas of Plâs Einon? But that had been the name of the poor devils into whose inheritance he was come! It seemed indecent to be announced to their relatives by the title of the dead. A sense of his own inadequacy caused Dick to look down at his feet; a shoe-lace was dangling; he stooped to tuck it in. Two Sealyham terriers came sniffing and waggling at him, their claws scuttering on the parquet floor. A warm tongue licked the tip of his nose. How easy it was to get on well with dogs! Then he stood up, threw back his shoulders as on parade, and strode past the shielding grey skirt. To leave it behind was like taking a plunge into cold water.

Three ladies rose to meet him. All were in mourning for his predecessors.

"I—I hope you don't mind," he stuttered, and shook hands rigidly with the widow.

She wore the usual little white collar and cuffs on a black gown, and an expression of decorous melancholy. Her large blue eyes were pretty but unprovocative. She seemed to have been very tired for a number of years.

"My calling, I mean," he hurried on, "I was awfully afraid, perhaps, that, that you'd think it rather soon after—" His voice trailed into silence.

Hot with shame, he gripped the next hand extended to him. It returned his clutch with a warm pressure. Some women's hands felt kind, he thought, particularly if they were broad and firm. But when he glanced up, encouraged, he was met by a frankly amused smile, which disconcerted him. He took the third hand. It was cold and glossy, and narrow, like a serpent.

"My sister-in-law, Mrs. Blake," the widow was murmuring. " And my other sister-in-law, Miss Einon-Thomas. She lives with us—that is, I mean— she—has always made her home here." There was a dangerous pause until she added with forced brightness, "I am trying to persuade her to pay me a visit at Cannes next winter. I mean to share a small villa with an old friend there."

"Oh, do you?" said Dick. And after a moment's travail he brought forth, "Jolly nice spot, I believe." "Oh very," she said, and began to speak in a flat voice, as though to gain time, about English clubs, and of how, by living abroad for half the year, one might escape Income Tax. But from that topic she shied away, not wishing to reproach him with her future poverty. Nice, feeling little woman, he told himself; and felt the more guilty in robbing her of her husband's estate.

She turned to her married sister-in-law.

"Mrs. Blake is only here on a visit...Won't you sit down? I'm sure I don't know why we are all standing....Her husband is in the Navy. At least he is actually resigning this week, isn't he, Frances?" "Yes," answered the lady with the large friendly hand. She dropped into an easy chair and crossed her legs. "He's going to give up the service and try his luck in Fleet Street. Unless I manage to get a job, too, I expect the children will starve."

That's a bit stiff! Dick thought, but the speaker seemed cheerfully unaware of having embarrassed him. She talked about employment, and the problems of the new rich and the new poor, as though she were alluding to a game of chess, and not to matters which touched them all closely. At length the widow intervened, bringing the conversation back to safe, dull ground: the weather, the state of the roads.

"They are terribly cut up," she said. "So much timber-hauling during the war, you know."

"Oh, of course," he agreed.

Watching her hands, small and white, which played with an antique mourning brooch of black enamel, he began to think of the family jewels which his wife might wear—when he had chosen her. It would be chivalrous to take over the widow with the estate and to let her wear the heirlooms to which she was accustomed. But the idea made him want to laugh. He would marry a dazzler, a real fresh pretty girl! This Mrs. Einon-Thomas was old enough to be his mother. Not quite, perhaps, but nearing forty. Still, she was the best of the three, the most womanly; though the others had appeared more striking in the flurry of his first encounter. He began now, furtively, to study them.

They were much alike, tall and dark. No doubt they were considered handsome a few years ago. But they weren't his style—too foreign, too much what you expected of the Welsh. It was odd that they should be his first cousins. Those boldly marked, level eyebrows, those almost Italian features with so little flesh upon them, suggested bad temper, or worse, fanaticism. He shouldn't wonder if they were rabid teetotallers, or religious, or something of the kind. The married one looked cheerful enough, and she was the younger, but she displeased him by being untidy. His mother and the Army had taught him to revere neatness in dress and to disapprove of those who were indifferent to it. Frances Blake's abundance of black hair, with its natural, unruly wave, seemed to have been tossed up in a hurry, and her dress was without precision. Dick turned away to her sister and tried to draw her into the conversation. Last night, in the bar of the Green Dragon, he had talked with a man in the Timber Supply Department. Now he quoted what he hoped was a well-informed remark on the supply of pit-props to the collieries of South Wales. Miss Einon-Thomas looked at him in silent disdain. Had the timber fellow been pulling his leg? he wondered; and he recalled hotly that Flash Frank had laid traps for his ignorance when first he joined the regiment. What was his cousin thinking of him as she sat there, not troubling to answer? At least she was not laughing at him, as they had so often laughed in the Mess. She was staring out of the French windows at the lawns and the tall trees beyond. Her profile would look well on a coin.

She was dressed, though plainly, with the care for exact order that he had been bred to admire. An uneasy interest in her stirred within him, not because she was a woman, for she was hard and dry, like well-seasoned wood, but because he guessed, by the stiffening of her body and the compression of her well-shaped lips, that, of these three, it was she who suffered most. I suppose, he decided, being un-married and a daughter at home and all that, she was wrapped up in her brothers, and he was sorry for her.

"I dare say you notice the difference," he observed, still relying on timber to keep the conversation from collapse, "but I've never seen this country before, you know, and to me the valleys look jolly well wooded. It's awfully pretty, anyway"

That would please her, he thought.

But Gwenllian's dark eyes flashed on him, large and beautiful as an angry cat's. He was startled.

"It's ruined," she said. "There's almost nothing left."

Was she thinking of men as well as of trees? His face burned as though she had slapped it; but an instant later she had risen, and he watched her go down the long room with the quiet assurance of movement that he had always envied. A faint glow of satisfaction at being in the intimate company of a gentlewoman whose dignity none could dispute warmed his being. How different she was in voice and carriage and manner from the girls he had taken on the river at Maidenhead before he was Einon-Thomas of Plâs Einon! As he studied her, he became aware for the first time that the large drawing-room at Plâs Einon fitted her as a frame its picture.

There were many portraits in oils of dark, handsome folk, evidently her ancestors, and beside the hearth was a case of miniatures mounted on black velvet. Several of the Persian rugs were threadbare, and the striped wall-paper was stained by damp. There was no means of lighting but by candles in mirrored sconces or by oil-lamps with shades of puckered silk flounced with lace—such shades as reminded him of ladies' hats in his childhood. There were people, Dick knew, who wouldn't like the room as he did, but even they wouldn't dare to call it dowdy. It was full of the flower-like gaiety of old china. Out of the darkness of walnut cabinets sprang the brilliance of apple-green, the bouquets and birds of Nantgarw, the rich gold of Crown Derby. "Pretty they are," he said, boldly picking up from the mantelshelf one of the many figures that posed there—arch little ladies and gentlemen of Chelsea and Bow. What a mixture! But he liked it. He was proud of being able to recognise so much—the harp of the Regency with its drooping strings, the Jacobean chairs with tapestried seats of faded blue and green, the fat bunch of wax fruit under glass, which, he guessed, dated from the 'sixties. Nothing here was out of place, for even the chintz covers on the chubby armchairs of King Edward's latter days were washed so dim that they also belonged naturally to this family museum. His mother had wistfully studied books on the applied arts, borrowed from the free library, and the habit of her early profession as a teacher had survived her marriage. What she knew, she imparted. Lucky, Dick thought; some fellows would be all at sea in a room like this. He would drop a remark about these treasures presently—perhaps about the fluted, handleless cups which, he'd bet, were old Worcester.

And suddenly, flattered by his kinship with the room and with his cousin Gwenllian, he imagined himself walking into a smart restaurant in London with her at his side. Flash Frank would be there. "Hello!" he'd say, trying to stare a fellow out of countenance, "What the deuce are you doin' here, Scrub?" Then, seeing the lady, he'd rise. His whole manner would change, conveying, as it always did, the precise measure of respect to which a woman was entitled. He would know Gwenllian for what she was. Dick saw his eyebrows go up a little, at the introduction: "My cousin, Miss Einon-Thomas." It would, of course, be very casually spoken.

The pleasing vision faded. Dick rubbed his small blond moustache. She had turned round, her hand on the bell rope, and was looking over his head as though he did not exist.

"Shall I ring for tea, Cecily?" and she had rung before the mistress of the house replied.

When tea was brought, it was to her that the parlourmaid turned for orders.

"Do pour out, dear," said the widow, as if this were a regular formula. "We always have an old-fashioned sit-down tea. Draw up your chair—Captain Einon-Thomas." She hesitated at his name.

"This is absurd," Mrs. Blake said. "We're all relations. What d'you answer to—Richard?"

"Dick," he answered, feeling that it had a foolish sound; but it was better than Scrub.

"Right," she said. "I shall start at once. And I am Frances. No-one asked you if you'd have preferred a whiskey and soda?"

He gave her a confused glance, and took a cup of tea from Gwenllian's hand. "Oh no, thanks," he said. "I'd rather this."

Frances's broad smile expressed her disbelief. "I'm used to Service tastes," she announced.

He struggled in difficult conversation with the widow on bee-keeping, gardening and poultry while Gwenllian remained silent, her fine brows drawn together. When tea was over, Frances again came to the rescue.

"What are your politics?" she demanded.

"Oh, Unionist, of course."

"Why 'of course'? I keep on changing mine with youthful optimism. I'm a good deal older than you are, but I still hope to find a party that combines a bit of honesty with a gleam of intelligence."

"Oh, I say," he laughed, "you don't really mean to use your vote, now you've got one, first one way and then another?"

" I mean to keep an open mind."

"But people who keep on changing look such asses."

"They're alive at any rate. When you can't change, you're dead."

Dick thought that annoyingly clever; and she made it worse.

"My husband's going to stand as a Labour candidate, if they'll give him a show."

"You don't really expect me to believe that," Dick retorted with a smile which turned to blankness on his face. Too late he perceived in the mild distress of her sister-in-law's look and the undisguised contempt of Gwenllian's, that Frances had been serious.

She began to talk subversive politics, like the young fools from Oxford and Cambridge who had no studs to their shirts and wore their hair long; and he grew so angry, recalling the discipline of his subaltern days and contrasting it with the licence permitted to civilian cubs, that he forgot his shyness and flatly contradicted her.

" Frances doesn't mean half she says," put in the widow in a non-committal tone.

"Does anyone?" Frances laughed, and she began to mock at the Prime Minister whom in the spring of 1919 it was still the fashion to applaud. She even derided the coming Peace Treaty.

Dick quoted the defence of Lloyd George that he had so often heard on his Colonel's lips. "If one can forgive him his Limehouse past, the little devil's done pretty well."

Frances shrugged her shoulders. "The verdict of history may prefer Limehouse."

Such perversity was too much. Dick made a gesture of impatience, and at once became aware that Gwenllian's eyes were on him. And how she had changed! Her resentful scorn had given place to eager speculation. He had caught her studying him from head to foot as though he were an object of supreme interest and curiosity. Deeply surprised, he tried to return her gaze. She stooped at once and began to pat one of the Sealyhams.

"You're a Unionist like myself, I take it?" he ventured.

"I?" she answered, her head still bent over the dog so that the light shone on the rich mass of her hair and the whiteness of its parting. "Oh, yes. Like yourself—more than a Unionist, a staunch Conservative, a Tory in all things."

He thought how pleasant it was to see a woman again with abundant and well-kept hair.

"Good," he said, "you and I'll agree better than I shall with your sister, Cousin——" but he could not for the life of him remember her outlandish name.

"Gwenllian," she said, raising her head, and at last according him a softening of the lips that was almost a smile. "Until you're used to our Welsh names, you'd better call me Gwen."

"Oh, thanks awfully," he said.

The ormolu clock struck half-past five. Afraid that he had stayed too long, he stumbled into apologies.

"Oh, but you have not seen the house yet," the widow said.

"We can go into all that later," he stammered with a return of his former distress. "You mustn't feel under any obligation, you know."

"But really you've been much too kind to us already— hasn't he, Gwenllian?—letting us stay on so long."

"Not at all. Not at all. I couldn't have got home from Mespot any sooner, or got clear of the Army. And if it's any convenience to you—"

"Much too generous," she sighed. "But my plans are all made—really—thank you so much. I shall be starting on a round of visits the end of next week. And Gwenllian too. Frances, of course, will be rejoining her husband."

"In that case," he said, much relieved, "you'd like to go over things with that lawyer chap and myself pretty soon?"

"Well yes," she agreed wearily. "Perhaps if you would both come to lunch on Thursday? We have everything in order, I think, haven't we, Gwenllian? There's the inventory, and the cellar book, and the keys and so forth. You'll be taking your time, later, over the gardens and the home farm and the estate. The agent, Mr. Lloyd, will present all the tenants to you— won't he, Gwenllian? We shall just have to tell you a few things about the indoor servants."

"Quite," he said, "quite."

"May I make a suggestion?" said a voice of quiet authority at his elbow.

"Yes, rather."

"Wouldn't it be pleasanter," Gwenllian continued, "if we showed you round first—just a family party? There are Einon-Thomas jokes and histories we shouldn't care to tell in front of little Price the solicitor."

Dick warmed to her instantly. "Capital," he said, more flattered than he cared to admit, and he turned with eagerness to the widow to confirm the invitation.

Her faded, pretty face wore a look of surprise. "If you really think it worth your while," she replied with hesitation.

"Come to lunch alone at one o'clock on Wednesday," Gwenllian said, "and again on Thursday, bringing Mr. Price with you. Will you ring up his office to-night from the Green Dragon? We aren't on the telephone here."

"Delighted," said Dick.

But still the widow murmured something about going over the same ground twice. "And then I promised to motor Frances over to luncheon with her godmother."

"That was on Tuesday, dear," Gwenllian told her.

"Are you quite sure, dear?"

"Quite. It is in the engagement calendar."

"Very well," the widow said, giving Dick her limp hand, "we shall have the pleasure of seeing you by yourself on Wednesday?" The arrangement still seemed to surprise her. Really, he thought, Cousin Gwen, who had been so standoffish at first, turned out to be the more considerate of the two! An Einon-Thomas family party—a capital idea!

Frances rose and stretched herself. "I think you ought to see the crocuses now, whatever you may see on Wednesday and

Thursday," she said. "This house is full of the worst art of every age. But the crocuses look gorgeous to-day—all their little faces open to the sun. It's sure to be pelting again by then. I suppose you've been warned that it rains here nine days out of ten, have you, Dick? Come on, everybody, for a stroll before the heavens descend."

Dick opened the door for them and the married ladies passed through. But when Gwenllian came abreast of him she stopped abruptly as though stayed by some new idea. "I'll say *au revoir* to you here."

"Oh come on," called Frances from the hall. "You were shut up with accounts all the morning." "It's not accounts," Gwenllian answered. "I've just remembered I ought to visit Ifor Cobbler. While you're taking Cousin Dick round the garden, I'll go down to the village…till Wednesday then, Dick."

"Till Wednesday," he said, and heartily shook her hand. But he felt too awkward to add, "Gwen." She was, after all, so much older than himself.

Chapter III

SHE REMEMBERS THE PAST

Centuries ago the yew trees had been planted in a circle. Their trunks had now the bulk of the piers of a Roman amphitheatre. Though set far apart, they were linked by their branches which met and interlocked, forming at the circumference of the arena a low, knotted aisle less than the height of a man. Towards the centre, the level, inky limbs stretched out, but did not meet there. Light from above, bleached by the surrounding darkness, fell in rigid arrows through the interval of the roof. No breeze entered here; no bird sang.

When she was a child, Gwenllian had said, in her father's hearing, that it was "a gorgeous place to hate in." He had laughed at her, and she, driven in upon her secret, had spoken of it no more, but she had continued to visit the place in all the bitter seasons of her life, and came to it now, with fearful eagerness, out of the flecked sunshine of the drive where the graceful winter tracery of beech was softened by a foam of green and the chestnuts were already putting on the first shrill gaiety of spring. Crouching her way under the boughs, she entered the inner ring and stood there for a little while, stiff and trembling; then, with lowered head and the smooth, rapid gait of a troubled animal, began to move upon the arc of the lighted circle, never completing her journey in one direction, but twining upon her own track, twisting always to and fro.

If she had been bred a nun, she might have ignored men; but

in her world, there was no power but through them; they were
in possession, hour by hour and generation by generation, of
all that she desired to possess; they invaded her integrity,
usurped the inheritance of her soul. Without them, how little
evil there would be in her, she thought, and how peaceful the
colours of her life—grey, with the formal piety that was
natural in her: green, with the calm hours she loved to spend
in the open air. It was they who streaked her quiet, decorous
years with hatred and passion—the black and the scarlet, and
they always who drove her into this cage.

She had come here first in flight from their injustice, her
small fists clenched, her cheeks scalded by tears, beside
herself in a child's tragic, impotent rage. She had been riding
the roan pony every day— since Easter she had ridden it,
and her father had allowed her to follow him round the estate
on Taffy, the new grey cob. She had been frightened of Taffy
but had mastered him; it had been a victory of her own
solitary determination. But Howel and Evan had come home
from school, each bringing a friend with him, and the four
boys had emptied the stables every morning and afternoon.
Howel had given her favourite a sore back: Evan had raced
the roan on the high road and lamed him. They were
excused, because they were boys. And when they were not
galloping over the countryside, they went ferreting with
Daniel Keeper. The white ferrets were hers, not theirs. For
months past she had fed them; she could handle them as her
brothers dared not. But the boys had the fun of them,
excluding her.

She must go for walks with Nannie and baby Frances at a
pram's pace, with no consolation, no chance to do and make,
except when she could escape to the shed where Ifor

Carpenter had taught her the use of tools. She was neat with her fingers as Howel would never be, but the day came when he snatched her work from her and tried to shut her out of the carpenter's shed. "Give it to me," he had commanded. "Girls can't carpenter." All the supposed disabilities of girlhood had rung for her in his voice. Girls can't shoot. Girls can't ride astride. Girls can't play cricket....Her long resentment was focused now. She hated him with a blind hatred as he thrust her towards the door, their feet scuffling among the chips and shavings, and suddenly with all her strength she had struck him and pulled his hair and kicked and struck him again. When he tried to ward her off with his hand, she had bitten it and drawn blood. There had been fierce delight in her power to hurt and frighten a boy.

Disgrace and punishment had followed. Her explanations went unheard; that she had been attacked was of no account. Boys might fight; her father encouraged them to use their fists; she must submit. In flight from that humiliation, she had come among the yew trees for the first time, to burn in solitude, to weep and beat her head upon the earth; then to grow calm, steel herself, re-order her battle.

After this, she endured in silence her brothers' invasion of her home three times a year. They shattered the life she built up round her father and she hated them more and more. But she learned to hide her detestation with increasing skill, until nursery quarrels were forgotten by all but herself and she was held up in other families as a model sister. If one of the boys had an unstrung tennis racquet, she lent him hers. It did not matter, she would say calmly, for in any case she could not play a man's hard game. Howel accepted her sacrifices as a matter of course. Women were by nature unselfish, their mother was for ever saying, with a sigh, and it was part of his romanticism that he should agree with her.

For years, while her mother half lived upon a sofa, Gwenllian had held the reins of the household. On the day when she walked with downcast eyes behind her mother's coffin, she was sorry to lose so harmless a presence, but she had not been touched by her brothers' sense of irreparable calamity. Howel mourned for two years with intense, lover- like grief; then married a girl with his mother's mild blue eyes. For Gwenllian there were from the first rich compensations. At the graveside she knew that henceforth she would sit at the head of her father's table, the acknowledged mistress of his house, and she glanced up at his handsome face, coarsened by drink, reddened by all weathers, sullen now with the solemnity of the burial service. There was no grief in it for the woman who had been his loyal and patient slave for more than twenty years. He was bored; and though Gwenllian loved him, though he was for her the very splendour of manhood, she cursed him and his sex in the name of the meek dead and of all women living.

Remembering that surge of bitterness against him, she checked herself in her pacing to and fro. She wanted to understand the rage of triumph and grief that confused her mind when she thought that he also was now in the vault where her mother had been laid. Reason told her that it was wrong to judge all men by him. There were good husbands and good fathers whom there was no cause to hate; there were men, perhaps, without his courage in the saddle or his bold fling at life itself, whom she might admire. But for good and evil her judgment of men was rooted in her judgment of him. He had been as careless of his children's future as of his wife's health. Though the estate had meant more to him than any human affection, he had encumbered it with debt. Her labour and economy had been pitted continuously against his extravagance. She had nursed him night and day through his last illness when, abusing her always, he would have none other to attend him. And when he died, she had nothing but her brothers' charity and what little her mother had left to her.

This was the justice of mankind and the penalty of womanhood. But in her father also had been the glamour from which even now she could not escape. She remembered the giant who strode into her nursery in his gay pink coat and picked her up with one hand. She remembered the hero of the 1906 election, and how the mob had cheered him in the market square at Llanon. She saw him presiding at a local eisteddfod, and smelt again paraffin, farm labourers, the dankness of a village hall. She saw the rows of lively Welsh faces upturned, laughing. He was chaffing the prize winners. Beside her, on the platform, a sly little minister was chuckling. "The Squire's champion! Yes, indeed! He's always the best speaker present."

The scene shifted: a steamy summer's day after heavy rain; the smell of trampled earth, pulped grass and wet canvas. Through the mud she skidded after her father as he strode round the ring. A trotting match was about to begin. The sporting crowd of dark, eager men was excited. Bets were being exchanged and children hoisted on to their parents' shoulders, the better to see the great event of the Llanon Show. Preoccupied as they were, all these people saluted her father. She enjoyed the smiles and nods, the raised hats and the forelocks touched. "There he goes. Look, man! There be the Squire. Ah, he's the most rash, fearless rider in three counties."

She was on the stairs at home, very cold in her cotton nightgown. Her naked toes were curled on the polished oak. How long she had waited, craning over the banisters to hear the buzz of talk that came muffled from the drawing-room! At last he appeared in the black satin knee-breeches and white lace of his High Sheriff's uniform—a hero of the cloak and sword romances she had just begun to read. He had promised to look up and wave. But he crossed the hall without remembering her.

Her father's failures to keep his word had often driven her out to these never-changing yews. She had come here, too, to think in secret of another man. Not far from this dark place he had overtaken her the night before he sailed for India, and had caught her in his arms and kissed her, not with tenderness, as always before, but so roughly that he bruised her lips. She had struggled for a moment, frightened and angry; then been still, feeling her heart, wild with pleasure, close to his.

"I won't take no for an answer, d'you hear?" he had said. "You've played with me for over a year. You've kept me dangling—"

"No," she protested, "it wasn't play."

"And now you've turned me down for the sake of a damned house—"

"It's not that only. There's father—"

"Much he cares! We've been into all that before. You'll be sorry when I've gone."

"Oh, my dear! My dear! Don't you think I know it?"

"Then come away now."

"I *can't*. Not yet—not till I've thought—"

"When I come back then, you shall say yes. If you haven't made up your mind by then, I'll burn the damned house down! I'm coming back the first leave I get—are you listening?"

Her father had died before that first leave and Howel had brought home Cecily to be the mistress of Plâs Einon. Gwenllian remembered how with mingled distress and relief, she had put the keys and account books into her sister-in-law's soft little hands. Then she had run up to her room, shaken with excitement, to write a letter to India. But he had not come back. This was the fidelity of men.

It was Howel she had hated for bringing Cecily home, not Cecily herself. Cecily was weak and amiable; she did not rule Plâs Einon long. An heir was needed. After two or three disappointments, the effort of trying to produce a living child had robbed her of interest in anything but her own condition, and government had passed again into Gwenllian's hands. She ceased to think then of her faithless lover. Instead she became once more busy, powerful, respected; in all but name, mistress of the place she loved. Her future seemed assured. Howel would live; if Cecily died and he married again, he would choose a girl as docile as she, as weak as his own mother had been. Evan was a morose widower; he had shunned women since the death of his bride. If by chance he inherits in my time, Gwenllian told herself, he will need me.

But the war came. Security was at an end. Evan was killed at Gallipoli; Howel in hourly danger in Flanders. Morning after morning, with tight lips and a sinking heart, Gwenllian searched the casualty list for his name. No man's wife could have dreaded news of his death more than she her brother's, and none worked harder to hold and improve his estate. But when Howel died of wounds in the last month of the war, she knew that, deep in her heart, there was no grief for him. Her youth, which in 1914 had scarcely begun to fade, abruptly left her. She went about her business, white as a ghost, and the neighbours were touched by her sorrow. All could see that it was real and crushing. But it was for Plâs Einon she mourned. It was not for selfish, overbearing Howel that night after night she drove her wet face into the pillow, but because she must leave the stately house she had ruled, the garden she had made lovely, the land she had learned to farm, the green hills and the woods where she had played and hunted all her life. For these she had denied her only love and concealed her wrath against the men of her race. Now, by the terms of her father's will, a stranger inherited.

Under the yews she brooded on him, this common little suburban with a pale moustache, this governess's son, whose father had been cut off from the family by his misalliance! She had intended to disregard him; to leave him to wreck Plâs Einon; never again to set eyes upon it herself. But something in his anxious young face, as though he were eager to be taught; some echo of her own mood in his hot defence of conservatism had pierced her despair and she had begun to watch him. He was no Einon-Thomas in appearance—like his third-rate little mother, she supposed—but, if she could win his confidence and become his adviser, she might save him from being a discredit to the family. Perhaps then, she would visit Plâs Einon— the woman to whom the next generation would appeal as to the oracle of their race. Even through him, the tradition might be handed on. Her quick brain, accustomed to contrivance, had sprung to a new determination while they were saying goodbye in the drawing-room. On Tuesday, by a trick of the engagement calendar, she would have him alone. She could test her material.

Through the yew trees, she heard a car coming from the direction of the house. In all her brooding on the past, she had been listening for this sound. Her lips parted in eagerness, but not to smile. Stooping beneath the dark branches, she went to meet another man in whose keeping was all that she loved.

Chapter IV

HE LISTENS TO HER

When Dick had been shewn the walled garden with its box-edged walks, and had explored the winding paths of the shrubbery, in which graceful nature was half tamed, he was more than ever pleased with his inheritance. It was agreeable to prod the spongy lawns with his stick and to let his imagination loose on tennis parties and girls in thin white frocks. In the honied evening light that turned raindrops to topaz, the sprouting grass, the flowers, the trees in bud, all looked their freshest and most lovely. He listened with pleasure to the song of a blackbird and the sweet whistling of a thrush. The melody of running water too, in Plâs Einon dingle, enchanted him. When a shower pattered down his neck off the glossy leaves of laurel, he reflected that it would be even better here at midsummer.

His spirits had risen so high by the time he jumped into his car that he forgot to be apologetic, and waved a jaunty farewell to the widow. Decent little woman, he thought, admiring her big blue eyes. If she'd been ten years younger—but a man in his position could take his pick of the best. He wasn't going to hurry over his choice! He meant to have a bit of fun first. And he drove away from Plâs Einon with a grin on his freckled face.

He went slowly, the better to look about him. The drive was suitably picturesque, curving to and fro along the side of a miniature ravine at the foot of which the river flowed. The eighteenth-century designer of the grounds had constructed the usual waterfalls and artificial ponds. He had built a summer-house or two in the style of a classic temple, and planted ornamental clumps of trees, arranging vistas through the beech woods. Coming to the sombre group of yew trees near the lodge, Dick felt that they were independent of the general design; these dark giants, tortuously interlocked, were never planted in the Age of Reason. They seemed, rather, to be survivals, like very ancient witches, of a time of faith and fear, when the land was still haunted by ghosts and demons.

This bit wants clearing, Dick decided. I shall have half of these chaps down, and let in some light.

A figure in black appeared on the road ahead of him.

Queer, he thought, I never noticed her when I turned the last corner. She must have been lurking among those dismal trees. Blessed if it isn't Cousin Gwen!

He pulled up sharp.

"Hello! Can I give you a lift anywhere?"

"Oh, thanks so much. As a matter of fact, I was going down to the village before dinner. But it's later than I thought. I could walk back if you'd just run me down."

"Right," he answered, set almost at ease by the friendliness of her manner.

She climbed in beside him and, after she was seated, exclaimed: "Oh, but I forgot. It's not on your way back to Llanon."

"That doesn't matter," he assured her. "I'm my own master now. I can dine at any old hour."

"I hope that doesn't mean you sometimes forget to dine at

all?" she said, and he was reminded of his mother, who had often lectured him on the care of his health. Cousin Gwen was a good sort.

"Oh dear no. I'm not at all a helpless sort of chap," he boasted, glad that there were still women who *were* women. It was pleasant to see her shake her head when he added: "I can take good care of myself." It made him feel warm and sheltered; it gave him confidence in a callous world.

They approached the lodge, and the keeper hurried out as fast as his rheumatic legs would carry him. He wore a respectful smile as he opened the gate, reviving in Dick the feelings of a second lieutenant acknowledging his first salute. But here there were no senior officers whom he must salute in turn. Plâs Einon was his. The people on the estate were his servants, to keep on, to promote, to discharge. Henceforth he was accountable to none for his actions, and need not associate with those who criticised or ridiculed him. A little song of emancipation sang itself through his whole being: "I can do what I damned well like." Not that he'd be a tyrant. He'd be popular as well as respected.

Suddenly he realised that he did not know which way to turn the car. "Where d'you want me to go?" he asked Gwenllian.

"Right. Our village is a mile further along the road by which you came."

He swerved at her bidding and began with caution to descend a very long steep hill. He was not sure yet of his command over the first car he had ever owned. Far away below them, he could see a church tower, grey, between elm trees. No houses were visible, but a few threads of bluish smoke rose into the still air.

"You call it *our* village," he said. "I don't remember any village on the plans they sent me of the property."

"No," she answered. "But that's our parish church. And we're buried under it—lots of us. We walk over ourselves every Sunday, going into the family pew."

"Good Lord! What a grim idea!" he exclaimed.

She changed the subject at once. "We're rather proud of our village, let me tell you. It's our nearest shopping centre though it has only one shop. But you've no idea what odd things you can buy in it. And then we've a real live banker and a butcher too, besides all the poachers who bring fish and game to back doors after dark—not to ours, of course. The banker only sets up shop once a week, and the butcher twice—when he's sober—for three hours."

"Good heavens," laughed Dick, "can you only cash a cheque once a week?"

"That's oftener than you'll need to. Everybody'll trust you here," she said, and smiled at him as though she already did so.

"That'll be a change," he was about to say with a rueful grin, but he thought better of it, and observed instead, "I like the sound of our village. Tell me more about it."

She told him, and he was relieved to find that she made her account amusing and intimate, as though the village were his indeed and she had ceased to think of him as an outsider. Next week's stocktaking would be less formidable than he had feared. And he was encouraged to question her about the villagers and the men who worked on the estate. Her replies showed an impressive knowledge of their characters, the wages they received, the rents they paid.

"You seem to have everything to do with the estate at your finger tips," he said in a tone of surprise.

She gave a laugh that sounded unexpectedly hard. "I ought to know a bit about it. I've only just handed it back to Mr. Lloyd—I flatter myself in better condition than he left it."

"To the agent?" Dick asked. "But didn't he always manage it?"

"He's been away in the Yeomanry since August '14"

"Oh, I say," Dick exclaimed. "And you've been running the whole show single-handed?"

She smiled at him—as though she liked him quite a lot, he fancied. "Cecily's had no business training and her health's bad," she said. "Frances is never here."

"But, hang it all, I shouldn't have thought you were brought up to estate management, either—not with two brothers."

A slight grimace twisted her lips downwards. "Father let me pick up a good deal, riding about with him." And she added: "In term time, when the boys weren't there."

"Well," Dick declared, "all I can say is, you must be jolly clever."

She looked into his eyes and slowly smiled in such a fashion that he became vividly aware for the first time of her sex. "It isn't so difficult to learn about what you love," she said.

He was embarrassed and replied hastily: "You ought to have been a boy."

To that she made no answer, but leaned forward so that he could see nothing but her hunched shoulder. "Stop here, please," she commanded. Her tone was abrupt. Hang it all, he thought, he wasn't her chauffeur.

He brought the car to a standstill before the first white-washed cottage of Cwmnant. Beyond it straggled the rest of the village, like a disordered flock of sheep along a winding lane. An amusing sort of hamlet, Dick considered it, but think of living clean out of the world like this! He'd have to get away pretty often.

When Cousin Gwen was in the road beside the car, she stooped and seemed to be re-tying her shoe-lace. She took a long time about it. What was the trouble? And, catching a glimpse of her face, he thought that the features were contracted, as if by a twinge of pain.

"Are you all right?" he enquired, peering at her.

"Perfectly, thanks," she answered, straightening herself. "My shoe-lace broke." She was smiling at him again and talking pleasantly about his homeward drive, but he had an uncomfortable feeling that it cost her an effort. He ought not to have said, "You ought to have been a boy." It seemed to have upset her. Perhaps she was touchy about not being more attractive. He stared at her feet. What serviceable brogues she wore! She had mended the lace neatly, though; he couldn't see the knot.

"I'd better be getting along," he said, his hand on the wheel.

"Thank you most awfully," she answered. "It's been such a pleasure to me to tell you just a few things about our people. I should like—if you'll allow me—" Then she broke off, and staring at her shoe-lace again, added, "Oh, by the way, I looked up our engagement calendar again to make sure. *Wednesday*, not Tuesday, was the day fixed on for the others to lunch out."

"Oh," he said. "Then you won't want me then?"

"But, of course. Just drop in whenever you like. It's your house now. And even if it weren't—Only, perhaps, Tuesday would be better. Can you manage it?"

"Rather. All days are the same to me," Dick declared. And he repeated with complacence, "I'm my own master now."

"You're lucky," she told him. When she became animated, she had remarkably fine eyes. Not that he had ever cared much for any woman's eyes unless they were blue. As he drove back past his new domain, he wondered why blue eyes should— but she did not remain in his thought. What interested him was his own future, with which she wasn't concerned.

Dickie, my boy, he said, your luck's just beginning, and he thought how glad his mother would have been. She would have been rather a fish out of water at Plâs Einon. Still, he would have been glad to have her there—or in the dower house at any rate.

Chapter V

HE IS AGAIN HER LISTENER

Getting to know his estate was not as agreeable as he had anticipated. The tenants were extremely polite, but they made him drink so much stewed tea and eat so many currant pancakes that his digestion became deranged. He had been told that they would be offended if he declined any offer of food or drink, and he wished at all costs to get on well with them. But it was difficult. He failed to understand half they said, and was at times unsure whether they were addressing him in English, or in the Welsh language which they used amongst themselves. When the good news had reached him that he had inherited an estate at home, he had not bargained for its being inhabited by a lot of jabbering foreigners. He had thought of the principality as a remote part of England where the miners gave trouble but the fishing was said to be good, and he had imagined tenant-farmers as red-faced fellows, honest but slow, quaint as rustic characters in a play. It was a shock to discover that most of his own tenants were sharp-featured, bright-eyed folk, whose swift speech and dramatic gesture showed that they were quicker-witted than himself, and he began to wonder whether the studied monotony of his own speech might not seem as comic to them as the chanting cadence of theirs was to him strange and irritating. Well, not comic perhaps. They would know of course that his way of speaking English was correct. But he was ill at ease among them. If his estate had been in one of the home counties, he would have liked it better.

The agent, too, was a most annoying fellow. He selected all the gateways where mud lay deepest and squelched through it as if it didn't exist. Dick had been bred on pavements. He had spent the first winter of the war in the trenches. He hated mud; it was associated in his mind neither with sport nor with agriculture, but with freezing hours of alternate terror and boredom. To clog through the foul substance, day after day, was not his idea of the privileges of ownership.

Nor was Mr. Lloyd's duck-like fondness for swamps his sole offence. He had begun by taking it for granted that Dick understood his technical jargon. He spoke of sweet land and sour, of pleaching hedges and of silage. For even so plain an animal as the sheep, he had a string of preposterous names: theaves, tups, ewes, wether lambs, rams, hoggs. Dick lost count of them. Pigs, when Mr. Lloyd spoke of them, became sows or boars, brims or gilts. At last Dick was forced to admit that all this was Greek to him, and the fellow was surprised. As though, thought Dick in sore self-defence, I were to plunge some poor devil of a civilian into Autumn Manoeuvres and expect him to know what everything was about! Probably the agent despised him.

On Tuesday, at the hour appointed for luncheon with the three friendly ladies, he drove up to the portico of his own house, telling himself that an Englishman's home, at any rate, was his castle. The parlourmaid who took his hat and stick from him in the hall, did not ask as before: "What name shall I say, please sir?" but gave him a deferential smile. He followed her into the pleasant drawing-room. Only his cousin Gwen was there, arranging a bowl of daffodils. He liked to see a lady at a pretty task like that.

"Oh Dick," she said, laying down the flowers, and advancing with outstretched hand, "I've been wondering whether I ought to have sent a man into Llanon to stop your coming."

"Why?" he asked. "You don't mean to give up my education, I hope? Not after all the stuff you began to tell me the other evening?"

"Of course not," she said, signing to him to take a seat beside her on the sofa. "If there's any way whatever in which I can be of use to you—It's the very least I could do, isn't it, after your letting me stay on here so long?"

"Rot," he exclaimed, and wished he had not done so. It was such a schoolboy word and rather third-rate.

"And you mustn't suppose," she continued, "I didn't realise how awkward that first meeting must have been for you— worse for you than for any of us."

"Oh, I don't know," he said.

"But I do," she persisted, "because you've shown yourself to be so extraordinarily generous since poor Howel was killed. I can guess just what anyone of your generous nature—"

"Oh I say," he protested, "please don't—" It was decent of her to credit him with generosity. There was nothing he liked better than being highly esteemed. But he wished she'd shut up. He stooped down and began to scratch the stouter of the two Sealyhams, who lay bolster-like, displaying a pink belly and waving short thick paws in the air. "I like your dogs," he said.

"I'm so glad. I shouldn't have liked you if you hadn't."

He looked up at her and they exchanged a smile.

"I want to ask your pardon," she said.

"What on earth for?" he stammered, tickling the terrier with such nervous vigour that she rolled about in an ecstasy.

"Well I'm afraid I'm always rather stiff with people at first," she explained, "until I know we're going to be good friends. Then I'm all right."

"I know you are," he declared with what gallantry he could summon. "I enjoyed that drive down to *our* village, and all the tales you told me."

"I'll tell you plenty more if you encourage me like that. We Welsh are famous talkers."

"Then why were you thinking of putting me off to-day?"

"Have a glass of sherry," she said, "while I tell you."

The decanter was of massive old cut glass and the sherry did it credit. As Dick sipped he warmed towards his cousin. Before he had emptied his glass he liked her as much as any middle-aged woman he had ever known.

"I breakfasted early," she said, "and went out before the others were down. There's a good deal of work with the poultry at this time of year you know. If I don't keep the men up to the mark they let half the chicks die of the gapes."

"I thought your sister-in-law was the poultry expert."

Gwenllian's smile disposed of that error. "She talks a lot about it. Well, I was busy till noon, so I didn't hear her and Frances making their plans for the day. Of course I thought they'd both be here to receive you. But when I came in, I found they'd gone over to Lady Llangattoc's—some stupid misreading of the engagement book. I'm dreadfully sorry it's happened."

"I'm not," said Dick, growing more at ease and able to pay compliments. "I'm glad, as long as you'll let me come again to-morrow?"

Luncheon was announced, and Gwenllian led the way across the hall, hung with trophies of hunt and battle and the travels of younger sons among savage people. The dining-room was large, more formal and less pleasing than the drawing-room. At first it seemed to Dick chilling that he and Gwenllian should eat alone at one end of so long a table, with two silent and watchful maids hovering over them; but half a bottle of the best claret he had ever drunk gave him confidence. The lamb, Gwenllian informed him, had been reared on the estate and roast in front of an open fire.

"I believe this is the last house in Wales where meat isn't thrust into an oven to bake," she declared. And when he was helping himself to pie, she spoke of the delicacy of her early forced rhubarb. "Such a vile stringy weed as most people eat it late in summer," she said. "Fit for trippers at a seaside boarding-house, like stewed prunes or tinned pears." Dick heartily agreed. The Einon-Thomas rhubarb melted in the mouth, and the vast loaf of bread that stood among the Georgian silver on the sideboard was another revelation to him. There were marks of wood ash upon it and, unlike baker's bread, it had positive flavour and moisture. It was surprising to discover that plain fare could be so good, for he had supposed that one could feed well only by paying a high price for dishes with French names.

"I say," he asked, when they were left alone, "how on earth do you get modem servants to do all these things in the old way?"

"I catch them when they leave school at fourteen," she answered, with a smile. "When once I've taught them that they know nothing whatever about anything, I can begin to train them."

"Sounds like shaking the raw recruit in the Service. But don't they desert?"

"Not once they're broken in," Gwenllian answered. "They begin to take a pride in the tradition of the house."

"What makes 'em stay at first?"

"Their parents. Plâs Einon still means something in this corner of the county. Frances's Labour friends are trying to set class against class, but they haven't succeeded in making our people look on us as enemies. The older ones know that for generations we've worked as hard as they—most of us, at any rate. We've kept them as well as ourselves in old age, long before L. G. was born or thought of. There's never been a faithful retainer we haven't pensioned off."

Dick watched the proud lift of her chin, and said to himself: I'm glad she's a relation of mine. Drinking his own excellent port and hearing his cousin talk thus, he felt every inch an Einon-Thomas.

His admiration for her grew throughout the afternoon. There was nothing she did not know, yet her knowledge never humiliated him. As she was showing him the dubious Romney of laughing great-aunt Lavinia, who went to London to see George the Fourth crowned and died there of the small-pox, she said: "You can't have had much time to spare for connoisseurship. How have you managed to learn so much about pictures and furniture and china?" "Oh, I don't know," he said, blushing with pleasure. "Fond of 'em, I suppose. But you know a lot more than I do."

"My dear Dick! I've had little else to do all my life; while you were fighting in the greatest war there's ever been."

He had made a mistake, he perceived, in avoiding middle-aged spinsters. The company of a well-informed woman, who wished to please, yet did not expect to be flirted with, was extremely comfortable, and he felt sorry that Cousin Gwen was to leave the neighbourhood so soon. He began to talk of the dower house, regretting that it was let. Gwenllian had some amusing tales to tell of its former occupants.

"But I'm boring you, perhaps," she asked, "with stories you already know?"

"Good Lord no," he assured her. "I know next to nothing about our family history."

"You have had every reason to think ill of us, too," she said. "Our treatment of your mother—"

He felt his face and neck grow hot. "Oh, well, I don't know. I suppose the old man had a right to cut off a son who married without his consent."

"When there was nothing against the match," Gwenllian protested, "except that the lady was not an heiress?" Dick stared at his feet. "That's true, isn't it?" she added gently. "Your mother hadn't much money of her own?"

"No," he said, "she hadn't." Was it possible that Cousin Gwen had never heard that his mother had been a nursery-governess whose father kept a chemist's shop?

"Of course," she continued, "Grandpapa belonged to the old school. When he was young the French Revolution was fresh in people's minds, and he had a horror of insubordination. He didn't marry until late in life, and brought up his children on the principles of his own boyhood. Father often told us how they never dared speak until spoken to, or sit down in his presence without his leave. He arranged a match between your father and Miss Emily Gwynne-Evans of Llanyre Abbey. She had a fortune of twelve hundred a year, which was handsome in those days. But she had the Gwynne-Evans impediment in her speech. One of her great uncles was promoted for the gallant stand his company made at Waterloo.

It was said in this neighbourhood that he'd given the order to retire, but that, as usual, his men hadn't been able to understand him."

"That's good," chuckled Dick.

"Anyhow, your father wouldn't marry the lady. Grandpapa was furious, but after a while he arranged another match which he fancied no sportsman could refuse. It was with Miss Lavinia Lloyd-Jones of Llandau Castle. She was the youngest of nine, and her fortune consisted of one diamond bracelet and a farm rented at eighteen pounds a year. But there were expectations from a godmother, and she was considered to have the most graceful seat on horseback of any lady in the county. Those were the days of long flowing habits, you know, when style was admired in the softer sex more than hard riding. Her mounts were trained to go straight from a walk into a canter so that Miss Lavinia might never be seen rising to anything so inelegant as a trot."

Dick guffawed. "I say," he interrupted, "you tell these old stories awfully well. And Father cut up rusty about the cantering lady, too?"

"Yes. Grandfather was livid with rage. So one day— Father used to make us laugh describing it, he was a gifted mimic, like so many Welshmen—the fierce old man stalked into this room where Grandmamma was going through her visiting list, preparing to send out invitations to an archery meeting, and Aunt Fanny was helping. ' Take paper and pen, child,' Grandpapa commanded; Aunt Fanny was thirty-six at the time. And when she had a pen in her hand, 'D'you know the name of every marriageable filly in every stable in the county?' he asked. 'Of every young maiden lady, Papa?' 'Yes, Miss Impudence! Don't mince words with me.

Do you, or do you not, eh? Can't you give a plain answer to a plain question, eh?' 'Yes Papa, I—I think so.' 'And I should think so too. What else do I provide you two ladies with a carriage and pair for? All this calling isn't likely to lead to a husband for yourself now, eh?' Poor Aunt Fanny hung her head, and Grandmamma took the smelling-salts out of her reticule. 'Well then,' the old tyrant went on, 'make me out a list of those who are still hopeful. See that it be writ legibly, and take heed you omit none.' When it was written in Aunt Fanny's exquisite Italian hand, he sent for your father. 'Now, Sir Hard-to-please,' he growled, 'here are Roses and Violets, and Marys and Margarets, and Henriettas and Harriets and Hannahs. You will go to the Hunt Ball next month.' 'But I don't dance, sir.' 'You will go to the Hunt Ball, d'you hear me? You'll see everyone of 'em there, waltzing for their living, as the late Lord Byron said. If you can't pick one of 'em out of the ring and get into double harness with her before the year is out, you shall have neither a father's blessing, nor a penny of his leavings.' But your father stayed at home on the night of the Hunt Ball. Grandmamma and Aunt Fanny drove off in tears. Grandpapa shut himself up in his study in a towering rage, but he could hear your father playing the piano—an instrument he despised as effeminate. And one of the tunes your father dared to play was— what *do* you think?—The Marseillaise!"

Dick laughed outright. "And what happened then?"

"He was packed off to a firm in Cheapside, through whom Grandpapa bought his Port. He came down here again only once, many years later, to announce his marriage to a lady— his own choice— a very pretty, charming one, I believe. Did you know that?"

"No," Dick said. "I was only seven when he died. Mother told me nothing except that he'd quarrelled with his family."

"Yes," Gwenllian said in a tone of sympathy. "It was terribly hard on your parents, and on you. And, unfortunately, Father became involved in the foolish unjust quarrel. But for that, of course, we should have made it up after Grandpapa's death." Dick scratched the Sealyham behind the ear and she knowingly put out the tip of her pink tongue. He and his mother had been all in all to each other, but he was glad that Cousin Gwen had never met her.

"It's a great pity," he said, secure in an ashamed knowledge that they could never meet now, "you and my poor Mater never got to know each other."

"Try to forgive us, will you?" said Gwenllian softly "If it's not too late?" His face burned, and she added in a lighter tone, "I forgot to point out the Richard Wilson in the dining-room. It's worth a lot. But I think I've managed to save so that you won't have to sell it to pay the death duties. By the way," she added, "don't think me impertinent— will you?—if I ask whether you have any debts?"

"No," he answered. "Never dared run 'em up." She smiled her approval at him. "Splendid. Now come and look at your most valuable picture."

The inspection of one led to another. They were half way up the wide, shallow stairs, jesting over their great aunts' watercolours, when Gwenllian exclaimed, "Oh, but I oughtn't to be taking the honours of show-woman on myself, while Cecily's out."

But the intimacy between them seemed now so well established that he urged her to show him the whole house. "I won't split on you tomorrow," he chuckled.

She laughed back at him. "All right. But we shall feel like two naughty children.…The pictures on the landing are only copies of Carlo Dolci and Sassoferrato. My mother's grandfather bought them in Rome when he was on his grand tour. A good many of our pictures came into the family from her side. That's her portrait, painted by John Collier not long before she died."

Dick saw a realistic painting of a very tired and faded lady. She was reclining on a green plush sofa, with her feet on a rest. Her hands were limp in her silken lap. Behind her was the striped wall-paper he had noticed in the drawing-room, less pale than it had now become.

"You're not a bit the same style of beauty as your mother," he hastened to say.

She smiled at him again. "No. I'm an Einon-Thomas."

Opening a door she led him into a severely furnished room. He glanced round it, noting the large roll-top desk, the shelves full of informative books, the pigeon-holes, the ordnance map. Her brother's room, he thought, and then: No, by Jove, hers!

A man would have caused more disorder, and have chosen more comfortable chairs.

"Father," said Gwenllian, indicating a large oil painting that dominated the room. "But it doesn't begin to do him justice. He was considered remarkably handsome. It was done by a local painter to be presented to the Shire Hall the year he was High Sheriff. I managed, with a lot of persuasion, to have this copy made. Nothing would induce him to sit again. He hated the tomfoolery as he called it. You can see from the expression how he disliked sitting." Dick looked at a muddy painting of a man with a heavy jowl and leaden brows. There was a tinge of purple in his cheeks. He was strongly built, with massive,

insensitive hands, which were clutching the stock of a shot-
gun. Dick resolved to banish the ugly thing to the attic or the
servants' hall.

"Not a flattering likeness, I should think," he said, for the
sake of being polite.

"It's an atrocious caricature," Gwenllian declared with an
anger that surprised him. If she didn't like it, why on earth did
she keep it here? And, answering his unspoken question, she
added "It's all I have of him." After a silence, she asked
suddenly: "Would you mind very much if I took it away with
me?" Well, thank God, that disposes of *that,* he thought.

"Naturally you must have anything—" he began

"Oh," she said, "but I must have your authority for moving
even a pin." She went close to the portrait and stared up at it,
twisting her hands together.

"You see, when Father had his stroke and made that will a
couple of months before the end, Cecily was expecting her
first baby. So was Evan's wife, too, as it happened. She died,
you know, and they couldn't save the infant. And then, just
after Father's death, Cecily—" Gwenllian paused. "Poor
Cecily's been unlucky. All her children have been born dead
or have died a few days later."

"Good Lord," exclaimed Dick, "I'd no idea."

"No," she said, with that downward twist of the lips which
had startled him at their first meeting, "Neither had Father
when he made his will."

Dick's face was burning. He could think of nothing to say.

"I believe Father was right, though, to do as he did," she
declared in a fierce tone. "It's only by leaving every sou to
heirs male, and demanding sacrifices of the others, that any
property can be held together in these days of murderous

taxation. We have been here since the legendary days of Welsh history. English people with French names who are proud of having 'come over with the Conqueror' can't show a pedigree that compares with ours. We fought the Romans, and the Saxons after them, and held on to our own. We can't go down now before a rabble of little Socialists, blustering in the House of Commons." He was startled by her vehemence. "Frances and I profoundly disagree. Her reforms would lead to the old families being yet more impoverished, the great houses and parks and gardens broken up. They used to be the glory of England. Now, because everybody clamours for an equal share, they are to be turned into chicken farms and allotments, covered with barbed wire and tin shanties. And all the art treasures stored in them are to be sold to the Jews and resold to America. It makes me *sick* to think of!" She was pale and bitter.

"I quite agree with you," Dick muttered, anxious to soothe her. It seemed to him extraordinary for a woman, who was out of the running herself, to be so passionate about property. But very unselfish, he told himself, very creditable.

"I'm afraid I grow rather warm on the subject," she said, after a pause. "It seems to me so base to be the weak link in a long chain—the first poor soft thing to let it break."

"I suppose a chain is a bit of a drag on some people," he said vaguely.

Her chin went up. "Oh, the *weak* links feel the strain, I dare say…"

Somehow that phrase made him ill at ease. He began urging her again to take her father's portrait.

Gwenllian's lips parted eagerly. "I'm not sure, though," she sighed, "that I want to take anything which belongs here, out of its setting. Don't think me ungrateful, please Dick, but I would rather not until I've had time to think it over... Some day, perhaps, I'll remind you of your generous offer."

Oh Lord, he thought, does that mean I've got to keep this hideous relic here until she makes up her mind?

"Now," she said, in her usual brisk tone, "you'd better go before the others return. Remember, tomorrow, not a word about our conspiracy." She smiled at him, a mischievous smile that made her look years younger. "Poor Cecily must be allowed the distinction of telling you all she knows, or imagines she knows, about our home."

Dick nodded. Cousin Gwen's an astonishing able woman, he told himself as he drove away. I like her, too. And she can be made devilish useful if I play my cards right.

Chapter VI

SHE DECIDES HIS FUTURE

The children's quarters were on the second floor of Plâs Einon, separated by stairs and a winding passage from the body of the house and by a pair of baize-covered doors from the attics where servants slept and lumber was stored. Here Gwenllian could be almost as safe from interruption as among her yew trees. In the old schoolroom she might put off her mask of composure and be free of her own mind.

For an hour she had been pacing up and down among the relics of her girlhood, finding in them a torment and an obscure consolation. She knew that she must be parted from them and from all that they represented; she knew it, but in their presence could not finally believe and accept it; and there was something delicious—a suspension of pain—in that unbelief. There was time yet. If she had been a woman of softer character, she would have added: Something will happen to save me. To her, tantalising hope presented itself differently. There is still something I may do, she said, and though her reason told her she was powerless, she felt within her that there was something she would do.

What bound her to this room was what she herself had done and made. Frances, on the rare occasions when she visited the schoolroom, would examine the pictures and laugh over them, remembering her favourites, rekindling old affections. But Gwenllian cared little for the ringleted children with their baskets of roses and their collie dogs, or for the Coronation of Queen Victoria, or for Nelson's too theatrical Death. Nelson had treated women as men always treated them—sometimes callously, sometimes sentimentally, but always to his own advantage. There was little difference between him and the rest. And as for the Bath of Psyche, which amused Frances with her modern ideas about art, Gwenllian remembered only that, if ever her father came to the schoolroom, he stared at it and would take no notice of the things she wanted him to admire. That little table, for example. She crossed the room and fingered it. How small it had grown since she made it! She lifted it up, remembering how heavy it had once seemed. It had been intended to stand beside her father's chair for him to keep his pipes on, but when she had offered it to him he had laughed—perhaps because he wasn't listening or hadn't understood what she said—and here it had stayed. How proud she had been of it! Her old crony, the estate carpenter, had stood by smiling while she insisted that the work must be all her own.

Trying to drag her thoughts out of the past and to direct her mind to her present necessity, she turned away from the table. At any rate, I have his confidence, she said, recollecting her little triumph of two days ago. If she postponed her visits and lingered in the neighbourhood, he would often come to her for advice. That would be something. That would be something, she repeated, feeling her way... But would it? She'd not deceive herself. There would be nothing but bitterness and disappointment in haunting her old home, without place in it, without authority. She might rule him while he was new to it and alone, but soon, very soon, he'd marry some young girl. Then there'd be no holding him.

These silly, pretty girls to whom power came without effort! She despised men for the ignorance and unfairness of their awards. She began to pull out here and there a drawer from the cabinet in which, years ago, she made her collection of birds' eggs—better than Evan's, better than Howel's, who was too clumsy to blow an egg without breaking it. Beside the cabinet hung a map of South Africa stuck with paper flags on rusty pins, still marking the position of Boer and British troops at the moment when her interest in the war had ceased. Each of these incidents of her childhood had been a thread on a closely woven fabric which, in a few days, would be torn uncompleted from the loom. This was the pattern of her life; she could make no other; she must preserve it. There must still be a way to preserve it.

She went to the window and opened it. Rain lashed in. The trees below were tossing their heads.

It was an angry, crying day; and she wished that she could be out on the hills, listening to the shrilling of the seabirds as they were swept inland. But in half-an-hour she must be composed and tidy to welcome Dick and the solicitor. Half-an-hour. She had no plan.

"Go on! Go on!" she said aloud, turning sharply from the window. There were footsteps in the passage; they seemed to check at the school- room door. "Go on!" she whispered. "Can't you leave me alone? Can't you leave me!" But the white china knob was turning—the loose knob that must be repaired—and Frances came in.

"Hello," she exclaimed, "I didn't know you were here. Am I disturbing you?"

"Of course not, my dear. But what brought you here?" Gwenllian asked, forcing a smile. "You were always in rebellion against Miss Dodds. I thought you disliked the scene of your shame."

Frances looked about her and made a grimace. "Oh I never really disliked Doddy," she answered. "But I knew the poor old thing's teaching was a farce. You were lucky to escape it—taking on the house-keeping so young." And, going to the bookshelves, she began to laugh. "Heavens! What in- credible survivals of the eighteenth century our parents were! They paid their butler three times the salary they gave the decayed gentlewoman supposed to educate their daughters! No science, no mathematics, no economics—nothing that gave us the least inkling of the world in which we were going to live."

"I taught myself what I wanted to know," Gwenllian said.

"Yes," Frances protested, "but people needn't positively hinder girls from finding out the truth about anything. It isn't so long ago since our parents did that to us. Yet here are Stanley and I pawning the last of our wedding presents to give Gill as good an education as her brothers. Heaven knows, girls' schools are still stupid enough, but at least parents aren't as blind as they were."

Gwenllian hated Frances when she spoke in dis- paragement of the past. "What will be the result of her expensive education?" she asked. "Probably she'll marry a poor man, as you did, and wish you'd taught her to be a good domestic servant."

"Oh but she *is* learning more practical things than ever I did, cooped up here," Frances answered.

"That may be. But you weren't intended to marry as you did. You were educated for your own position in life. It was your choice to abandon it. Gill won't be able to choose."

"She may not wish to marry," Frances said. "You think my married life has been one of degradation, don't you?" she added with a good- humoured smile. "Well Gill may think so too. There are other careers open to her now."

Gwenllian tried to conceal her contempt. Frances had always talked nonsense since, as a young girl, she had gone to stay with friends in London of whom her father disapproved and had refused to return. She had taken a post in the secretariat of a suffrage organisation, and persisted in her view that life in a comfortless hostel at twenty-five shillings a week was "glorious freedom." After a year or two, she had become engaged to marry a young naval officer without means or prospects, and was married, "like any little shorthand typist," in a London church of which no-one had ever heard. Since then, she had moved from lodging to lodging in the home ports, surrounded, as Gwenllian said, by fumed oak and bamboo. She had three children and was happy. She would be, Gwenllian thought, and despised her the more for her happiness. When she had visited Frances in Southsea, it had entered her mind that her sister was an echo, perhaps, of some forgotten note of ill-breeding far away in the Einon-Thomas pedigree. If Frances hadn't been born one of us, she said to herself, she might have become a popular barmaid. I can imagine her, with that wide smile and high colour and altogether excessive amount of hair, leaning over a counter, chatting amicably to all and sundry. And Gwenllian looked now at the good-humoured woman beside her with the mingled disdain and envy that many a virgin feels for a "joyful mother of children."

"I suppose," she said, "that you'll bring Gill up to your own ideas until she thinks, as you do, that I'm half-criminal to have spent my life in keeping the property together."

It was useless, Frances knew, to argue with Gwenllian when she was in this angry mood of defence and self-justification. Argument would widen the breach between them—a strange breach, Frances said within her, for we are more alike than many sisters, alike in appearance, alike in our streak of fanaticism. But all Gwen's fanaticism has dragged her inward and inward on to the property; she's given up everything for that. And mine has forced me outward, away from this property and all property. I want my life to be an adventure, full of love. I've flung away everything else—even things beautiful in themselves—things I do love and prize, though Gwen thinks I don't see the value of them— for fear they'd become more precious than human affections—growth— change of ideas. She wants her life to be set, like a frozen stream. There must be no warmth in it, for then the stream would melt, and begin to flow, and carry her away. I want my life to flow and carry me away.

Poor Cousin Dick, she thought. I wonder what he wants. I don't suppose he knows. Probably he thinks he can have it both ways—property, without going to prison in it. He ought to look at Gwenllian; she's serving a life-sentence.

"That young cousin of ours will be here directly," she said aloud. "What did you make of him? He didn't strike me as over intelligent."

"What makes you say that?" Gwenllian asked. She was sore against her sister and quick to resent whatever she might say. Why should she criticise Dick? He was not more undistinguished than her penniless husband and was at least free of Stanley's socialistic delusions. "What do you see wrong in him?" she insisted.

"Stupidly conventional, I thought," Frances answered.

"More so even than most Army men. He didn't utter a word that suggested his ever having faced a problem for himself since he was born."

"He's been too busy fighting to spare as much time for meditation as some of your subversive friends," retorted Gwenllian. "Men who preferred a safe prison to the front line seem to impress you more than a soldier."

Frances laughed. How perversely young she still looked, in spite of her three children! "Your attitude to the head of the house has undergone a quick change, hasn't it?" she said. "You could scarcely bring yourself to shake hands with him the first day he called."

Gwenllian bit her lip. She must not be provoked into confessing the secret friendship between herself and Dick. "Naturally I hated the idea of handing all this over to a stranger," she said, as casually as possible. "But since I've heard him talking to Cecily, I've ceased to dislike him."

"Oh," Frances interjected, "one can't *dislike* the boy. He's so inoffensive."

Her sister's tone roused Gwenllian yet further to his defence. "Well, I thought he showed great good sense in not laying down the law as so many of your young friends do," she answered, and she added tartly, "You expect people to be original, or at least to be forever showing off, like pert children who need smacking."

"Like my own, I know you mean," laughed Frances.

Gwenllian disregarded the interruption, though it increased her anger. "I prefer a young man to have some modesty and reticence," she said, and, in an excited tone cried out: "Here he comes." Dick was climbing out of his car, and, the window being open, she leaned out. It was his small, slightly receding

chin that had given him an air of indecision, but the collar of
his coat was now turned up and she could see only the upper
part of his face. Though his nose, straight and short, might
have been called pretty in a girl, and his cheeks, stung by the
wind, were a girlish pink, he looked more soldierly than
before. He carried his head well, his shoulders were square,
and set back. He had evidently been drilled. Gwenllian
approved of his brisk movements as he helped his passenger
to alight. His appearance of fragile youth was made the more
pleasing by its contrast with the sallow complexion and stiff
gestures of the lawyer, who now emerged from the car.

Mr. Price had been for years her tongue-tied adorer. She
had thought the family solicitor beneath her consideration as
a husband, but remained woman enough to enjoy masculine
admiration. Poor little Price, she mused, looking down on him
with compassion. If I had ever given him the least
encouragement, he would have proposed to me. He would
still, I believe. But she turned her gaze from him with distaste.
He looked like a tallow candle that had melted into a crooked
droop, as he mounted the steps beside her cousin.

Frances had joined her at the window. "You mustn't think
I've a down on that harmless boy," she said.

"He's not a boy," Gwenllian answered.

"Well, youth then. He's so undeveloped, so like a nice little
pink fledgling, you can't call him a man."

"Nonsense, Frances! He's twenty-eight; and he has a fine
war record."

"I never heard of it."

Gwenllian's smouldering resentment blazed into fire. Her
eyes flashed at her sister. "Why must you always disparage
people who do their duty? If anyone's sent to prison, you're

the first to defend him. But you grudge a word of praise to a loyal soldier. If Dick were some long-haired poet, you wouldn't try to find fault with him."

Frances tried to protest, but Gwenllian rode her down.

"You've no use for loyalty—to country or to family tradition. But, thank goodness, Dick isn't one of your moderns. He knows he has a lot to learn. And he wants to be taught."

"Well, if it's his modest ambition to be moulded into the traditional Einon-Thomas shape," Frances retorted, "he couldn't go to a better teacher than yourself." And turning away to light a cigarette, she added with a careless laugh, "Why don't you marry him?"

Gwenllian leaned out into the rain. The pungent, moist scent of the earth and the trees she loved almost made her cry aloud with emotion. She would have known from any other smell in the world that of the ferny dingle below her father's house. There is that one way, she thought. Strange that Frances should have shown it to her. He was weak; and suddenly she felt very strong, stronger than she had ever been and more resolute. The rain was cooling her forehead and the parting of her hair. Dick could make her mistress of Plâs Einon. She clasped her hands, gathering her strength together. There was a singing in her ears, like the shrill sound of wind in telegraph wires. She knew now what she must do.

"Well, why not?" Frances mocked.

But Gwenllian was not touched by her mockery. I can make him do what I wish, she was thinking. She closed the window and latched it; then crossed the schoolroom towards the door.

"You had better come down to meet him, too," she said.

"In a moment," Frances replied. She was on her knees

beside the bookshelf, turning over the leaves of an old picture book.

"Don't forget your cigarette," Gwenllian said. It was smouldering on the edge of the table. It might start a blaze not easy to put out.

Chapter VII

HE ACCEPTS HER DECISION

Throughout the summer Dick spent many instructive hours in Gwenllian's company and was grateful to her for teaching him a landowner's craft. Their relationship was easy and unruffled. In a motherly way she showed affection for him, and it did not seem to him at all strange that she should stay all these months at the Vicarage and have reason to visit Plâs Einon every day. She was a well-informed, sensible woman, and he was always glad to see her.

It was Lewis Vaughan, the noisy tenant of Llanddwy Hall, who disturbed his peace of mind.

"She's set her cap at you," Vaughan assured him.

"Rot—at her time of life!"

"She's only forty. A dangerous age. You'd better look out."

"Oh, you go to hell," Dick replied. He enjoyed using such familiar speech to other country gentlemen. But few were as friendly as Vaughan, whom Gwenllian considered a bounder. "I ought to know my own cousin. She's harmless enough. Fond of the old place, that's all."

"And of its new owner, so they were saying at the County Club yesterday."

Dick made a gesture of impatience but he was secretly flattered. "We get on pretty well," he said. "That's all there is to it. And why shouldn't we? We're interested in the same things and we're first cousins."

"You'll look more like aunt and nephew, if she catches you."

"D'you think I'm such a fool as to be caught?" Dick raised his voice because his confidence was a little shaken. "I shall marry a peach, I can tell you, when I've had time to look round."

He put away drink that night. Vaughan's cellar was well stocked and there were no ladies present. Next morning, when he awoke with a headache, he was ashamed of having boasted of his experience of women more freely than would have been possible if he had been sober... Poor old Gwen! He ought not to have discussed her with that cad. She was quite right to despise the fellow; he wasn't of the same class as the Einon-Thomases. He didn't even own the house he lived in, and his people had made their money in trade. Gwen's my own flesh and blood, said Dick to himself. I won't have it said that she's husband-hunting.

But it's true, he reflected, that she has taken to dressing better since she went into half-mourning, and he remembered, almost with alarm, that he had lately begun to admire her hair. Had it always been waved? Surely not. Why, then... That simpering goose, the vicar's wife, must think there was something between them, for whenever he visited the Vicarage she would leave them alone together. But Mrs. Evans was a busybody; and as for the County Club—well, the Army had been bad enough, but, for malicious gossip, a quiet country district was hard to beat! He'd pay no attention to any of 'em. Still, what Vaughan had said wasn't pleasant. Perhaps for Gwenllian's sake, he had better clear out for a bit. So he went to London, and did not reply to her letters.

For a week after his return, he avoided meeting her. Staring at her pretty grey hat in church on Sunday morning, he wondered whether he had been unkind. She might not understand that he was protecting her from gossip. A new hat? he thought during the Creed. It was the smartest he had ever seen her wear. Poor Gwen, how she'd hate leaving the neighbourhood! Her becoming hat and the handsome, decisive profile beneath it consoled him for a dull sermon. He'd miss her when she was gone. After the service, he found her in the graveyard. "Hullo, Gwen!"

"Hullo, Dick. You've been a long time in ' foreign parts.' Weeks and weeks."

"Oh, I say. It was only two."

She did not say that it had seemed longer to her, but he had little doubt of what was in her mind. She had missed him, and it was years since anyone had missed him. Her unanswered letters smote his conscience.

"And why haven't you called on poor Mrs. Parson Evans and me, and given us your news of London?"

He grinned. "I never thought there were two ladies in the world who took so much interest in my doings."

"You knew there was one," she said so that he did not know whether she was still teasing him or in earnest; and when the doctor's wife came up with a gush of enquiry for his *adventures*, though he was glad that her coming relieved him of embarrassment, he was annoyed with her for having inter-rupted Gwenllian.

"I haven't been to London for seven years," Mrs. Roberts cooed complacently. "They poison you in the hotels and restaurants. I do like to know what I'm eating, don't you? Weren't you glad to escape from the horrid place alive?"

"Can't say I was," Dick answered. "I wish I could have stayed for a few more shows."

"I don't believe you," she said looking very knowing and holding her head on one side. "We're sure he couldn't bear to stay away any longer from the charming society he enjoys down here, aren't we, Gwenllian?"

Silly ass! Dick thought. Here was yet another of them on the same track! And when she had trotted away, pleased to have caused embarrassment of the kind that was supposed to forward match making, he was left cross and ill at ease.

"Dick," Gwenllian said simply, "you know I'm leaving this week?"

"No! So soon? That's too bad."

"It won't be any easier two months hence—or two years," she answered. "I'm determined at last to get it over, and not to trade on your kindness by hanging about the place like a ghost any longer." He made deprecating noises. "No," she insisted, "you've been a brick." He liked her best when she talked like this, with a frank affection that seemed to ask no return. But her next remark was disconcerting. "I'd like, though, to spend the afternoon taking a last look round with you."

"Today?" he asked.

"If you don't mind. I mayn't have the heart as the time for going draws nearer."

"But I'm afraid I've got the Williamses—the old lady and those two pretty daughters from the place with the unpronounceable name—coming to tea. Lewis Vaughan threatened to drop in too. He's keen on the younger one, Megan."

"Is he?" asked Gwenllian, her dark brows raised ironically. "I heard that you were."

"Oh, rot! Who told you?"

"Never mind. I heard all about your playing tennis with her and no-one else at Lady Llangattoc's."

"She's a good player."

"Was that why you took her into the kitchen garden to gather gooseberries after tea?"

Dick was flattered by any woman's jealousy, even though he supposed it to be no more than half serious. "Sorry the lovely Megan's being there this afternoon will spoil the party for you," he grinned.

"I don't want a party at all," Gwenllian said gravely. "Don't you understand? I want to say good-bye."

His mood of complacency was dashed. "I understand," he murmured. "I say, I'm awfully sorry, my dear."

For a minute or two they were silent, nodding to the villagers who passed the churchyard on their way home from the chapels. Then she asked, "May I walk back with you now to lunch, and leave before your guests come?"

"Of course you may," Dick had to answer.

As they walked together towards Plâs Einon, he admired the courage with which she recounted anecdotes it must have hurt her to recall.

"I remember so well the first time I played hostess at a shooting party," she said. "Mother was ill. She was a great invalid, you know, but Father wouldn't have the guests put off. And it was to be a married couples' party—lots of formidable wives. I was only just sixteen. I put up my hair for the occasion, and was terrified of its falling down and giving me away. Of course they all knew that I wasn't out, but they played up with great gravity, and so did I. I wore a gown of Mother's—lavender moiré with black velvet bows at intervals down the front. There was a vast difference between a school-girl's dress and a grown-up lady's in those days. What trouble I had with the train! And I hung myself, like a Christmas tree, with *all* the family amethysts." She had made Dick laugh, and his suspicions were lulled. "I sat up half the night before, getting people's relations off by heart in Burke, in case I should make a mistake in precedence, and I nearly drove the poor old cook out of her wits with last minute improvements of the menu. The servants tried to treat me as a joke, but I put that down with a firmness which has stood me in good stead ever since. *Can't* one take oneself seriously at sixteen?" Dick had a vision of himself at that age, very secretly and ineffectually, trying to grow the first blond hairs of his moustache. He used still to be caned at a time of life when she was learning to be a hostess.

"How did your *tamasha* go off?" he enquired.

"So well that father gave me a whole half-sovereign—a golden half-sovereign! It was riches to me, I can tell you. I had only twenty-four pounds a year to dress on even after I came out."

"Good Lord! I thought girls in your position spent that on a single frock."

"Not when they have two brothers at Eton and a mortgaged estate."

"But there's no mortgage on it now."

"No."

He bit his lip, realising, as never before, how much she had sacrificed for the home from which he, a stranger, had turned her out.

"You might let me come back to sit at the head of the table once in a way," she said giving him a wistful look, "if you give any but stag parties in the shooting season. I'd come from wherever I was." He promised to send for her, and together they turned in through the drive gates under a golden shower of falling beech leaves. Dick was reminded with half humorous misgiving of the flowers that used to be strewn before a bride and bridegroom; and like a small boy he shuffled through the dead leaves, kicking them aside. The lodge-keeper, seeing his former mistress pass, darted out after her, crying, "Well indeed, Miss Gwennie, 'tis good to catch a sight o' your dear face again! We've all o' us old 'uns been moping here the last few days, like a lot o' poor sheep with the rot and no shepherd. Wherever was you gone, Miss?"

"I was only shut up in the Vicarage, Isaac, hardening my heart to go."

"Oh *duwch*!" he wailed, raising gnarled hands to heaven. And there he stood disregarding his new master, throwing his arms about like a thorn tree in a gale. "Oh, goodness gracious!" And he broke into a lament in his own tongue. Gwenllian could speak Welsh as fluently as he. Her voice became more resonant and flexible when she spoke the language of her race. Dick had often been amused to hear her in dramatic conversation with the people.

Now as he listened to the dirge to which she was supplying mournful responses, he grew ashamed of being present. "I damned well *ought* to marry her," he told himself, "or give her back this place. She's a right to it—almost." He tried to put the idea from him, but throughout luncheon it persisted, making him uneasy.

The meal was not a good one. When Powell, the parlourmaid, was handing a burnt sago pudding, she murmured in Gwenllian's ear, "Cook's terrible upset, Miss, she didn't have warning you were expected. She'd have had something more suitable, if she'd known."

"Tell her I expect her to do as well for her new master as she did for me," Gwenllian answered.

Powell flushed, and Dick scowled at his plate. He wished that he knew, as Gwen did, just how to be friendly with servants when it was expedient, and how to put them again in their place.

When he and she were in the drawing-room, drinking coffee out of the fluted Worcester cups, she remarked, "You've changed the blend."

"Not my orders," he grumbled. "The coffee's been rotten lately. I don't know why."

She sipped, wrinkling her nose. "They've palmed off some cheap ready-ground blend on you."

"D'you think that's it?"

She gave him a pitying smile. "I'm sure of it... I always think it takes a lady to arrange flowers," she added.

He looked sheepishly at the dahlias, crushed into vases by a servant's hands. "Perhaps I ought to try and do 'em myself now," he said.

"But you're far too busy with the estate," she answered. "You will have to employ a responsible woman to relieve you of all household cares. By the way, I hear you're losing Annie?"

"Yes," he said, frowning. And the thought crossed his mind that a fellow need not regard himself as specially quixotic who married a good housekeeper, even though she were a few years older than himself. A good housekeeper was needed as mistress of such an old-fashioned place as Plâs Einon, he thought, and he wondered whether a young girl like Megan Williams would ever be able to cope with it. The lamps had smelt and smoked abominably since he had come to live here. When he rang for a fire in his study on cold evenings, the logs were damp and would not kindle. Powell was for ever coming to tell him that cook had forgotten to order this or that. Neither the grocer's nor the butcher's cart would be calling again for three days: would he please send the car seven miles into Llanon for five mutton chops or an ounce of pepper?

"Annie's gone to pieces since you left," he told Gwenllian. "I used to think her a rattling good cook."

"So she is, with judicious management."

"That's all very fine," he growled. "But when I tried to ginger her up, she burst into tears and gave notice."

Gwenllian smiled. "You need firm but very light hands with these spirited Welsh cobs."

"You seemed able to master 'em all right," he sighed. "They bolt with me, whether I try the curb or the snaffle."

"Would you like me to make Annie stay?"

"Indeed I would—if it's on to do. It mayn't be easy to find another cook who'll stay in the depths of the country in a stone-flagged kitchen as big as a barn."

"Very well," and she went towards the door with that quiet decision of movement which he most admired in her.

While she was gone, he smoked cigarette after cigarette in nervous haste, thinking of her, now with gratitude, now with envy of her ability, now with pity, because she was poor and homeless, and sometimes with mistrust. He would look a fool if he were to marry her after his boasts to Lewis Vaughan. Yet she was handsome; she was fond of him; she'd make the place comfortable.

When she returned, there was a becoming flush on her cheeks. Her large dark eyes were bright and soft. Dick stared at her in admiration. How her looks varied, and, with them, his feelings towards her!

"Annie's staying," she exclaimed, "and she's promised to turn over a new leaf."

"I say, you're a wonder! How on earth did you do it?"

"Oh," Gwenllian said, "I scolded her in Welsh and made her cry. And then, at the sight of the old kitchen with its copper and brass skillets arranged as it was when I was a child, I'm afraid I cried a bit too." She gave a husky little laugh. "Powell joined in, and the housemaids, and the kitchen-maid— like the chorus in *The Trojan Women*. Altogether we gave a most affecting performance."

She was trying to speak lightly, but he could see that she was deeply moved. His sense of obligation towards her increased. Too agitated to sit down, she went over to the French windows and stood looking out upon the lawns.

"Don't let them get mossy, Dick," she entreated. "I managed to fight moss and plantains even during the war, when one felt it wasn't right to put men on a job like that. The true patriots about here ploughed up their. tennis courts to grow potatoes; but I stuck at that. I did everything else we were supposed to do, but I wasn't going to have the beauty of Plâs Einon spoiled. Oh, and Dick," she said, after a pause, turning to look at him with eyes still brightened by emotion, "you know that picture of father you offered to give me? I told you I'd think it over. I'm sure now I'd rather it stayed where it belongs." The drawing-room faced west. At this hour of day it was radiant with October sunshine filtering in through the golden leaves of the beech trees. Close to the windows were beds of chrysanthemums, amber and orange and rich russet-red. A reflection of their colour, like warm kind firelight cast a glow on Gwenllian's face. She is lovely still, Dick thought. In that gentle grey dress, which he liked for reasons deeply buried in his childhood, she was more feminine, and more desirable by far than he had ever supposed her to be.

"I—I wish you'd accept a few presents from me," he stammered. "It's awfully unselfish of you, and all that. But, don't you see, it makes me feel pretty rotten?"

"I can't spoil Plâs Einon, Dick dear," she interrupted him with quivering lips, "not even to please you. Don't ask me to destroy my picture of it —the picture I shall carry with me always in my heart, wherever I go, whatever I may do—my Plâs Einon—with each detail precisely as it is to-day, as it was when father was still living."

She could say no more. With consternation, Dick saw her handsome face crumple into a grimace of misery. She hid it in her hands. Her fingers writhed; her shoulders were shaken with sobs.

"Gwen," he gasped, "Gwen, for God's sake, don't cry like that!" He had never been able to endure a woman's tears, even when they were facile and their cause was mere pettishness. And Gwen was not weeping for nothing. She was brave and self-controlled. Her breaking down thus, melted him to pity because she was a woman; it shocked him also, as though she had been a man. He patted her on the back and made incoherent noises of sympathy and comfort. But she continued to sob, hard sobs that tore her whole body. At last he put his arm round her.

"Gwen," he implored, "do stop. Do, please, *please* stop, there's a dear, good girl! I'll do anything—*anything*—"

Suddenly she twisted herself round and hid her wet, distorted face against his shoulder. She had to stoop a little. He held her close. She was warm and surprisingly soft; grief-stricken and a woman. His heart began to beat fast. He felt his neck burning as though he had sat too near a fire.

"Dick, I can't bear it." The sound of her voice was muffled by his coat. "You don't know—all this place has meant to me—all that I've given up because of it. I think it will kill me—leaving."

"Then don't leave, my dear," he blurted out "Are you listening? Stay on."

He felt her shiver and press still closer to him. "How can I?"

He moistened his lips with the tip of his tongue, seeking for words. Her shivering increased, and he said, "You might marry me, for instance." He thought that sounded a weak proposal. A man ought to be ardent and passionate. He tried again. "I'd be awfully glad if you would, you know."

She drew a long, quivering breath, and her crying ceased.

"Will you?" he asked after a pause during which she had released him and brought out a pocket handkerchief. She was making small, angry noises, blowing her nose. He felt less hot and excited now that he no longer held her in his arms. She looked round at him at last, her cheeks pale, her eyelids pink and swollen. Her face seemed to have aged. It wore a strained, anxious expression.

"Oh, Dick," she said, "*dear* Dick!"

He took her hand limply. Her fingers gripped his with convulsive eagerness.

"For better for worse, for richer for poorer, in sickness and in health, till death us do part." The sombre words of the marriage service tolled in his brain. "Good Lord," he thought, "that's final!"

Half-an-hour later Mrs. Williams was announced. She

marched in dressed in tweeds, brogues and woollen stockings, but her two daughters were light and gay in frocks that reminded Dick pleasantly of the vanished summer. They were both ready to flirt with any man, particularly with so eligible a bachelor as the new owner of Plâs Einon; but the elder had a good-natured air of withholding the full battery of her smiles and glances in favour of her sister. She and her stout fool of a mother, thought Dick with irritation, seemed to imagine that he had compromised Megan with his attentions—as though a fellow couldn't say a civil word to anyone without being tied to her for life! He sat on a sofa beside Megan and felt angry and a fool. On the ladies' heels came Lewis Vaughan. Every speech showed that he was determined not to let his new neighbour cut him out. Mrs. Williams smiled discreetly, and Gwenllian smiled also, watching the farce. Vaughan persisted in paying Megan compliments and in trying to monopolise her in conversation, but she turned away from him to Dick. Her mother and her sister alternately came to her aid, attempting by flank attacks to keep Vaughan from interfering between the young lovers. At tea-time they drew together round the table and there fell an embarrassing silence. All at once Gwenllian set down the silver teapot, folded her hands in her lap, and smiled at Dick with undisguised tenderness.

"Dick," she said, speaking in a clear voice, "shall we tell them our news?"

He saw four pairs of eyes turn, startled, from Gwen's face to his own. "Yes," he said, because it would have been ungentlemanly to answer, "No! For heaven's sake don't rush me into it like this!" While she told them, he sat rigid on the edge of his chair, aware of his two hands and his two feet, and wondering what the hell to do with them all. He suffered inside from the hollow sensation he had once experienced in a lift that was dropping too fast. How humiliating it was to be so very very hot!

When she had made public his engagement to her, he stole a glance at each of the listeners' faces before they had had time to assume the mask of politeness. Lewis Vaughan was contemptuously amused, glad to be free of a rival to better game. Mrs. Williams was very angry, her bland mouth for once tight shut.

"Fancy throwing over my lovely little girl for a dried old spinster," Dick fancied her exclaiming. The elder Miss Williams was disappointed and embarrassed, avoiding her sister's eye. And Megan, with whom he had flirted so enjoyably, who had seemed such a good-natured girl, gave him a look of disgust.

"I say," he exclaimed, jumping up and seizing the first plate of cakes that came to hand, "you're not eating anything, any of you."

At that, with an awkward rush, they broke out into smiling congratulations.

Chapter VIII

HE AND SHE FACE LIFE TOGETHER

Call on Gwen he must, Dick told himself next day. He went down to the village on foot, that the going might be longer. Swerving, irresolute, into the general store, he bought a ball of string he did not need and lingered to turn over a pile of fly-blown postcards. Some of them represented actresses dressed in pre-war fashion. How silly such finery seemed now —those tucked blouses, those flowers and feathers in the cart-wheel hats! Three little children' came into the shop and stared up at him, solemn as owls.

"Like some sweets?" he asked.

The eldest dimpled, but the toddler hid its face in her pinafore.

"Let's have six penn'orth of those," Dick said, pointing to a large bottle of coagulated raspberry drops. When they had been dug out with a knife, he thrust them into the little girl's palm.

"Go on! Eat them! Don't be shy!"

He would have liked to suck one himself. They used to be a solace at school. But the stout woman behind the counter was watching him. She nudged her husband and winked.

"The Captain 'ud like to stand the whole world treat to-day," she chuckled.

What the hell…! Dick thought.

"Our Megan's in service at the Vicarage," she continued,

beaming at him. "She was telling us last night as we might look for a happy event."

Dick muttered something and hurried out into the road. Women were watching him from cottage doorways. He almost ran past them. But once safe inside the Victorian Gothic porch of the Vicarage, he began to loiter, staring at the bicycle, the perambulator and the goloshes. When at last he had pulled the bell, its faint tinkling at the end of a long passage sounded mournfully in his ears.

In the empty drawing-room he gazed at the photographs of plain people ranged upon the upright piano, and wondered why ebonized furniture had been fashionable about the time his mother was married. Ugly stuff! Then he heard footsteps approaching. They were a woman's, light, swift, decisive. He braced himself to smile. She opened the door and, closing it softly behind her, leaned against it.

"Hello," he said.

And she said, "Dick!"

He saw that her embarrassment was as painful as his own. It was a bond of sympathy between them. He took a step towards her. She smiled nervously and looked down at her tightly clasped hands.

"I've come to ask you up to tea," he stammered, "at Plâs Einon."

Then she looked at him, smiling, with tears in her eyes, and he was moved to pity—she looked so very grateful. How she must love him! Poor Gwen, he thought, dear Gwen! I'll be jolly kind to her. And hurriedly he gave her cheek an awkward little kiss.

He had hoped that the continuance of Gwen's half-mourning might enable her bridegroom to escape publicity. Didn't she think they might be quietly married at once? he asked, wishing her to suppose that ardour was the reason of his haste. She was not reluctant. "Then I could wear my going-away dress—no wedding gown and so forth. Yes, it would save a lot of expense." A woman economising on her trousseau surprised him, and he told himself that she was doing it for his sake; but the explanation was not quite satisfactory. He didn't know what to believe, so swift and so conflicting were her decisions.

There would be no reception after the wedding: she agreed to that. But no sooner had he escaped this ordeal than he was faced by another. Friends might be denied their entertainment and champagne, but tenants and retainers must have their customary tea and be allowed to make their traditional speeches.

"Good Lord! But why?" asked Dick.

"Because, dear, they always have. And they're planning a presentation. The parish is frenzied with excitement about it. The illuminated-address-and-rose-bowl party is waging war on the inkstand-and-album-with-views-of-the-estate opposition. I'm not supposed to know, but rumours of the battle came to me through my spies."

"Can't we choose what we'd like?" Dick ventured.

She laughed at him. "What a revolutionary idea!"

"Oh well, we can always pawn what we're given," he remarked, trying to sound cheerful.

To his astonishment, the smile vanished from her face. "Dick, how can you! We must keep whatever we're given all our lives, and in a prominent place too, or the servants will tell their relations."

"Oh Lord! Need we always consider what the servants will say?"

"You have to when you've a position to keep up," she said. "And you must be ready with a speech of gratitude. You'd better go along to the study now and prepare it."

He made a wry face. "Couldn't all this fuss be put off till we come back from abroad?"

She shook her head. "It's always been the custom—"

He could have shouted at her—"I wish to heaven you wouldn't use that damned phrase so often!" Thrusting his hands boyishly deep into his pockets, he took a turn about the room. When his irritation was a little cooled, he said, "I say, Gwen, let's get married in town. You could run up there to-morrow on the pretext of buying clothes, what? And I'd slink off and join you."

"And disappoint our kind vicar and his wife, when I've been their guest for so long?"

"Hang it all," he grumbled, "it's not *their* funeral."

"What a way to talk of our wedding," Gwenllian exclaimed and set him an example of laughter. But he could not laugh. A childish desire to stamp assailed him, as she went on speaking with the firm brightness of a nurse exhorting her little charge to obey. "My godfather expects to officiate. He'd be shocked if I rushed off to London to get married in a hole and corner fashion."

"I thought a Bishop was supposed to be so busy nowadays that he wouldn't mind missing a wedding," Dick growled.

"He's a very old friend of the family," she answered with dignity. "And it isn't often that our poor vicar has the chance of meeting his Bishop. Our parish is so out of the world. Besides," she added, running her fingers caressingly over Dick's sleeve, "we mustn't be selfish and think only of our own wishes, now that we're so happy, must we?"

"If you put it like that," he stammered, shamed into compliance, "go ahead. Make what arrangements you think fit for the Bishop and this infernal tenants' beano. I'll foot the bill."

The last sentence compensated him for much.

Next day he was turned out of the dining-room. "Miss Gwennie's orders was to serve your meals in the study, sir," he was told. He disliked eating surrounded by leather-bound books; they reminded him of his schooldays and of his inability to win prizes; but he submitted. For days the maids were too busy cleaning silver and washing china to attend to his comfort, and whenever he entered any room, the chair in which he wished to sit was always being carried out of it. He became increasingly nervous and restless until the tenants came, ate, made speeches and were at last dispersed.

"Thank God," he swore to himself; then, "*that* shan't ever happen again."

He went into the study, and having mixed a stiff whiskey and soda, flung himself down on the horsehair sofa. It was the only downstairs room that the women had left undisturbed. The sporting-prints, the guns and fishing-rods of his predecessors encumbered it. Must chuck out this old junk, he thought, twisting his body about. What's the good of having money if you can't make yourself comfortable? All these antiques may look jolly fine till one comes to five with 'em. I don't blame impoverished families for letting the Yanks have 'em. If any Yank makes *me* an offer—*God,* he was tired! His throat ached with so much talking: his hand from being wrung so often and so hard. To play the country gentleman and to be married were not the soft jobs he had imagined. Today had been hell. Tomorrow, too, there would be the commotion of restoring the house to its normal order. The next day packing must begin for the wedding tour. Why couldn't newly married people get used to each other in some familiar place instead of having to endure the additional embarrassments of foreign hotels? He had heard too many funny tales of other men's honeymoons not to fear that he would be made to look a fool on his own. Meanwhile, there'd be orders to leave with the servants and financial arrangements to make with the agent. He didn't look forward to his interview with Mr. Lloyd. "I intend to act as my own agent in future," he would say. It had sounded easy enough as Gwenllian had put it. But it wasn't easy at all. Not only would Lloyd resent losing his job, but he'd know well enough that the new owner of Plâs Einon was incapable of managing his own estate. He wouldn't say: "So Miss Gwenllian's taking charge of you is she?" but he'd think it, and a sarcastic, contemptuous—yes, by God, a pitying— look would come into his eyes which Dick already knew too well. In the discomfort of the horsehair sofa, he planned rebellion. He'd go to Gwenllian now and say, "Look here, Gwen, don't you think we'd better keep Lloyd on after all?" or perhaps he'd say decisively but casually: "Gwen, I've decided that for a little while at any rate…" But it was useless. She'd say they must economise. She'd say they could do it much better themselves. She'd remind him that, during the war, when Lloyd was away with the Yeomanry, she'd done it single-handed. "Then why on earth did you ever hand it back to him?" he'd ask, and she would answer that of course when the estate had passed from her brother to a stranger different arrangements had had to be made. "But you're not a stranger any more, are you, Dick!" she would add. "I am entitled to work for you now, as I did for my own people." They would

go over the old ground again. It was useless to argue with
Gwen. Easier to face Lloyd and get rid of him, he thought,
and the rebellious leg which had been dropped over the side
of the sofa was submissively returned to it. When Lloyd was
done with, he reflected, there'd still be the lawyer with the
marriage settlement; and even on the eve of his wedding,
when a fellow expected a lively dinner with his bachelor
friends to buck him up, he would have to entertain Gwen's
old fogey of a Bishop. What the devil did one talk about to a
Bishop, and a Welsh Bishop at that?

Little Johnnie Smith, the last of his school friends left alive,
was coming down to be best man. Captain Smith, he was now,
with an M.C. and a toothbrush moustache. He had no job and
no particular place in society—just "blueing " his gratuity, like
so many of his class, Dick thought with superior compassion,
but what good company he'd been that night at the Troc!
Afterwards they'd both gone on to a night club of which
neither was a member. Dick, sprawling on the prim Victorian
sofa, in his quiet study, grinned over his memories. Amusing
chap, Johnnie! He'd shove his way in anywhere. But perhaps
it had been a mistake to invite him down here, where
standards were different. And yet a man must be loyal to his
old pals. But what would Gwen and her county matrons and
her blessed clergy think of Johnnie? Dick's mind swerved
away from the harsh expressions "ill-bred," "bad-form,"
"suburban." He substituted *modern*. That was it, he told
himself, trying to justify his former choice of friends. Gwen
and her circle were a bit behind the times. They expected
people still to talk and behave like characters out of that dull
writer's novels his mother used to read —Strumpet or
Trollope—something of the kind. Absurd in 1919. Like caged

mice, his thoughts scuttered hither and thither, and he grew weary of his attempt to reconcile the claims of old friendship and social advancement. Flash Frank was the fellow he ought to have asked to be best man. No-one could accuse *him* of not being a sahib. But would he have deigned to come? Old wounds in Dick's pride began to throb. When he had been a country squire longer and felt more sure of himself, then he would show Plâs Einon to the man of all others he had most dreaded and most idolised. Now his thoughts fled to the less distinguished and subtle bullies of his Dulwich schooldays. How they'd have jeered, damn them, if they'd seen him— "Little Scrub "—blushing like a girl, this afternoon while his tenants made speech after speech addressing him as if he were a Ruritanian royalty about to espouse the world's most beautiful princess! How the Welsh laid it on! And what a grotesque looking lot they were—some of the older ones bearded, some whiskered, some more like dagos than Englishmen! They had seemed to him a people, not only of a foreign race, but of a past age, having gargantuan appetites and Shakespearean humour. Their use of biblical phraseology would have shocked his Bible-reading mother, and their frank talk of the breeding of animals have discomforted his town-bred acquaintance. He himself was repelled by their toil-blunted fingers and their sweaty smell of earth and farm. They puzzled him, too; for though they expressed a feudal devotion to the house of which he was become the head, they were not curbed or ill at ease as common soldiers were in the presence of an officer. Beneath both their flattery and their joking familiarity—broad, sometimes, as that of Juliet's nurse—he had been aware of keen observation and criticism. It seemed that they revered the name of Einon-Thomas, and that Gwenllian had won their unbounded admiration. But of himself, what was the opinion forming behind those shrewd, watchful eyes?

What did it matter? A parcel of ignorant yokels! His mind tried to escape from its cage of self-distrust. But it was caught by the knowledge that without Gwenllian he would not have known what to do with his party. She it was who had seated the guests in order of precedence, so that none was affronted; she who enquired by name after all their absent relations; she who pressed them to eat, with an inconceivable urgency and persistence. She had capped their local anecdotes throughout what had seemed to him an endless afternoon, and had never ceased to laugh, chatter and gesticulate with the best of them. Silent and constrained, he listened to her in astonishment, using their dialect, rolling her Rs, raising her voice at the end of each phrase. Why ever did she do it? To put these common people at their ease, he supposed, though, heaven knew, they all appeared more at home in his own house than he did! Gwen was a marvel of tact, he told himself. I ought to be jolly grateful to her. *Ought* to be!

While he was helping himself to a second whiskey and soda, she came into the room.

"Hello," he said, putting down the glass with a feeling of guilt, "I thought you'd gone."

"My *dear"* she exclaimed, closing the door behind her and coming to him with outstretched hands, "as though I *could,* without saying good night and thanking you for your lovely, lovely party!"

Rebuked, he felt himself flush. He must try to be civil, though his head was aching. "You must have thought me beastly rude," he forced himself to apologise, "shutting myself

up here. I wouldn't have done it, only I saw you walking down
the drive with that awful female who dug me in the ribs and
said—" He stopped abruptly, wishing that he had not alluded
to the incident. He could not repeat what she had said in front
of Gwen. It had been something coarse about twins—all very
well for a music-hall, but before a gentlewoman about to
marry—

To his astonishment she laughed. "You mustn't mind what
they say, Dick. They haven't left the eighteenth century. I hope
they never will."

His eyes widened.

"Well," she challenged, "aren't they better than the betwixt-
and-betweeners who live in cities—all alike, cardboard
dummies cut by the million to one pattern?"

There was a glow in her cheeks. Dick had never seen her
more handsome or animated than now, when he was throbbing
with the fatigue and annoyance of the past few hours. Could
she really have enjoyed what he had so much disliked? He
stared at her dumbfounded.

"Why are you so solemn?" she asked, seizing the lapels of
his coat and playfully shaking him. "Because of what dear old
Mrs. Jones Cefn-Coed predicted? You must learn to laugh at
our people's humour, Dick, however crude it may seem. You
must practise cracking that sort of homely jest yourself. Father
was an adept at it, and they adored him. ' A merry gentleman,'
they used to say, ' no pride on him at all.' English people think
we're a gloomy race because we are religious. But let me tell
you, you'll never win a Welshman's affections, unless you can
crack a joke with him. He has the great heart of the ancient
Greek, Dick," she went on with increased vehemence. "Yes
indeed! Don't look so unbelieving. He doesn't keep his heart

in his pocket, whatever his detractors may say. He likes money, like another, and he loves a bargain. But it's the prosaic English who put money first. Better than gold, we love music and song, poetry and rhetoric, the history and traditions of our race, and, above all, our land."

"Oh," said Dick. He had never known her declaim like this, though she always seemed to him to become unnecessarily enthusiastic when she spoke about the Welsh. He tried to bring the conversation down to a saner level. "Why did you go off with that old woman?"

Gwenllian let go the lapels of the coat and sighed. "Oh, she wanted to confide in me about her daughter's trouble. She's in terrible distress, poor old darling, though she hides it heroically under a lot of nonsense. Nobody guesses in the parish. She's managed to keep all the prying neighbours at bay. But she trusts us, of course."

And suddenly the woman he was going to marry flung her arms round Dick's neck. The warmth of this unexpected embrace startled him. A chaste kiss was all they had exchanged since the day when she had wept in his arms and he had found himself pledged to marry her.

"Oh, Dick, Dick," she cried, "aren't you proud? Aren't you glad?"

"What of? What for?" he had it on his tongue to ask. But discretion kept him silent, staring at her, his arms clasped, rather limply, round her waist. Hers were tight about his neck. She had thrown back her head and was looking intently into his bewildered face.

"Isn't it splendid," she asked him, "that our people love and respect us so? Still, Dick, though taxation has made us so poor. You wouldn't change places with an upstart millionaire, would you, Dick? Or with any man on earth who draws a fortune from dividend warrants without personal power or family prestige?"

Dick looked confused. Only that morning, going through his rent-roll, he had wished that his money were invested in the funds.

"Dick," Gwenllian persisted, "it *does* mean something to you to keep going what has gone on for so long?"

He grinned and tightened his hold on her waist. Her emotion made her look superb, but it appeared to him slightly ridiculous.

"Say something, Dick," she urged. "Tell me it's going to mean to you all that it means to me. Promise, Dick, promise!"

"Of course, my dear," was all he could say. He felt extremely foolish. But she was so close, so warm, so vibrant, that her passion communicated itself to him. Suddenly excited, though not by the subject of her appeal, he buried his face in the mass of her hair, and kissed it. He kissed her ear, then her neck. He pulled back her head and kissed her mouth. His kisses were not dry and quick as they had been hitherto. Fatigue and boredom were swept away. For the moment he was eager, who had been reluctant, or at least indifferent. "I love you," he told her, "I love you," because, for an instant, his pulses were throbbing with desire for her or for any other comely, responsive woman.

But she believed what he said. She looked up at him with an expression of mingled tenderness and triumph.

"Oh my dear," she whispered, "my darling! I want to be so proud of you—always. We're going to make a success of it, aren't we, you and I, for the sake of the place?"

He was too excited to read the omens.

BOOK II

Chapter I

HE FORESEES HER TRIUMPH

Softly, steadily, day after day, the rain had been falling. It pattered on the window-panes whenever the crackling of log fires was hushed. For hours there would be no other sound but the quiet footfall of Gwenllian's disciplined servants, and the scurry of mice behind the wainscot. After Christmas so few people came up the drive beneath the naked, dripping branches of the trees, that to Dick any visitor would have been welcome. He had bought a gramophone and been delighted with it in the South of France, but when its dance music clashed with the quiet of Plâs Einon, he became, against his will, ashamed of it and turned it off. The small voice of the rain rose through the following silence. He awoke at night, and heard it gurgling down the pipes below the eaves. He stood in the portico, tapping the barometer for promise of change, but always there reached his ears the same hissing and whisper from among the laurels.

Gwenllian would come in from the garden, shiny and stiff as a laurel leaf, in her oilskin and sou'wester. "You haven't been out to-day, Dick."

"I was hoping it might clear."

"No use to wait for that, dear. This is 'February Fildyke.'"

"By Jove, it is. I tried to plough round the home farm to please you yesterday. It was a morass."

"That won't hurt you, if you're properly shod. I've got the

dubbin for your boots, and I've ordered those rubber ones I was telling you about."

"You're determined to have me out in all weathers," he grumbled. "Why can't you leave me alone?"

"Because you've been growing depressed and liverish, my dear, with not enough to do. I go out, wet or fine, and I'm never ill. I haven't the time."

To be proud of one's own tough constitution, he decided, was the most annoying form of self-righteousness. Since he had had rheumatic fever and a piece of shrapnel in his chest, he had learned to be interested in the variations of his health. His wife would not have been so monotonously well nor so brisk at breakfast, if *she* had fought in the war.

"I wish we'd stayed a bit longer on the Riviera," he sighed.

"We couldn't holiday-make all our lives," she would answer, taking up a seedsman's catalogue and beginning to compile one of her many lists.

Why not, he often wondered! There were plenty of retired Army men, like himself, who led a care-free existence in well-warmed hotels, enjoying the sunshine, enjoying golf, dancing, a game of bridge every night, and the society of their own kind.

Lucky devils! However good a woman a fellow's wife might be, he didn't want to see no face but hers, meal after meal, to hear only her improving conversation throughout long fireside evenings. Plâs Einon was all very well for a month or two in summer. But if it were not for Gwen, he would let it for the rest of the year. He might get a good price for it from some stout hero with a taste for standing at drenching covert sides waiting to pot pheasants, or for wading icy rivers with the patience of Job. Dick liked the friendliness and the pretty setting of a cricket pitch or a tennis court. He was a moderate batsman, and a good enough tennis player to win garden-party applause. Having no purpose in life, he craved for amusements as a child for sweets, but in sports that were chill, damp and solitary, he found no satisfaction. Already he had discovered with regret that his fine sporting estate was going to give little pleasure to him. The worst of it was he dared not tell his wife so. She seemed unable to understand that he suffered miserably from cold. She herself was capable of changing for dinner in a bedroom as big as a barn with a couple of sticks smouldering in one corner of it. His dressing-room hadn't even a fireplace.

When he spoke of installing central heating, she provided him with a tiny oil stove and banished the subject. Secretly he had consulted the plumber and the builder at Llanon, talking valiantly of having electric light, a telephone, more and better bathrooms. When Gwenllian heard of these boasts, as she did of everything which was said in the district, she laid account books before him.

"Just go through these," she said in a tone of authority, "before you talk any more about spending hundreds of pounds."

For the moment he was quelled. But after next quarter, he reassured himself, I shall insist on having my own way. Hang it all, the money was his, not hers! Of course, a wife must be consulted in matters that concerned the house; and for him it was more difficult, as the house was his wife's old home. Still, he thought, that's no reason for her vetoing every suggestion I make as though she were my landlady and I her lodger.

One morning, while riding the cob that he was bound to exercise, he made a resolve to "have it out " with Gwen before another day passed; but as he was composing phrases of manly firmness with which to overcome her obstinacy, he heard his name shouted. Blinking the raindrops off his lashes, he saw Lewis Vaughan cantering towards him over the sodden grass in a skelter of mud. By Jove! It was good to exchange masculine gossip again of the kind to which the Service had accustomed him— racing tips, news of winter sports from pals in Switzerland, politics treated as a sour joke, and a smoking-room story or two. Moreover, before they parted, his cheerful neighbour gave him a particular piece of news which delighted him. Flash Frank was in the district, staying at Cefnllys. Eager to share his excitement with Gwen, Dick splashed home, flung the reins to the groom in the stable yard, tossed his soaked mackintosh to Powell in the hall, and ran upstairs, two at a time, to the room where he was sure of finding the lady of the house at work. There she sat at her official desk, beneath her father's portrait.

"I say, I have news," he cried from the doorway. She did not look round, but he refused to be chilled by her indifference. One-stepping across the shabby carpet to her Chippendale chair, he perched himself on its arm. He felt affectionate towards her, and being in an exhilarated, optimistic mood, he resolved, here and now, to laugh her out of her pig-headed opposition to modernising the house.

"Aren't you going to pay me any attention?" he asked.

She raised her head, but the smile she gave him was abstracted.

"Must you finish that letter before hearing my news?" he enquired, hoping to see her put away the sheet of paper.

Her pen began to move again. "Yes, if you don't mind, dear," she said, intent upon her writing.

"The queen must attend to her dispatches, what?"

But she was too absorbed to notice his little joke. From over her shoulder he read the words, "very pleased to address the Women's Institute, if you know certainly that Lady Llangattoc will be prevented from doing so—"

Dick made a grimace and rose from the arm of his wife's chair, without bestowing the kiss he had intended for the nape of her neck. He could never come close behind her and look at her abundance of dusky hair, without wishing to pull it down; for when it fell in a cloak of feminine softness about her face and breast, it almost made her seem a girl. To run his hands through it excited him. But she required him to wait until she went to bed—punctually at half-past ten every night. And even then— A fellow felt an ass, kissing a woman's hair, winding the strange electric stuff round his tingling fingers, burying his face in it, when she looked at her wrist-watch and asked, "D'you know how late it's growing?" And he remembered that the jolly old writer, Sterne, whom his mother did not think it proper to read, although he was "set " in school, had written something comic about a husband and wife in bed and the winding of a clock.

Grinning ruefully, Dick walked over to the window and watched the falling rain. He had had a friend, since killed at Mons, poor devil, who had married young, in spite of his Colonel's disapproval. She was pretty and a sport, didn't seem to mind being poor, and spent her time on the links caddying for her husband. He said he was awfully happy, but he seemed gay, rather than content—grew jumpy, took to smoking a hundred cigarettes a day.

At last he confessed to Dick that, though he and his wife were first-rate day-time companions, she could not bear "*that*

side of marriage." Dick had blurted out the confidence to
Flash Frank, and, too late, repented. How clearly the scene
came back to him now—his admired and dreaded senior
astride a chair, laughing cynically! "Let it be a warning to you
never to get hooked, Scrub, my lad," he had scoffed. "If you
marry a chaste woman, she won't respond to your advances.
If you marry a hot 'un, yours won't be the only ones to which
she'll respond. And the devil of it is, you'll never know what
on earth you're in for until it's too late to get out— unless
she's the sort you needn't have married at all. That's the safest,
Scrub, if you're careful of your health. Consort with the kind
little ladies of the town, who'll give you a good time without
chasing you into matrimony." Since his marriage, Dick had
often recalled that saying. Good women, perhaps, were never
very responsive. But then, he argued, in loyalty to Gwen, they
had been married only three months. She loved him very
much, he was sure—in her way. And her way might improve.
At Nice, where he had wished to dance and she had failed in
the rhythm of jazz music, there had been no sign of jealousy
in her when he left her to knit and look on. She had seemed
unselfishly glad that he should enjoy himself. When he took
her to the Casino, too, he had been proud of being seen with
her—so much more handsome in her severe clothes than the
flashy, painted women surrounding her. After all, he told
himself, I haven't much to complain of, if only she wouldn't
live the whole year round in this damp hole, and would have
the house brought up to date.

"Are you ever going to finish that letter?" he demanded,
nerving himself for good-humoured battle.

"Oh, my dear Dick," she answered, laying down her pen, "I
quite forgot you were in the room."

"Forgot I was in the room," he repeated, pretending to be amused, and he forced himself to perch once more on the arm of her chair and to hug her more roughly than he would ordinarily have dared.

She disengaged herself—with annoyance, he fancied; but a moment later she wore her usual composed smile, and asked, "Well, what's your news?"

"I met Vaughan as I was out exercising the cob."

"Which Vaughan?"

"Oh, you know who I mean. The other's only a farmer," he said, thinking her wilfully stupid.

Her brows came together in a frown. "He's by far the better man," she answered. "Mr. Lewis Vaughan seems to lie in wait for you, Dick. Do take my advice and snub him. You're far too indiscriminate in your friendship."

"Vaughan's a jolly amusing fellow," he protested, "the only one who is about here."

"My dear! You know he drinks."

Dick tried to laugh at her. "You see to it that he doesn't put away much in *this* house!"

"He was never an intimate of ours. Why should he become so now?"

"Because I like him."

"My brothers didn't," she said.

He felt himself growing hot and flurried. "Well never mind that now. He's met an old friend of mine, a Major Stansbury. You've heard me talk of Frank, haven't you?"

"I've heard you speak of someone nicknamed Flash Frank," she said, with a lift of her eyebrows. "He certainly sounds like a friend of Mr. Vaughan's."

"They aren't friends in the least," Dick burst out. "I wish to goodness you'd let me tell my story without interruption!" And he got off the arm of her chair. "Vaughan met Frank the other day by chance. He's staying with some people called Goldman. I don't suppose you've ever heard of them."

She smiled in an ironic, irritating fashion. "Jews, who have rented Sir Evan Lewis's place, Cefnllys. I hear the girls go out with the guns, made up like a musical comedy chorus. Everybody is laughing at them. They offer you these mixed American drinks, before lunch, even. We don't want to get involved with guests of theirs."

"My dear girl," Dick exclaimed, "try not to be so provincial! Everybody drinks cocktails since the war. And Frank's most awfully well connected. I daresay his family is as ancient and stuck up as yours—"

"As *ours,*" she corrected.

He hurried on. "There he is, staying within twenty miles of us, and I might never have known it if Vaughan hadn't mentioned casually what an amusing chap he'd met! I've arranged to run over with Vaughan in the car—"

"But Dick," Gwenllian cried, "don't you understand? I don't wish to know these Goldmans."

"Well, you needn't. I didn't suggest taking you too."

"How can I avoid getting to know them, if you call?"

"Call! It's not a call."

"They won't miss their chance. They'll treat it as such and return it. I shall have to receive them."

"Well … and if you should have to bow to the lady when you see her, what does it matter?"

"In the country, Dick, one either knows people or one does not."

"Look here," he shouted at her, "Frank's staying under their roof. That's good enough for me. I don't care if they are Jews. I'd go and ferret the dear old boy out if they were black men. So there! Vaughan's afraid he's leaving in a day or two," he added in a calmer tone. "I'm going over this afternoon."

"You can't go this afternoon. Have you forgotten that the Vicar and Dr. Roberts are coming to discuss the War Memorial?"

"*You* do all the talking on these occasions," he grumbled. "I should only sit and twiddle my thumbs, if I stayed."

Gwenllian looked up at him with an expression of pain and entreaty. The curbed composure of her normal look, the scorn which her face expressed whenever she spoke about people of whom she disapproved, were swept away. "Dick dear," she said earnestly, "you've opened the subject now that I've been longing to speak of ever since we came home." "Why so portentous?" he asked, trying to laugh off a feeling of uneasiness.

"You make it difficult," she said. "You take everything so lightly."

"*You* don't," he grinned.

"No," she agreed, unsmiling, "certainly not your position in the county. I take that very seriously indeed, my dear. You have a great tradition to uphold."

"One might think I was the last of the bally Hapsburgs," he scoffed. Frank would have known how to laugh a woman out of her solemnity; his own attempt was a failure.

"I know you needed a holiday and deserved it," Gwenllian continued, "but it's nearly a year now since you left the Army. It's time you settled down. The county expects"

"Oh come," he protested. "I'm not Nelson. Anyhow, I've only been asked to go on half a dozen rotten little local committees. That sort of thing bores me to death."

"Doing one's duty often *is* a bore," she said.

"Why should it be my duty, anyway?" he asked with an impatient gesture. "There are plenty of busybodies in every parish who like having a finger in the pie. Let 'em do it."

Gwenllian shook her head. "There are not enough of the right people in public affairs today, Dick, and you know it. Taking your part in minor parochial affairs will lead to your being elected to the County Council."

"But I don't want to be."

"That's beside the mark."

"Look here," he cried, "it's all rot you're wanting to turn me into a public man. You know I'm a damned bad, nervous speaker."

She forced a smile. "You could overcome that. There's the classical example of a stammerer who trained himself for the sake of the state—"

"Well I don't propose to spend *my* time on the seashore with pebbles in my mouth," he answered. "And I've done my bit for the precious state already. I've had a more rotten time than you realise in the war. I've never talked to you about all I've seen and suffered. It isn't fit to tell a woman." He heard his voice growing shrill as it always did when he spoke of this section of his past. Hastily he added, "I've been poor all my life. Now I've got a bit of money, I'm damned well going to enjoy myself in my own fashion."

She rose and, coming to him, laid her hand on his arm. "Dick," she said softly, "this is the first real difference we've ever had. I wish it hadn't happened to-day."

"Might as well have it out now as postpone it," he said, turning his head away to avoid her pleading eyes. "I've been meaning to say something to you, too. There's the question of making this house comfortable, and of where we're going to spend next winter."

"I shall spend it here," she answered, with a quiet, self-confident smile.

"But why? When you know this damp cold disagrees with me?"

"Because, my dear, I'm almost sure that I'm going to have a child."

He stared at her, open-mouthed. He had never contemplated the possibility of their having children. The prospect seemed to make her younger and to threaten him with middle-age. "Oh Lord," he gasped.

"Aren't you *glad*?"

He hastened to parade the proper feelings. "Well, yes, of course I am, if *you* are. It's your trouble, dear, isn't it?"

She dismissed his pity. "I'm not afraid," she said, and began to pace about the room in growing excitement. "I've been trying to keep calm," she told him, "to say not a word, for fear it shouldn't be true. It's not a fortnight since I began to hope, so we mustn't build too much on it yet. But, if it goes on all right—oh Dick, my dear, do you realise that we may have a son of our very own to inherit after us?"

"Well, yes," he said. "I suppose we may." What would it matter who stepped into his shoes after he was dead? He stared at her in amazement, as she walked to and fro, clasping and unclasping her hands. The eyes she would scarcely raise to his when he kissed her were bright and fierce now, with a passion he did not understand. Her cheeks were flushed, but not for love of him. She talked and talked, her voice rising and falling in a dramatic lilt. As the torrent of her enthusiasm flowed on, he felt himself crushed beneath it. He had no spirit left for resistance. Motherhood, he perceived, would be no quiescent state in her, but an active passion. That puts the lid on my plans for the winter, he thought. It wasn't right to thwart a pregnant woman. Until her child was born, he must submit to her whims, leave the cold, inconvenient house as it was, make a show of performing whatever she considered to be his duties. He must avoid quarrels by never contradicting her, no matter how trying her demands. He foresaw the slow months crawling by during which he must be consistently kind, patient, considerate, and for ever on his guard. That was how his mother would have expected him to behave; for she had taught him, in speaking of the sweet girl her boy would choose for his bride, that on these occasions all the virtues of chivalry were required of a husband. He shook himself out of a gloomy trance, took Gwenllian's arm, and agreed with everything she said. The words "heir," "estate," "economy," were continually on her lips. Not with regret but with fervour, she spoke of the sacrifices that must be made by parents in their position. "Have you insured your life yet, Dick? You must insure it."

"The truth is," he said, "it's not insurable." That, he thought, will make her think of me. It did, indeed, check her. She halted and gazed at him. "Poor Dick!" he expected her to say. "Is that true? Is it really true?" And perhaps she would add that doctors were often wrong. He didn't believe they were wrong in this, but he would have liked her feminine consolations.

"Not insurable," she repeated. "Are you sure?" "Quite sure," he answered, almost proudly.

"I've tried. They all say—"

She interrupted him. "That makes it the more important," she said, as though speaking to herself.

"Makes what more important?"

"That I should have a son now," she answered. "There must be an heir."

Chapter II

HE AND SHE GIVE HOSTAGES TO FORTUNE

For days he had hated the starched nurse in the house. The sight of her tautened his muscles and dragged at his nerves. She reminded him of the bleak passages of a military hospital, the hard swift fingers that probed and bandaged tight, the stringent whiff of antiseptics, a prelude to pain. When the doctor was at last sent for at dawn, Thank God! he said to himself. Now it will soon be over.

It was not soon over. Whenever he ventured out of his study, he met the scared face of one or other of the maids. Powell had burst into tears as she set before him an unappetising lunch. "Oh, the poor lady," she had sobbed, hurrying from the room and slamming the door. He suspected her of hating him because of her mistress's suffering, and he took a gloomy pride in leaving the cold meat untouched. It had always been the same with these Welsh servants — devoted to Gwen, as nearly insolent as they dared be to himself. He'd like to chuck out the lot of 'em.

He prowled about and fingered his gramophone records, longing for the blatant tunes with which the wounded had kept up their spirits. But these women would consider it indecent of him to play music or to read a novel or doze in an armchair. They hated to see him make himself comfortable. Better look at the paper, which could be dropped at the sound of an approaching step. The news was dull and he had read it over and over again since five o'clock this morning. Today's paper would not arrive until tea-time. He smoked cigarette after cigarette, and stared at the decanter. But society was not tolerant enough nowadays to pardon a husband who became drunk during his wife's confinement, though, God knew, there was excuse enough. In the good old days—but then he remembered that until modem times women had endured their part of this ordeal without the relief of anaesthetics. He shuddered, and began to ask himself why those butchers upstairs were withholding chloroform from poor Gwen? Callous brutes, doctors and nurses. He knew what the Army ones were like. He ought to go up and insist that something was done to slacken her agony; and he drove his unwilling feet to climb the stairs, his trembling hand to knock at her bedroom door. While he waited for an answer, he clenched his fists, anticipating one of those heart-rending groans that had spoiled his breakfast. The room was quiet. Could she have been delivered?

The nurse peeped out.

"Is it all over? "

She laughed in his face. "Of course not. D'you want to see her?"

"No," he exclaimed, "no, no!"

"You can. It'll be quite all right just for a minute. Doctor's gone off to visit another patient. He won't be back for an hour."

"He oughtn't to leave her," Dick cried. "What's he thinking of?"

"There's plenty of time," the nurse answered, her hard lips set in a smile. "You can't expect a first confinement to be over in half-an-hour."

He longed to run away from all this, back to the little house in Streatham where he had been sheltered from the cruelty of the world. But it was like "going over the top"; a fellow couldn't retreat. He entered his wife's room at the nurse's heels, fearing that he might have to see blood.

One nervous glance reassured him. Everything was in its usual precise order. On the draped Victorian dressing-table the silver gleamed. The stiff chintz curtains and chair covers were unrumpled. An austere single bed, suggesting a ward, had been set beside the four-poster, and on it Gwen was lying, a white coverlet drawn up to her throat, a white pillow beneath her head. Her eyes were shut. Her stillness frightened him.

Seeing him flinch, the nurse said brightly, "Things have slowed down a bit. Go and cheer her up." Obediently he went, and looked down on her in bewildered compassion, as on some stranger he had found half dead by the road-side. Was this the well-preserved woman of forty whom he had married only a year ago? Twenty years could not have added more to her age. Her face was thin and haggard; the sharp nose and chin seemed drawn together; there was a deep furrow between her brows.

"Buck up," he muttered. She opened her eyes slowly, as if the lids were heavy to lift. Even those flashing, eloquent eyes of hers were dulled, like the repulsive eyes of a dead fish, he thought. He could think of nothing to say but, "You poor thing! You poor thing!" But that would not be in accordance with the nurse's orders.

At length he managed to stammer, "You're not in much pain, now?"

"No," she said in a whisper, "unfortunately not. The pains have slackened off. It's disappointing. They've been trying to make me sleep." And there stole back into her eyes a gleam of their former fire. "Sleep," she said contemptuously. "As though I *could,* until he's safely born!"

She was trying with dry creased lips, the lips of an old woman, to smile. A valiant grimace. Dick continued to gaze at her, fascinated. Suddenly he started. Her mouth had twisted with pain and her hands appeared, writhing, to clutch at the bedclothes.

When the spasm had passed and Dick was wiping away the sweat that had broken out on his forehead, he heard her say, "Nurse, that was a better one. They're coming again."

"Capital," the nurse answered, as though she, too, were pleased by this horrible torment.

Dick turned, incredulous, from one woman to the other. "I say," he pleaded, "can't you put her under an anzæsthetic?"

The nurse forgave his ignorance. "We haven't reached that stage yet." And turning to her patient she said, "That's splendid, you're helping the pains along fine." Over her shoulder she said to Dick, "You'd better go."

Thankful to be dismissed, he fled. To witness torture was abhorrent to him. He wanted a world full of bloodless pleasure, like a perpetual seaside holiday, with nice young people strolling up and down, well, cheerful and good to look upon. Ugliness and pain should be hidden, as civilised nations hid the floggings and hangings considered necessary within their prisons. How he pitied poor Gwen! But he pitied himself more. He was proud of being so much upset on her account, but he was ashamed of the harsh words that tolled in his mind—old and ugly! Old and ugly! There was no escaping from the truth. He was married to an old and ugly woman. Old! Old and ugly! And he didn't love her. What a caddish thing to admit, even to himself, when she lay upstairs in torment! He would be kinder to her in future, he vowed. He remembered, with contrition, having made a like vow when she told him of her pregnancy. Well? Had he not refrained from making the alterations to which she objected? Hadn't he done many boring things to please her? At first he had; but soon he had wearied of well-doing, and had motored off to the County Club, day after day, leaving her alone. From this hour he would turn over a new leaf. She should never again have to complain of his neglect. But would his good conduct hide his feelings from her? She was devilish astute... Old, ugly, unloved... She'd know.

"I'm an unfeeling brute," he muttered, and mixed himself a stiff whiskey and soda. "No. The trouble is that I'm too damned sensitive."

An hour passed; and he thought: Supposing she were to die, while I'm pitying myself because she's lost her looks?

Contrite, he rushed into the hall and upstairs. At her door his heart again failed him. From within there came the moan of an animal in pain. He hurried off. He came back. He stood irresolute. At last he knocked.

"Who's there?" he heard Dr. Roberts's angry voice exclaim.

He slunk away without answering, but was too late to escape. The old doctor's frowning face looked out.

"Oh, you," he said, and followed Dick downstairs.

He commanded respect, this tall, blunt-spoken man with eyes set far apart in a face rough-hewn, like a chunk of seasoned oak. Dick, who always felt small, young and useless in his sturdy presence, had sometimes tried to get even with him by mocking his Welsh accent. "Pretty rough and common," he had once hazarded to Gwenllian, but she had swept his criticism aside. "You don't understand. He comes of old yeoman stock. They used to take pride in being provincial before the railways came." Everyone but Dick spoke of him as The Doctor, as though there could be no other.

Some day, Dick thought, as he heard the heavy footsteps overtaking him, I shall fall ill and have to be attended by him. There's no choice in this desert. He'll stride up to my bedside, sodden with rain, splattered with mud, reeking of the horse he's ridden, and shout at me to follow my wife's example, to be strong and brave, to make an effort. He despises me, I know, because I haven't nerves and a constitution of iron. If some of these opinionated blighters had been through the war—!"

He was trembling with nervous irritation as he turned to face his pursuer in the hall. Out of the corner of his eye he saw with sharpened perception the wide stretch of polished floor and the trophies of chase and battle which displayed his family's credit. The great front door stood open, and through it flowed the sunshine of an October afternoon, gilding his many possessions. You shan't hector me, he wanted to tell the taller man. Your house is little more than a cottage. A wasp came buzzing in, and he shied away from it with a flap of his handkerchief. "They're dangerous brutes when they're sleepy," he muttered, excusing himself. There it went, curse the thing, hovering over a vase of crimson dahlias—the colour of blood. Why would Gwen have red about the place? She had arranged those flowers yesterday. His mind jerked back to her with a fresh pang of remorse. How little she had allowed her condition to interfere with her household duties! How courageous, how unselfish she had been!

"Is she going to pull through?" he asked with difficulty.

"Now look here, my boy," the Doctor said, "this won't do. Pull yourself together."

"I'll try," Dick promised, forgetting the difference in their stations. "But you don't know how I feel." A large steadying hand descended on his shoulder, and the Doctor growled: "There isn't a man, woman or child in this parish who doesn't love her."

Excepting myself, thought Dick.

"You don't imagine," the Doctor challenged, "that I'm going to shirk anything that can be done for her safety or comfort? Believe me, I knew that girl before you were bom or thought of. I've seen her nurse both her parents through their last illnesses. No man knows her worth better than I. But I've got my work cut out. I can't have you ill, too. Go out and take a good walk."

"I couldn't," Dick protested. "Suppose—just suppose—" The fact that he wasn't in love with her, that he wouldn't miss her much if she died, made the thought of her death the more pitiful.

"Don't be a fool, man. It's a perfectly normal labour, so far: only likely to be protracted on account of her age."

Her age again! She looked old enough to be my mother, Dick thought, older than I ever saw my own mother look—a poor old hag they were torturing to death because she looked like a witch! He loathed and despised himself for insulting his wife with his fancies. His eyes began to prick, his throat to contract, his mouth to twist into unmanageable shapes.

"Now then, steady," he heard the Doctor say. "That's not the most useful way of showing your love for her."

The irony of it was that his tears were not for Gwen, but for his own dead affection, the little affection he had ever had for her! If she died, he would reproach himself bitterly. But if she lived, how bitter to be tied to a wife he didn't love!

As he was wiping his eyes, a two-seater car stopped before the door. Glancing round over his handkerchief, he saw a pair of very long, thin legs in plus-fours and sporting stockings of an uncommon pattern thrust themselves forward. The body of a man slid into view after them, and Dick uttered an exclamation of delighted surprise. "Frank!" he exclaimed.

"Hello, Scrub, old boy," Major Stansbury shouted across the hall. Then, on a lower note, "I say! Is anything the matter?"

Dick went to him and gripped his slim fingers, but could not speak. There was no need; for the visitor, patting him on the back, turned to the Doctor; and it was the Doctor who made apologies and explanations. Dick heard the others in consultation; but was himself powerless to intervene. He was listening to his own past, to the man who had been his hero then and whose voice profoundly stirred and excited him. "Perhaps I'd better go?" Frank was saying.

No, no! For God's sake stay and give me some of your confidence, Dick yearned to cry out, but not a sound could he utter.

"On the contrary, I'd be much obliged to you for stopping," the Doctor replied; and Dick had a twinge of liking for him. "You might hold on to this young husband. He wants taking out and exercising."

Then came the cheery, commanding voice Dick had so often tried in vain to copy. "Right you are! I'll try him up and down the gallops half a dozen times."

They were making a jest of his misery, but he did not resent it.

He looked up at Frank and, recovering control of his tongue, made a feeble effort to assert himself as the principal character in the tragedy.

"I must stay within call till it's over."

Dr. Roberts told him brutally that it would be long yet.

"Tell you what," Frank suggested. "We needn't go far. Let's have a look at the stables and grounds. I've not had the honour of seeing your place yet, you lucky devil! Last time I was staying in this neighbourhood, Doctor, I didn't hear till the day I left that Scrub had set up as a landed proprietor." Dick was pleased by the familiar bantering tone. It warmed his vitals to find that someone could be lively and normal in this house of sickness and fear.

"Come on, then," he exclaimed. "If you'd like to, let's get out at once. I'll show you over the house when things are less upset."

"Of course. Of course. This won't be my last visit."

It was a blessed relief to see the Doctor go back upstairs and to escape from the house. He found it encouraging to have his arm taken by Frank, and a precious flattery to hear those often scornful lips praise his gardens, his buildings, his timber and the view from his terrace. The pride of ownership rekindled in him, the satisfaction of those few possessive months before he married Gwen.

"It's jolly pretty, I must admit," he said, as he and his visitor leaned on the grey stone balustrade and gazed down through the speckled gold and copper of the beech trees to where the river gleamed in the dingle far below.

"It's perfectly charming, my dear fellow," cried Frank. "You're too modest about it. You always were too modest by half."

Dick did not remember that his senior officer had told him

so in the old days. Frank must have liked him better than he had dared to suppose.

"Shooting and fishing well preserved?" Frank asked.

"Pretty fair. I'm not much of a sportsman myself, I'm afraid. Can't stand hanging about in the wet since that go of rheumatic fever. It left my heart dicky, so the medicos say. I've got to take care of myself. But you can have all the sport you like if you'll come and stay here."

"Nothing I should enjoy more," Frank answered, and Dick relished the sensation of conferring favours upon him.

When he had been subjected to a catechism on the sporting resources of his estate, he saw his guest swing round and contemplate the facade of the house.

"Good place for parties. I suppose you have them pretty often?"

"Well, no," Dick admitted, his face falling. "My wife doesn't care for a lot of people, except her old friends."

"Oh come, you must shake her out of that, as soon as she's fit again. Doesn't do to get into a rut in the country. One soon grows unsociable—miserly and all that. What's the use of having money if you don't share it out?"

Dick looked at him in wistful longing. If only this prince of good companions, with his irresistible charm, his determination to be gay wherever he was, were a near neighbour, what an ally he would be against Gwen!

And, as though in answer to his wish, Frank said, "I'd rent a little place hereabouts if I could find one going for a song. I don't mind telling you I've run through nearly all my fortune since I left the Service. The old story," he explained making a grimace, "fast women and slow horses. But this ought to be a goodish neighbourhood to lie low in, what?"

"Couldn't have a better," Dick grinned ruefully. "It's dull as ditchwater."

"Splendid," Frank cried. "Suits me down to the ground."

Dick laughed—his first laugh for days. "You must have changed then, Flash!"

"No, But my bank balance has." And Frank began to make plans for a life of economy at somebody else's expense. He would not have to entertain or to belong to clubs if he lived in the depths of Wales, nor to tip his friends' servants on the scale they had learned to expect. "Then there's a soft billet waiting for me at the Goldmans'," he chuckled. "The old boy doesn't know a thing about sport, really, and he likes to pick my brains on the quiet. I could potter about his place with a rod or a gun any day I liked, *and* drink his champagne, too, if only I could find somewhere to live."

"I know," cried Dick, in a glow of excitement. "There's the dower house."

"Whose dower house?"

"Mine." There was warmth in the word.

Frank looked at him through narrowed eyes. "Is it empty?"

"Why, yes. The old girl who rented it died a month ago. Her relations carted off the furniture and the place is shut. I've got the key in my study. Like to see it?"

"You bet I would! I say, Scrub, old man, what a lark if I became your tenant, what?"

"And I your landlord," said Dick.

"You haven't anyone else after it?"

"Oh, my wife talked of someone. But nothing's signed yet, luckily."

As he spoke, he saw a greedy look flash across the Major's lean face, with its wide, thin-lipped mouth, and its eyes set close together. He had often likened his friend to a graceful, fine-bred greyhound. Now, for a disconcerting moment, he was reminded of a lurcher closing on a silly hare. The comparison flattered neither himself nor his guest.

"Come on," he cried, dismissing it. "Let's see if the house will serve your turn."

It served exceedingly well. The prospective tenant suggested a few improvements, and the landlord agreed to make them.

"Well, that's as good as settled," Dick exclaimed in triumph when twilight drove them to abandon their measuring and tapping in the empty rooms.

He wasn't sorry to be in the air again, for the dower house—though Frank hadn't noticed it—was full of echoes and, he had felt, of hostility. Were the ghosts of malicious, dispossessed dowagers laughing at him? Each succeeding bearer of his name had turned them out of Plâs Einon to end their days here. Was he the hereditary enemy of them all? And were they laughing at him now because he was sliding, as he knew, into a damned bad bargain—failing even to keep his own end up. Nonsense. He was Einon- Thomas of Plâs Einon and they were dead. He was too sensitive—that was the trouble. He'd do as he pleased.

"New drainage will be an investment, Scrub," Frank was saying, "And the new heating apparatus." "Still," Dick answered, "it will cost a bit. You don't want to pay much rent."

"Can't afford to, my dear boy."

"Oh, I daresay we shall come to terms," Dick went on, looking sideways in expectation of gratitude, and he felt an arm linked with his own.

"I shouldn't be surprised if we did," Frank said. They went

in step up the long avenue in cheerful talk. The air was bitter with a frost that was killing the last of autumn's flowers, and stars were cold in the darkening sky. For an instant as they were passing the inky circle of yew trees, Dick felt threatened by the majesty of nature. The nakedness of his own soul appeared to him, making him long for the companionable noise of cities. Afraid of the words that might have expressed the terror of space and silence that gripped him, he fell back on a phrase that Stansbury would accept without surprise. "I find the country pretty dull," he said.

"Trust me to liven things up, if I settle here,"

Frank answered, and Dick was reassured. God's imminence wouldn't trouble him in the company of jolly old Flash.

Not until he came within sight of Plâs Einon, ghostly pale among its crouching black laurels, and saw the lighted window of his wife's room stare at him like an accusing eye, did he begin to feel again unhappy. He left Stansbury and ran upstairs without a word. Soon he stumbled down again, feeling weak at the knees.

"I say, Frank, I'd be grateful if you'd stay the night with me. I know it's asking a lot—the servants in a stew, and nothing ready. But you'd save my reason if you'd stop and go on talking. She's about as bad as she can be, though the stubborn old fool of a doctor keeps on telling me it's only a question of time. I wish to heaven she'd taken my advice and gone up to a nursing home in town. Then we shouldn't have had this awful upset here. But she would insist that the child must be born in this house. She's cracked about it, positively cracked." He moved about the study picking things up and putting them down again. "What will the Goldmans say to your staying, though?" he asked.

Frank stretched his long legs before the fire, and gave a lazy smile. "Oh, nothing. They eat out of my hand, Pa, Ma and the whole litter of daughters. You can send 'em a wire in the morning, if you like." He chose and carefully nipped one of Dick's best cigars. "I say, you do yourself well."

"I rarely smoke those myself," Dick said.

"Well sit down quietly, there's a good chap, and smoke one now. You fidget me, hopping about. Your old medicine man put me in charge of your case, remember, and I'm going to prescribe for you. Keep a cellar book?"

For a moment Dick forgot Gwen's sufferings as he answered proudly, "You bet I do."

"Out with it then," his guest ordered. "And we'll pick a bottle of the best."

They drank far into the night, and came down sleepy-eyed at half-past ten the next morning. Still Gwenllian was in labour.

"This is frightful," Dick groaned, after another visit to her door. "I don't know what to do."

"I'll tell you," Frank declared. "Does your estate run to a carpenter and a mason? Then let's have 'em along at the dower house to estimate for our improvements. We'll take sandwiches and a flask. Agreed?" Of course Dick agreed. And the day passed pleasantly enough, until at dusk a wide-eyed stable-boy came running from Plâs Einon to remind him once more of his wife.

"The Doctor do want partic'lar to speak to you, sir," the lad gasped. "It's about wiring to London, I do believe."

"Oh Lord!" groaned Dick, hurrying towards the house.

When his guest joined him at dinner, he was even more flurried than on the night before.

"The specialist can't be here till to-morrow morning," he complained, "even if he catches the night-mail. She may have died of exhaustion before then. Thank God you're with me, Frank. I shall never forget your kindness during this time."

"Oh, that's nothing," Frank answered. "It's no good worrying yourself into a panic. You had better decide on our drink."

"Choose what you like. I couldn't touch a drop." But over his best port that night, Dick gave away the dower house at a rent of thirty pounds a year.

"Thank you for sitting up with me," he said again and again. "I shan't be able to sleep a wink." Soon after one, his head sank on to his shirt-front: his eyes closed; his mouth dropped open. The Major helped him upstairs and into bed. Dick reached up to clasp him round the neck. "You're my best pal, Flash," he said very loud and slow. "My very, very, very best pal. There's nothing I wouldn't do for you after this."

He seemed scarcely to have fallen asleep when that meddlesome fool Powell, standing at his bedside in full daylight, awoke him with hysterical chatter.

"It's a boy, sir! Oh, sir, do listen! It's a boy! He's *lovely,* the nurse do say. He weighs over eight pounds! He's the spit and image o' his mother! Oh, sir, get up quick, and come and look! Oh, *duwch*! Aren't you thankful to God it's over, and the poor lady spared to us?" And she broke out crying afresh, though Dick saw with disgust that her silly face was already swollen and blotched with weeping.

Damn these emotional Welsh! Of course he was glad, he answered her. Where the devil was his dressing-gown? Who had hidden his slippers? His head was aching and his mouth seemed to be full of fur. He blundered into the passage where

Dr. Roberts was leaning against the wall, his big hands hanging at his sides. Sick and cross though he felt, Dick had a spasm of pity for the old fellow, for he had the appearance of a veteran who had been long in the front line. A greyish pallor showed beneath the weathering of his skin, and his big shoulders were bowed.

"Well," he said, without moving, "you have your heir, at last."

Dick blurted out the truth. "I never wanted him." The Doctor's wide-set eyes grew hard as slate. "Don't go saying that to your poor wife, young man."

"Of course not," Dick answered in a sulk. "Is she all right?"

"May have to lie up for two or three months. Her heart's a bit strained."

Dick surveyed this dismal prospect in silence. Then, because he could think of nothing else to say, he asked, "Will you have a drink?"

"Thanks," growled the old man, eyeing him with scorn. "Now my job's done, I can do with a drop of the liquor you and your friend found so cheering last night. You haven't asked to see your wife yet, I notice."

Dick felt his face redden and cursed the Welshman's insolence. "No," he said, very stiff and on his dignity, wishing that his attire were more formal. "May I?"

"No, you may not. She's too exhausted."

"Oh," said Dick, and led the way down to the dining-room.

When Dr. Roberts had swallowed his brandy, he looked more genially upon his sullen host. "Well, I hope you'll be happy," he said. "I'm sure I hope you'll be happy." He seemed on the point of saying more, but to Dick's relief, thought better of it. "You'll have something to live for now," was all that he added.

"Yes," answered Dick, busily mixing himself a "prairie-oyster." That would clear his head if anything could. "Yes, I suppose I shall," he repeated mechanically, and glanced at the clock. Frank would be down soon. Then there'd be someone to talk to, thank God!

Chapter III

SHE MEETS AN OBSTACLE

As Gwenllian opened the front door, the wind strove to wrench it from her grasp. She held fast, enjoying the tussle and the victory. Wisps of hair were flicked into her eyes. Her skirt flapped against her legs when she struggled down the steps. This wild weather exhilarated her. She would not get into the car until she had stood with head raised, breathing deep. The air was moist with rain that had come down in angry squalls for days past, and with yet more rain that lowered from the dark sky. She glanced up at the grey ribbons of cloud, taut and ragged on the gale. A black flight of rooks swirled overhead, and one white seagull uttered its desolate cry. The soul of a drowned sailor, she thought. There'll be wrecks at sea tonight. She wished she could fly, like a witch on a broomstick, to the fiercest part of the coast where cliffs of iron dropped sheer into deep water, and gigantic waves were splintered into a steam of spray.

But she would go, instead, to meet Dick at the station. It was her practice to be on the platform to greet him with a set smile whenever he returned from his costly, foolish trips to London. She allowed no word of reproach to pass her lips, but tried to shame him into repentance by telling in a cheerful manner of how she had been working and saving for their estate and their child. Dick was not proving as easy to mould as she had hoped, but today she had renewed hope, for, in his absence, she had given battle to his false friend, her enemy.

From the moment she had set eyes on Dick's new tenant, installed with such deceitful haste while she lay ill, she had known she would have trouble with him. He was more dangerous than their noisy neighbour, Lewis Vaughan, or Dick's common little best-man, whose visits her ridicule had soon made impossible. Major Stansbury was her equal in breeding and self-assurance, and Dick feared his sarcasm more than he feared her own. Silly little Dick, she said to herself, to be overawed by a waster! But for months after her baby's birth, she had been too tired to do more than warn her husband and her warnings had failed. Dick needed a firm hand. Now that she had regained her health, she would apply it.

Her plans for routing the intruder had been carefully matured. She had made sure that no other house within his means would be let to him in the district. Secretly, she had sought and found a tenant willing to pay a hundred pounds a year for the dower house. Then, having seen Dick off to London, she had told Major Stansbury that he must go. The duel had been fought in her own study, beneath her father's scowling portrait. There, standing up so that her visitor might not sit down, she had apologised with frigid dignity for having to put the interests of her family before those of an acquaintance. As she recalled her carefully chosen words and his sneering, mock-deferential replies, she put up her gauntleted hand to her face. It must be the wind which was making it so hot, for she was not Dick to be humiliated by such a man's irony. Thank goodness he had only a yearly tenancy! She had made it clear that the moment a more profitable tenant offered, a man of breeding would cease to trade upon his landlord's generosity. The word charity had slipped into her speech. No man, unless he had a hide too thick to feel the lash of any verbal whip, could stay after what she had said.

Smiling to think that she would soon have Dick again under her influence, she climbed into his car and set out to greet him with feelings of good-will. She had ordered him the dinner and the wine he liked and the extravagant fires for which he craved. She herself found them suffocating, but Dick was about to turn over a new leaf under her guidance, and for those whom she governed Gwenllian spared herself no pains.

On the drive she met the new nurse pushing the heir in his large pram. Nurses had come and gone during the year since Illtyd's birth, for his mother would suffer no will in the nursery but her own. The baby was hers, and his attendants her servants. She stopped the car, jumped out, and peeped under the pram's hood at the sleeping infant. Very gently she touched his wrists, where the white woolly mittens she had knitted for him ended. His tiny hands were warm. She bent lower, careful not to awaken him, and sniffed. He smelled sweet as a flower. Straightening herself, she gave a sharp glance at the frilled pillow with his monogram embroidered on it, at the fleecy, satin-edged blankets, the quilted silk coverlet. The nurse stood by with an expression of resentful apprehension. Gwenllian gave her a nod of encouragement.

"You keep him very spick and span, Nannie."

"I hope so, Madam. I try hard enough, I'm sure."

"D'you find me terribly particular?" Gwenllian asked with a smile, for this nurse promised to be worth keeping.

The stolid face could hide nothing from her. Nannie did not like her, but she was respectful, and that was of more importance. "I shouldn't wish to complain, Madam," she said.

"I'd rather a lady what knows. What I mean to say is, when one does one's duty—"

Gwenllian bestowed another smile. "We both mean my baby to be the best cared for in the world, don't we?"

The nurse's thick lips moved in a grudging smile. "That's right, Madam."

"But, Nannie," the mother added with a swift glance at the wildly swaying trees, "you mustn't ever bring him here in a gale like this. A branch might fall."

"Oh," the nurse protested. "I don't think there's much danger."

"I'm not going to run any risk with him, or any shadow of risk," Gwenllian answered in a tone that quenched dispute. "Take him round the walled garden where he'll be perfectly safe."

Safe! The soft word sang in her ears as she drove up over the desolate tableland towards Llanon. With her beloved child's safety went that of the inheritance. It must never, never go to her sister's ragamuffin children, trained to despise property and tradition, nor must Dick be suffered to dissipate any fraction of it, before her son stepped into his father's shoes. She had come to think of Dick as a Regent; of herself as a Queen Mother. What they possessed they held in trust.

Below her, far away on the right, a leaden sea, flecked with white horses, stretched to the paler lead of the horizon. On her left, the mountains frowned in purple majesty against a sombre sky. All around her tossed the wintry gorse bushes and stunted thorn trees. The wailing of the storm through sodden sedges and heather was shrill above the throbbing of the car. Water and mud spurted up as she jolted along the road, rutted, and pocked with puddles. Rain had begun to fall once more, driving against the windscreen, shooting in icy arrows through chinks in the hood. As Gwenllian turned up the collar of her old leather coat, she thought the more complacently of her baby's sheltered warmth.

He was not strong, Dr. Roberts feared. She mustn't try to harden him too soon. But she was confident that under her care he would grow into a tall, tough Einon-Thomas, and she remembered her madly pulsing joy, torn and feeble though she had been, when the doctors told her that she had brought into the world a living child—a son, and with dark eyes!

"Like yourself," they had said.

"Like my father," she had corrected them.

Every day for over a year, she had watched her baby continually, asleep, waking, feeding at her breast. In his features, as they began to develop, she looked for a mirror of the past. She made plans for his future, entering him for the public school at which her father and her grandfather had been educated. She invested money in his name. What she had suffered in her body to bring him to life, had been more than repaid in the pride and pleasure she had in this exquisite small creature of her own substance, this promise of a material immortality, this gift of hers to the race she worshipped.

Well pleased with herself, she drove along the desultory main street of Llanon, past square stone inns, and cosy whitewashed cottages, and the trim, unlovely villas of retired sea-captains, each with a flagstaff in its garden. She knew who lived in every one of these houses, and whether or not they were "deserving." Life in a city, it seemed to her, must be lonely and dull. Dick's pleasure in being where his name commanded no respect astonished her. At each of the small shops at which she stopped, an obsequious tradesman ran out, and stood bare-headed in the rain to take her orders.

"You'll get wet, Mr. Jones."

"No matter, Ma'am. 'Tis always a pleasure to serve you, wet or fine."

She enjoyed spending money on sanctioned necessities. Smiling, she returned compliment for compliment in regal fashion. "It's a pleasure to us, too, to deal with anyone who has served us well for so many years."

"Oh, the best my small shop is stocking, Ma'am, is always for the Plâs."

Then she would ask, "How's Minnie getting on at the Post Office?" Or, "Is your wife's rheumatism better?" And Mr. Jones-Butcher, Mrs. Grocer-Evans or Mr. Edwards-Co-op. would continue to risk rheumatic fever while asking for news of the Einon-Thomas heir.

When Dick's train had been overdue a quarter of an hour, Gwenllian remarked, "I shall be late if I don't get on to the station."

"No need to sweat yourself, Ma'am! We can see from here when the old train's coming, by Mr. Pugh-the-Coffin's hearse-horse galloping round his paddock."

As the grocer had foreseen, Gwenllian was there before the train, but the mistress of Plâs Einon neither fidgeted nor beat with her foot, as they are apt to do who are not bred to wait with composure. She stood quite still within the door of the general waiting-room. It was fireless and smelled musty. The rain tapped on the pavement outside and on the roof overhead, and cluck-clucked down the water-pipes. There was not another sound on the dreary little station but that of the solitary porter stamping his feet to keep them warm. But Gwenllian smiled, considering how to make Dick laugh over dinner. There were some droll new sayings of the villagers, bless them! And who could tell them so well as herself?

Afterwards, when he and she sat close to his wasteful fire in the gently lamp-lit drawing room, she would explain that it had become imperative to find a profitable tenant for the dower house. She would make it appear that an offer had come to her by chance and that Major Stansbury had instantly recognised the propriety of quitting. If Dick was angry, she would be patient, appealing to his sense of obligation, his affection as a father. "*Our* child," she would call Illtyd. "You've scarcely begun to take an interest in him yet; but as soon as he starts running about, you'll feel towards him as I do." It was not true, but she would say it. "And then you'll be glad," she would press her point, "that you've made sacrifices for his sake. An extra seventy pounds a year on the dower house will help towards his schooling. Let's begin from to-night, my dear, working together for our boy's future." And if Dick's face still wore that sulky schoolboy pout which of late had so exasperated her, she would kneel down beside him, and taking his hands in hers would summon all her resources of forbearance. "Dick dear," she would urge, "let's start afresh. Let's make this evening the first of a happier life, of mutual help and understanding." She was so touched by the tenderness of her own words that she forgot that their purpose was to bend him to her will.

At last the train came panting in, swirled about with its own smoke and steam. Gwenllian's face grew eager and she hurried along the platform, looking into each compartment. Half a dozen passengers clambered down, stiff and shivering from the unheated carriages. Dick was not among them.

Suddenly Gwenllian became aware of the cold, which it was her habit to defy. Was ever anything so sad, she asked herself, as an emptying railway station on which one is left forlorn, where one had hoped for a hand-shake and a kiss? And her heart cried out in pain that her young husband did not like her any more. He had never been in love with her, she knew. But once he had found her company agreeable and when she chose she had been able to arouse his desire. Now she remembered that she was two and forty years of age and that, like a working woman, she had been too busy to give thought to the preservation of her looks. Dick will be thirty next month, she said, staring into the puddle at her feet. There would be no scene of reconciliation to-night. Tomorrow or the next day she would have difficulty in reconstructing her loving speeches. Her eyes began to smart; her throat to feel raw. If her self-control had deserted her she would have burst into a passion of tears. But here was old Ben Morris, the guard, trotting up the platform towards her. She must act her part.

"Oh, Miss Gwennie—I beg your pardon, Ma'am," he panted, "the Captain stepped off the train at Carmarthen. He told me to bring on the luggage. Here it is, Miss. How's your little boy, Miss? Doing fine I do hope?"

"Fine," she replied, and repeated, "Stepped off the train? Then he was on his way here?"

"Yes, Miss Gwennie," the old guard nodded. "But the gentleman as is a tenant o' yours met the Captain. He said as they'd be motoring home together in a hired car after dining at the County Club."

"All the way from Carmarthen," she exclaimed, and, setting aside her personal disappointment, she began in anger to reckon the cost.

"Yes indeed, Miss Gwennie," the guard sympathised. "The Captain himself told me to tell you." Slowly her dazed mind understood Dick's treachery. So he knew I'd be here waiting for him, she thought. "It was Major Stansbury you saw meeting him, wasn't it, Morris?" she asked, with a bitter twist of her lips.

The old man's pink face, crumpled like an apple that has been stored too long, shewed such distress that she made a resolution to keep her feelings better hidden in future. She would not be pitied for her husband's neglect.

"Yes, Miss, yes, Ma'am," the guard answered. "'Twas a tall gentleman, whatever, with one o' them single glasses in his eye. The gentleman as is going to all the race meetings."

"Thank you, Morris," she said. "I remember now, the Captain had some business to talk over with him." She gave her old crony a considered tip, not so large that it might seem to compete with those of the new rich, but enough to show that the right people were not grown mean.

He kept the train waiting, that he himself might carry her husband's suitcase to the car, while he was reminding her of the mistletoe he had brought for her every Christmas when she was a child, and of how she had once kissed him under it.

"It's a lucky job as the Captain isn't here, Miss Gwennie, to hear me making so free with his lady," he chuckled, looking at her in tender anxiety to see whether he had succeeded in cheering her.

The station master and the porter stood by, grinning and touching their caps. They, also, enquired after Plâs Einon's heir. How kind they were, her dear Welsh country folk! But how intolerable it would be if she should see in all their eyes the compassion she had seen in those of Ben Morris! It was her place to be compassionate, not theirs. She nodded good-bye and drove away, fighting with tears of affronted pride. The common people pitied her! No wonder! She had lowered herself to make love to the insignificant son of a nursery governess. She had borne him a child, yielded to every whim of his except when he wished to fling away money in alterations of her home. With infinite patience she had taught him all that he was capable of learning—God knew it wasn't much! She alone had his welfare at heart, and could help him to take his place in the county. Yet he preferred the company of riff-raff, and, chief among them, of the man who had insulted her with his sneers.

She drove back at a reckless pace over the darkening moorland. The crying of the wind had risen to a shriek and aerial hands were tearing at the hood of her car. It lurched sometimes so that she feared it would overturn. The Cwn Annwn are out tonight, she told herself, the pack of fiends, hunting the souls of the wicked.

It was two o'clock on a black morning when Dick returned to his home. Gwenllian was in waiting for him, crouched over the embers of the fire that was to have warmed them both. When she heard him fumbling at the door, she sprang up and went into the hall. Would he beg her pardon when she told him that anxiety had kept her from sleep? He burst in with a torrent of wind that set the lamp swinging. Giant shadows of a man and a woman rushed towards each other and fled away, in a fierce dance across the armoury on the walls. He slammed the door, and she cried out, "For goodness sake think of others! You'll wake Illtyd!"

"Oh, rot," he said.

She could have struck him. For an instant she thought with

furious pleasure of the red mark her hand would print on his sottish face. But she forced herself to offer her cheek for the customary kiss. He scowled and brushed it with his moustache. His breath was hot and rank with whiskey. She shrank back, looking hard into his face. It was of an unwholesome pallor and the mouth was loose. She knew now, admitting it to herself for the first time, that she had always loathed his mouth—his soft, weak, red-lipped mouth, and little girlish chin. His eyes were very bright but vacant, their pupils much enlarged.

"You've been drinking," she exclaimed, too angry now to hide her disgust.

"And what have you been doing, I should like to know?" he retorted, in a querulous voice. "Insulting my best friend—talking about charity. It's a charity to me his staying in this damned hole. Trying to drive him away while I'm not there to take his part! I call that a sneaking dirty trick." He seemed to her more like a contemptible schoolboy than ever before—a tipsy schoolboy to whom she had been married in a nightmare. It was shameful and indecent. She turned her back on him and tried to fix her attention on the candles she lit, the lamp she was blowing out. It was not easy to perform these simple tasks, for her hands trembled.

"Look here," he brawled, "I won't have you slinking off like that! You'll jolly well stay and listen to me."

"We'll discuss the matter in the morning," she said, without looking at him again.

"There isn't going to be any discussion," he shouted. "I've put my foot down. I'm sick of being preached at and ordered about by a woman. There's no one more ridiculous than a hen-pecked husband. People are laughing. D'you know what they're saying? There's the soft chap who married a woman without a penny—married her out of kindness of heart, 'cos he didn't like to turn her out of her home. And now he lets her boss him as though the property belonged to her."

She knew that he was quoting her enemy. Major Stansbury had kindled him against her. You weak, suggestible little fool, she said in her heart. But fighting down her fury, she went towards the stair- case. "It's very late," she said. "We must go to bed. Please try not to wake the whole household."

"I don't care who hears me," he persisted, following her. She felt his hot breath on her neck and with a shudder hastened on upstairs. But he kept close to her heels, bragging noisily, "Frank is going to stay, in spite of you. ' I won't have you turned out,' I told him. 'I won't stand it.' And he said, 'No, I knew it wasn't any of your doing, my boy. You said you'd stick by me, when I stuck by you through that awful time, d'you remember?' As though I could ever forget it! That's why he wrote and asked me at once for a seven years' lease, and had it made out, too, to avoid the possibility of any more upsets. Luckily the lawyer chap—what's his name?— was in the club. Oh, I believe good old Frank had asked him there on purpose. So we signed it—signed, sealed and witnessed, stamped —before we sat down to dinner. So that's that."

She had reached the head of the stairs, and swung round on him. The flame of the candle she held in her clenched hand threw a quivering light on to his white face a step below the level of her own. He had let the candle she had given him go out, but still, at a slant, he held the silver stick. Beneath his fitfully lit, unsteady figure, was the black gulf of the hall. She could hear the gale raging at the windows, beating on the doors. The home she loved was beleaguered. Hissing draughts, cold as snakes, shot along the dark landing and the carpet rose under her feet. She curved a hand round her shuddering spear-point of light.

"So that cad wrote to you in London, behind my back," she said. "Intercepted you on your way home, fuddled you with drink, had a lawyer—not our Mr. Price, he'd never have been a party to it— and a lease that's positively dishonest, all ready prepared, and tricked you" She could not finish her broken sentence. Her teeth had begun to chatter.

"There was no trickery about it," Dick cried. "I won't have you turning my tenants out. I'll keep old Frank about the place if I choose."

"He will not enter this house again as long as I am mistress here," she cried.

"Don't suppose he wants to," Dick retorted. "You make the place like a reformatory. But I shall be able to go and have a jaw with him whenever I'm bored to death here."

"And get drunk with him, I suppose?" she said, "as you have to-night. And play cards for stakes you can't afford? And fling away money on racing? And give him seventy pounds a year, for seven years, so that he may sponge on you and teach you to destroy your child's inheritance."

"Oh shut up!" Dick said, "and get out of *my* way."

She let him stumble down the dark passage to his dressing-room, then went swiftly into her own bedroom and locked the communicating door.

Chapter IV

SHE MAKES SURE OF THE INHERITANCE

It was neither light nor yet quite dark when she became aware of the bedclothes' pallor, and of the ceiling, luminous, grey, unearthly, over her upturned face. Shadows and firelight had been chasing across the walls when she fell asleep in the afternoon. Now only a faint glow, dull red and sullen, lit the room. How deathly still it was! She began to count her heartbeats and the tickings of the clock. Was the world without still muffled in the heavy white of a sea fog? Or had night fallen, turning it to impenetrable darkness? Something ominous, of which she was afraid, had hung over her all day in the clammy unmoving air. Before long it would have to be faced. But she was scarcely awake yet. Her body was warm and craved for more repose after so many sleepless nights. She was sorry for her body, and her pity for it was dimly connected with her fear. Had not her flesh suffered enough two years ago, she asked in a vague rebellion against she knew not what? She did not want to be awakened by forebodings of further pain. Let the fear rest, whatever it might be, for just a little while longer. The pillow was soft. Her head sank back upon it; and she allowed memories of the past week to flicker across her slackened mind, as the firelight had been flickering when the Doctor sent her to bed.

"Won't you take my word for it?" he had growled, "the child's perfectly all right now. One would think no youngster had ever had croup before. Can't you trust me, or your excellent nurse here, for a single minute?"

For answer she had squeezed his big kind hand and tried to smile at Nannie. Of course she trusted them both. Dear old Dr. Roberts could not have been more skilful nor Nannie more untiring. But what did they know of the importance of her son's life to her? To them he was a sick child, like another, to be saved if possible. To her he was the only hope and reason for her future, the sole justification for her self-suppression, her suffering of mind and body in the past. If he should die, who had been so dearly borne, the story of her struggle to save and keep Plâs Einon would never make the epic she had planned. It would degenerate into the sordid tale of a woman who denied herself to no purpose, refusing the man she loved, marrying late in life one whom she despised, for the sake of a property and a house of which, in the end, he would rob her. For if I lost my only child, thought Gwenllian, beginning to turn and toss on her bed, I should lose the strength and courage to fight Dick's extravagance.

Her battle had been continuous since she had begun to wage it fourteen months ago. Led by Major Stansbury, Dick had been the winner. He had spent faster than she could save: not much faster, but fast enough to imperil her position. All her energies had been given to devising new economies, and she had finally wrested the management of the home-farm and the estate from his incompetent hands. As long as he stayed at Plâs Einon she had been able to check his expenditure. But the stern rule she found it necessary to exercise was driving him more often away from home, and when he was safe from her in his London club, he drew more money out of the bank than her labour and contriving could pay into it. And the better

I keep him in order here, the oftener he will escape, she told herself in despair, as she flung back the hair that was fallen over her eyes. She had made a mistake when she cut Major Stansbury and refused to entertain him. Subtler methods of attack might have done more to undermine his influence over Dick. If only she had not been too angry to disguise her feelings! And sitting up in bed, she said to herself with weary conviction; I must learn to act a part. I must contrive to keep Dick here. He's not safe except at my apron-strings.

She lowered her feet over the edge of the bed and began to grope with her toes for her slippers. Nothing was ever quite where she expected it to be in this room. She was not accustomed to it yet, though she had slept in it alone for a twelvemonth and more. It was a bleak room. The woodwork, painted white, chilled her, but she would not spare money to change it. In the midst of the empty floor stood a prim little bed. Here the widows and the spinster ladies, who came to visit, had been wont to sleep, for the White room was considered too large and imposing for bachelors. It was at the foot of the nursery stairs, thus giving Gwenllian a decorous excuse for her removal into it after her first violent quarrel with her husband. "In case Master Illtyd should be ill in the night," she had told the servants last winter. And since Christmas, pretence had ceased to be pretence. She had been creeping up those steps continually, candle in hand. The icy terror of losing her child had made her spirit shudder with her flesh in the small chill hours of morning, when the wind moaned in the chimneys and cold draughts slid along the dark passages. The old house seemed then to be quick with ghostly sighs and voices of foreboding. "Not strong! Not strong!" Gwenllian had heard them whisper. The heir was delicate and

Plâs Einon knew it. One day last week a picture had fallen: the maids said it was a sign of death. Annie, the cook, had heard knockings from unseen hands at midnight, and Powell told how a robin had flown in at her pantry window. "There's glad I was, Ma'am," she confessed, "next day, when poor Mrs. Pugh-the-lodge was taken so simple, sitting in our kitchen and died before they got her home." In tense silence Gwenllian had looked at the speaker. There was no need to ask, "why should you be glad of a harmless old woman's death?" The mistress knew that she and her maid, bred up in the same superstitions, had shared a common terror lest these signs should herald the death of Illtyd.

Huddled in a wadded dressing-gown, Gwenllian went to the fireplace and threw a log into the grate. It fizzled and spat. Then the dry wood caught fire and golden tongues of flame licked upwards, re-lighting the room. On the hearth stood an ancient cradle of oak. It was used for the wood that Gwen-llian burned when she allowed herself any heating at all. As she crouched beside it, warming her hands at the little blaze, she noticed the gleams of light dancing along the dark polished side of the cradle. To make them shimmer the more, she gave it a push. Weighted by logs, it could not swing easily upon its rockers. She thought: There ought to be a baby inside there. And suddenly she knew, with a shock that stiffened her, what it was she must do: what it was that, in waking, she had feared.

It was long before she had will enough to move, but when she could command her cold, numbed limbs, she forced them to raise and carry her to the window. Draw back the curtain, she said to her right hand, as though it had belonged to another, for her spirit and her body seemed to have been separated. They were no longer composed in the living unity that had been herself. Her will had become the detached and pitiless tyrant of a shrinking slave that was her flesh. She saw her hand extended. Her fingers felt the coldness and the gloss of the calendered chintz; but their sensation was an occurrence from which she stood aloof. She was remote; aware of the nerves and muscles in her body uttering their shuddering protest, of the heart's laboured beating, of the tightening of a throat that swallowed with difficulty, of the drumming noise in her ears, of the hot trickle of fear down her spine, of a disgust that tasted nauseous on her tongue—she was aware, but indifferent. She would compel this slave to her purpose. Though it shrank from the humiliation of an embrace it loathed, though it would be weary of the burden, though its delivery should rend it in two, yet it should obey. And it would survive, that the epic she had planned might, in her own seeing, be fulfilled.

When her hand had pulled aside the curtain, she looked out upon the night. It was opaque, but its darkness did not hide the shapes of the nearer trees. They loomed through the denseness of a sea-fog, their branches furred with the tentacles of hoar frost: wan ghosts of trees, like an army of skeletons. "Horrible," she whispered, shrinking back, "horrible!" And she remembered Frances's saying: "When things die, they should be given swift burial. Churches and traditions and marriages that go on in form after the spirit is out of them, breed poison. They remind me of gaunt dead trees on which venomous fungoids grow—dismal while they stand, and certain to fall some day on those who shelter beneath them." Gwenllian had mocked at Frances.

"How far-fetched!" And how like Frances! But she had

thought: Frances is an Einon-Thomas, as I am, with a streak of passionate mysticism in her. Her sister's dark eyes had shone as she answered, "Far-fetched? I wonder. My similes are from nature. Growth is beautiful but decay foul. Nothing is sweet that lingers on when it has ceased to grow."

"Not sweet," Gwenllian muttered, thinking of her own unhappy marriage. Love there had never been; affection and respect were dead now; but lust might survive and be made to serve her. "It is necessary," she said, half-aloud.

Shut out those ghosts, she ordered her hand. Light all the candles. When it was done, she drove her still reluctant body to the wardrobe. Here were hanging the shabby tweeds that she wore every week-day and the neat coat and skirt of serge that went to church on Sunday mornings. Searching beneath a pile of woollen garments, washed, darned, and folded in dried lavender, ready for next Christmas and the deserving poor, her fingers touched at last something smooth and sleek, and brought out a Chinese robe. Fierce golden dragons were embroidered on a heavy silk that had the gleam and colour of liquid blood. When she had received it from Hong Kong as a wedding-gift, it had seemed too grotesque, too theatrical for her to wear, but it was fitting that she should wear it now. She put on the graceful, ruby coat, the black trousers, the patterned shoes, and, standing before her mirror, gazed at the reflection of herself transformed. The woman in the mirror was brushing out a curtain of thick hair, and Gwenllian remembered that, in the early days of their marriage, Dick had loved to play with this hair. She had been still and submissive, a trifle bored, her thoughts far away from his caressing fingers.

Since last November he had not seen her hair loosened. To-night he should see it—no longer in the tight braids she wore by day. He should see and touch it; its soft web should fall again over his face and throat: and she took from a cupboard scent which Frances had given her at Christmas. The bottle was still unopened. She broke the gilded seal, and, dipping in a finger tip, put a drop of the fluid on to the parting of her hair. The perfume was of orange blossom—"The most aphrodisiac in the world," Frances had laughingly declared. Was it this sensuous sweetness, or her sister's words, or knowledge of her own plan that filled her now with an angry, unhappy excitement, an eagerness without joy? She despised her body for its half-willing response. Ashamed and derisive, she groped in an old chest that had once held the dowry of a bride. Here she stored the properties used when she organised theatricals for her Sunday School class. Sometimes she had wondered whether making up the little girls did not "put ideas into their heads." Now, finding the rouge and the hare's paw, she put a soft blush on her sallow cheeks and red upon her lips. She looked with shame and defiance at the result. Dick would prefer her thus—like a streetwalker; he was ill at ease in the presence of a gentlewoman. *She Stoops to Conquer*, she thought with a bitter smile, should have been the title of a tragedy.

When she was ready, she glanced at her watch. It was ten o'clock. After dining at the dower house, Dick seldom came home before midnight. She went up the narrow flight of stairs to the day nursery and softly opened the door. In the warm, still room there was no light but that of a merrily burning fire and one bright streak from the night nursery, whose communicating door stood ajar.

"Is that you, Madam?" Nannie whispered. She appeared in petticoat and corsets, her abundant person nipped in at the waist, like an hour-glass.

"Yes, Nannie. But don't mind me. I'll watch here, while you go on undressing. How has he been?"

"Sleeping lovely. I hope you've had a rest too, Madam?"

"Oh yes," Gwenllian answered. "I've had all the rest I need—all the rest I'm going to allow myself, anyway."

She knelt down beside the cot and gazed at her sleeping child. She had almost died that he might live, and she grudged neither peril nor torture. But by how little he seemed to hold the life she had given him! His face was the colour of an old wax candle; and a vision that had of late often appeared in her dreams returned to her—that baby face motionless among lilies waxen as itself. And she heard the whispered comments of the gossips who came to gape: "The only child!" ...."Of course there'll never be another. She married too late in life…"

"Who will the property go to if she doesn't have any more children?"... "Her sisters, I suppose. But the entail's gone. Her husband can will it where he likes."

If you die, thought Gwenllian, staring at the sick child, I may as well die too, unless I bear another son. She pressed her head against the bars of the cot. Unless I bear another son, she repeated again and again.

She had long been repeating these words to herself when she heard a timid, hesitant knock on the door. Dick! With hot excitement she sprang up and went to him.

They stood together on the landing, her hand drawing to the door behind her, his holding a little lamp whose light shot flames of scarlet among the crimson she was wearing. He stared at her robe and her coloured cheeks, and when she forced her lips to smile at him with the semblance of affection, he stared the more. She was seized by a wild desire to laugh. Dick's stupid, startled face—her own bedaubed one! What a mad-house jest, ludicrous and obscene, respectable, legal marriage could be! She wanted to laugh and cry and scream, to liberate herself in an outburst of hysteria. But she must not scare Dick away. She must win him, keep him, use him.

She said: "It was nice of you to come up."

"Oh," he answered, visibly embarrassed, "I only wanted to ask the nurse if the little beggar was better."

"Yes dear. He's much better. He'll live now, I think."

"Good Lord," exclaimed Dick, "you never told me his life was really in danger."

She clutched at his shoulder. "I didn't dare trust myself to speak. Oh, Dick, you don't know what I've gone through. Be a little nice to me. Comfort me, please. Please comfort me."

A flush spread over his face. "There, there," he muttered. "Better have a hot bath and go to bed. That'll do you good," and he began to retreat downstairs.

"No," she cried, following him. "I couldn't possibly sleep. I must have you to talk to till I'm calmer. *Please,* Dick, stay." He waited for her on the landing, looking more than ever embarrassed. "Is there a fire in your bedroom?" she asked, taking his arm. "May I come in and warm myself for a little?"

"If you really want to," he answered, averting his eyes. "But I think it would be far better for you to get to bed."

"Can't you understand," she answered, making her voice low and pleading, "that I'm lonely and miserable."

"I'll get you a hot drink," he said.

As soon as she entered the room they had shared, he left it, muttering about a saucepan. He was a long time gone; and while she crouched on the hearth, hugging her knees, pressing her chin against them, there dawned on her the humiliating conviction that he knew she had dressed up to woo him and that he wanted none of her. He had been intermittently ardent and she constantly cold during the first months of their marriage. When the birth of her child had separated them, when their quarrel over Major Stansbury had made her deny herself to Dick altogether, she had supposed that he would be glad enough to return at her summons. Now she hated him as never before, and with her hatred was mingled a fierce pride that demanded his submission.

At last he entered, the collar of a jaeger dressing-gown hunched up to his ears.

"Here," he said, "I heated this milk for you while I was undressing. Come on. Let me take it along to your room, and tuck you up. Do you good to drink it in bed. No use staying here moping."

"Oh Dick," she implored, "need we go on like this?"

His face became more purposefully stupid. "Like what?" he asked.

"You know what I mean—torturing ourselves with loneliness, living apart, keeping up hostilities, just because we once had a quarrel."

"You began it," he said. "And you kept it up. It wasn't I who suggested" He left the sentence unfinished and scowled fixedly at the floor. She had held out her arms to him and he was pretending not to see.

"Yes dear, I know," she persisted, though shame and rage burned within her. "But I'm sorry now. I'll even make it up with your friend, if you wish it. To please you, I'll—oh, Dick, say something! Try to meet me half way. I've been unhappy this last year."

"You haven't shown it."

"I don't show everything I feel," she said, and a voice within her cried out, "or I would strike you dead at this instant for daring to scorn me!" But aloud she pleaded, "Let's not keep up this heart-breaking estrangement. Let's start ail over again."

He thrust his hands deep into the pockets of his dressing-gown and stood sulky and stubborn, his feet far apart. "I see no reason for changing the arrangement you made yourself. We jog along quite comfortably as we are."

"No," she exclaimed, "we don't. You know we don't. It's unendurable. How can you pretend? Oh Dick, am I so old that you have ceased to think of me as a woman?" She went close to him, swiftly, before he had time to withdraw, and drew his face down upon her hair.

"You didn't appear to think much about me, or my feelings as a man," he sulked.

"Dick! Dick," she cried, "don't harp on the past. It's been a wretched, stupid year. And it's been my fault. Forgive me, dearest. Look at me."

As she passed her arms round his neck, she felt him stiffen and shiver. She nestled closer, and slowly his right hand moved round her waist. But suddenly he withdrew it and, raising it to his neck, tried to loosen the clasp of her arms.

"No," he said, as if in argument with himself. "No. You and I don't care a row of pins for each other."

For days she had been holding back the tears that could so readily have flowed because of her child's peril. Now her tears might be of use. Her head dropped against Dick's shoulder and she wept as though her heart would break.

"Don't," she heard him say from time to time. "Don't,

Gwen, please don't... I didn't mean to be such a beast... I didn't think you'd take what I said so hard ... Gwen, old girl, I say, I'd no idea you were so keen on me still." He said that! Hysterical laughter mingled with her sobbing. "Gwen dear, I didn't really mean it."

To weep was so great a relief that she wept on, though now Dick's arms were round her and he was holding her close. After a while, her speech coming in broken gasps, she said, "Your handkerchief, please, dear."

He let go of her with one hand to search in a pocket and to wipe her face. She saw wet pink stains upon the white silk.

"Don't look at me, dearest," she besought him. "I must be hideous."

"You're not," he whispered into her ear. "You're all warm and soft again, as you used to be. How did you manage to keep it up for a whole year? . . And, I say, Gwen, why did you never wear this silky red thing before?"

"D'you like it?" she asked, rubbing her head against his chin.

"Rather! It's as jolly to touch as your hair."

She felt his fingers steal over her. When she had ceased crying, she closed her eyes, and raised her face to his. His lips closed upon hers. She returned his kisses hotly, until she felt his ardour grown, and suddenly he forced her body backwards and leaned over her, his heart beating fast against her breast.

"Come on," she heard him say in the thick voice that he used when Major Stansbury had made him drink more than his weak head could stand. "Don't let's be such fools as to quarrel again."

Again? What did it matter if her purpose were served?

"Come on," he urged.

"Dick," she said, "you're trembling."

"So are you," he told her.

"Yes."

It was true, and it surprised her.

BOOK III

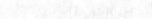

Chapter I

SHE LEARNS TO KNOW HERSELF

"The Doctor to see you, Ma'am."

Bran for the cows' mash. Maize for the poultry— surely they need not have so much? Horley's cattle cake—is that really needed? The vet to attend the setter—what's the use of keeping sporting dogs when Dick is away for half the shooting season? *More* boot polish! *More* knife powder! *More* lamp oil!… Gwenllian raised her eyes from the thumbed slips of paper on her desk and saw Powell standing in the doorway. "The Doctor?" she repeated, dazed with fatigue. "I hadn't an appointment with him, had I?"

"I can't say, I'm sure, Ma'am."

"Oh well, one more or less—"

Nathanial Vaughan, the tenant of Dolwern, had left but a few minutes ago. He had been pleading for a new roof to his barn, and the masonry of his ancient house was again in need of repair.

"If you could put us on a cement face," he had ventured, leaning forward eagerly from the edge of his chair, a gnarled hand on either knee.

"Indeed and indeed, Mrs. Einon-Thomas, Ma'am," his wife had quavered, "the rain it do be pouring down on to our bed, rough nights. There's sitting up with an umbrella I am, and these nasty old rheumaticky pains ketching me something dreadful!"

Gwenllian had looked at the old woman, dressed in her unpretentious gown of black. An antique gold watch chain was hung round her neck to show how important an occasion she considered a visit to the Mansion. She and her husband, with his grey side whiskers and his Liberal-Conservatism, were of the old-fashioned, respectful yet independent type that Gwenllian approved. It grieved and shamed her to have to say no to them. How patiently they bore the discomfort she could have relieved but for Dick's wastefulness! It was his fault that these hard-working people were sent away dis- appointed; his fault that the plumber had called pressing for settlement. She ought never to have yielded to his continued demands for "improvements." But when Richard was born she had been even more weakened than after the birth of her first child. And Dick had again shown signs of repentance during her pregnancy. If she were always in that condition, she thought with a grim smile, she might keep him in order, for he could pity her body when it suffered. For what he caused her to suffer in mind by his spendthrift ways, his drinking and idling with people she despised, his neglect of his children and his home, he had no care. A year ago, when she was still an invalid, though months had passed since her confinement, he had hung about the house, bored, sulky, but ashamed to leave, and she had hoped that, by making him more comfortable, she might, perhaps, win him to stay. Throughout the past summer her extravagances had in conse- quence been added to his. She had allowed the cream to be eaten at tennis-parties instead of having it turned into butter for market. When Dick invited his hotel acquaintances to Plâs Einon, she had raised no objections, but had wasted her time in playing hostess to them. Against her judgment, in desperate hope that he might settle down and cease to be a drag upon their fortunes, she had yielded to his whims and follies. But in the autumn, in spite of her costly concessions, even his interest in his own alterations of the house had begun to flag and his idle need for society to grow.

"Why not shut up the damned place for a couple of years?" he had suggested. "Do the children good to winter in Switzerland."

"Dick, will you never learn that where your duty lies there you must stay?"

"Oh, all this harping on duty—" he had begun to grumble.

But she had cut him short. "However much it may bore their father, I intend to bring up my children in the place to which they're bound. They will inherit, Dick; they must know their own people."

"Go ahead then," he had retorted. "Bring 'em up as you like. You never consult me."

"You haven't shown much interest in them."

"How d'you expect any father to, when he hears his wife all day long: '*My* children!'…"*My* nursery ' … ' *My* son ' … *My* heir'!" And, with a shrug of his shoulders, he had slouched off towards the dower house.

In January, in spite of his new radiators, he had had bronchitis.

"I warned you," she had said as she gave him his medicine, "that they were dangerous, unhealthy things."

"Oh, for God's sake don't stand gloating over my bed, repeating like a parrot, 'I told you so! … I told you so!' "

He had been as nervous about his health as he was irritable; and, as soon as he could travel, had gone off to the South of France, leaving her to settle the doctor's and chemist's bills.

These things she remembered with a resentment that bit into her mind. Her thought was full of them as she went down to the drawing-room to meet the Doctor, but she forced a smile of welcome to her guest. He was standing with his back to the meagre fire she allowed herself when she was alone. To-morrow would be the first of April, and she would give up fires altogether. She took the large hand that looked so uncouth and had so healing a touch. Lucky Dick to have been ill, she thought as she let her palm rest in the Doctor's, to lie quiet for two or three weeks, to be taken care of!

"How are you getting along by yourself?" Dr. Roberts asked. "Don't you find it a bit lonely? Like to have the wife over to spend a couple of nights here?"

"I should be charmed to see her," Gwenllian answered, making her smile more bright. "But you're not to worry about me. I'm far too busy to have a dull or a sad moment."

He growled like a faithful dog. "How's that absentee young man of yours?"

And again, pride compelling her, she lied. "Oh, quite recovered, thank you, and looking forward to coming here. He writes me cheerful letters every day." He had not written for a fortnight. She was surprised at her own glibness, and she thought: I used to despise liars, but Dick has made me one.

Ringing for tea, she urged her old friend to stay, for she longed to cling for a little while to someone who was fond of her. He sat down, watching her from under grey brows that hung over his eyes like the thatch above cottage windows, and, as he explained the reason for his calling, she knew that he also was concealing the truth. He had called often of late, making one excuse or another to have a look at her.

"Evans Cross-eyes is laid up again. That's what brought me out here," he declared.

"I'm sorry," she said. "Is there anything needed?"

"Could you lend him a bed-rest?"

"Of course. And shall I have some of our famous chicken jelly made?"

"I never say no to that for any of my patients, do I?"

She took a pocket book out of the leather handbag that held her many keys and made a note. The Doctor's eyes were still fixed on her when she looked up again. "I know what you're thinking," she laughed, "that I'm losing my memory. I've such a host of things to remember."

"I was thinking, my dear," he said, "that you are working too hard. You did in the war and wore yourself to the bone. It's a pity. There never was a handsomer girl than you were at nineteen."

She winced. It was when she was nineteen that she had fallen in love. "You can't expect youth to last," she said as lightly as she could.

"No. We're none of us getting any younger. But that's another reason why you should slacken off. Something will snap if you keep the tension so tight."

"Nonsense." She laughed again, but his words touched her with fear. Something would snap! Not her self-control? Not her ability to do right?

"Yes," he persisted, "you shouldn't risk a breakdown. It's harder for you now even than it was when your poor brother was at the front, for now you're saddled with—"

A husband, she ejaculated mentally.

But the word he said aloud was "children."

"I like work," she assured him. "Sugar? And milk?" How heavy the teapot seemed!

"Yes," he growled, "both, and plenty of 'em. But you ought not to do more than one person's work—not two or three."

She tried to change the subject. "This is the cake I invented in the days of rationing. There are no eggs in it. You put in a teaspoonful of vinegar to make it light."

"Don't think I'm trying to poke in my old nose where it's not wanted," he persisted, "but can't you teach your husband to pull his weight in the boat?" At that she was shaken by a blast of fury and despair. "No," she wanted to scream, "No! No! I can teach him nothing, I tell you, nothing! He's hopeless, useless, a drag on the estate, a burden, an encumbrance!" She bit her lip, though the hot words seethed within her. After a moment of tense silence she took out her handkerchief and, pressing it into a tight ball, passed it across her mouth. "Doctor, *bach,*" she said in a small voice, "do you mind if we don't discuss my husband? He's been wounded and ill. He's not strong."

"My dear girl," Dr. Roberts exclaimed, setting down his tea-cup in haste and sucking at his moustache, "I didn't mean for a moment to wound your feelings by implying the least thing against him. I realise, of course, that he's not robust. But you mustn't be so anxious about him. There's no occasion in the world to fret."

And until he left, half an hour later, he tried to allay her supposed fears for Dick. Men whose hearts were slightly defective often lasted longest. There was no reason why her husband shouldn't live to be eighty. "Bless your soul," he declared, "there's no reason why he shouldn't see us all out!"

When the Doctor was gone, blustering his sympathy for her well-acted concern, Gwenllian lay back on the sofa and closed her eyes. A laugh came from her lips—a jerk of sound with no mirth in it. Jenny, the Sealyham, scrambled up from her place on the hearth, where she had been roasting her stomach, and began to paw at her mistress's feet. Something must be wrong, her wrinkled twitching nose seemed to say.

Gwenllian took the comforter on to her lap. Something *is* wrong, she thought. But the Doctor doesn't suspect it. None must ever suspect. We're not the class of people who wash our dirty linen in public. A hot tongue licked away the tear that was beginning to trickle down Gwenllian's cheek. Dick may live on and on, she said, and outlive me and ruin the children and undo all my work. Sometimes I can't help wishing that he'd die—that he were already dead.

Powell came in to carry out the tea-tray. Her mistress had heard her approach, and was pulling the dog's ears in seeming good humour when the door opened.

"How the day flies, Powell! Is it really the children's time already?"

"Yes, Ma'am. Nannie was putting on their drawing-room suits when I looked in."

As she spoke Illtyd appeared at the door, made the dancing-class bow expected of him, then slid across the polished floor counting very laboriously, "one, two, *three-turn*! One, two, *three-turn*! Is that right, Mummy?"

"Quite right, darling. Come and give me a kiss."

"Mummy, why must the lady start off with the right foot and the gentleman with the left? When horses trot you watch their right shoulder—"

"Their *off* shoulder," she corrected.

"Yes. Their off one," he repeated in his painstaking drawl. "That's same thing, isn't it?"

"That is the same thing—try to articulate clearly, darling."

"You have to watch and rise with it," he persisted. "Or else you go bumpetty-bump. Do all horses start with the right—the off—foot? Or is it only the lady horses?"

"*Mares*," she corrected again. "Come and kiss me."

"Mares," he murmured. "Do gentleman horses, start trotting with the left foot, Mummy?"

"*Near,* not left, when you're speaking of a horse," she told him.

She saw a worried look, followed by one of resignation, pass over his pale little face. His big eyes brooded darkly on the mysteries of the universe.

"You haven't kissed me yet," she insisted. "Come here, and I'll try to explain."

But he had lost heart. He put up his face, but only, she perceived, because he had been trained to obey. Soon he wriggled away from her embrace to make discoveries of his own in a distant part of the room.

"This is a dog that has been very, very naughty," she heard him whispering as he pushed great-aunt Emily's beaded footstool into a corner. "He chasted sheep, and chasted and chasted them, 'cos it was fun to see them running and running with their silly tails wagging. And he wouldn't come when he was called. Now he's going to be shut up in prison like people who steal jam and tell fibs, and never, never let out again."

Anxiety about her children gnawed at the root of Gwenllian's love for them whenever she was more than usually tired. She feared that Illtyd was going to prove imaginative, dreamy. Frances loved him and urged that he should be left alone to develop in his own way. He must not be left alone.

"Fetch your bricks from the toy cupboard," Gwenllian commanded, "and I'll shew you how to build a house."

"I can't leave this prison door," he objected, "'cos you see, I'm a shepherd. And I've got to punish this naughty dog for doing what he was told not to."

"That's a silly game," Gwenllian said. "Come along and we'll make something together."

"I don't want to make anything. I'm a shepherd like Dan Owen. I order dogs about and drive sheep."

For once his mother did not insist. She rose wearily and, going over to the French windows, stared out, feeling more than ever forsaken and miserable because her child, like his father, wished to play his own games. Since her husband did not love her and she was too virtuous a woman to have thought of a lover, she craved morbidly for her children's attention. Often she felt a stab of jealousy when she saw them caress their nurse. They were hers, hers alone; all that she had left in life except the property she was fighting to save.

I deny myself everything for Illtyd's sake, she told herself as she pressed her forehead against the cooling glass. It's only for him and in a lesser degree for baby that I struggle on as I do. So often had she said this that she believed it, forgetting that for her the estate had come first and that her children had been called into existence only as heirs to the estate. He ought to be very grateful to me when he's old enough to understand, she thought But would he be? She knew what men were—what her father had been—and the child did not greatly love her.

She was overwrought tonight. He was a dear, good little boy, though not demonstrative. His love for her, and his ability to show it, would grow. Illtyd *shall* love me, Gwenllian vowed, clenching her fists. He shall be all in all to me, and I to him. But she knew that there was room in her hungry heart for a lover as well as a son. Her child should have been the fruit of married love, not a substitute for it.

Memories were tormenting her. When she pushed open the windows, there flowed in upon her the melancholy of a chill evening after rain and the restless scent of growth. A blackbird was crying over the past: "Sweet, sweet, sweet." Somewhere she had read a poem—was it of Mary Magdalene or of some other wanton shut out of Paradise.

She is sorry, sorry, sorry, piped the blackbird. Let her in.

The lines might have been written of herself. She, too, had let the gates of Paradise close against her long ago. "Let her in," sang the blackbird. But though God might pardon all the repentant harlots, and heaven be full of them, a good woman, who had denied her love for the sake of a house and a position, would never enter into her bliss. Never in this life. "Never, never, never," mourned the blackbird. And in the next life there would be neither marrying nor giving in marriage. "Sorry, sorry, sorry," cried the blackbird. And once his song had been a song of gladness! Once, such a spring twilight as this had seemed lovely, peaceful, full of promise. Now she felt only the weariness of the day's close, of the grey sky washed pale by rain and the approach of night. The air was laden with the fragrance of wallflower and hyacinth, drowsy as that of lilies on a coffin. Beneath the shelter of the house, daffodils hung fragile and pale on their slender stalks, and primroses looked up, glistening. The blackbird sang no longer "Sweet, sweet, sweet," for a spring that was over twenty-five years ago, but "Sad, sad, sad," for the present and the future.

With a deep sigh, Gwenllian shut out the haunted evening

and turned to meet the nurse who was carrying in Richard. She criticised the new smock he was wearing and stroked the fair fluff on his head, telling herself that she need not fear he would grow up like Dick.

"Children's colouring changes so," she said. "He may be quite dark when he's a man."

"Oh no," Nannie protested with the truthfulness that had won her testimonials and lost her situations, "he's the living image of his father."

Gwenllian was glad when an hour later the children had been kissed and were gone. It was hard to do a man's and woman's work as well, and she was tired. Lying on the sofa she closed her eyes, hoping that it might be long before the solicitor came. She was almost asleep when Powell's voice disturbed her:

"Mr. Price to see you, Ma'am."

Once more Gwenllian put on her smile and extended her hand. "How kind of you to come all this way! You ought to have sent for me to your office."

"Not at all," he protested, fidgeting with a dispatch-case. "It's a pleasure. I so rarely have the privilege of meeting you now. In the old days we often had a chat out otter hunting. Now nobody seems to have the time or the heart. I don't know what's come over the countryside."

She saw that he was nervous and distressed. More worries, she thought. But not until the curtains were drawn cosily, the gentle lamps glowing within their pink silk shades, and Powell gone from the room, did she cease to make polite conversation. Then she asked wearily: "What was it you wished to consult me about?"

He cleared his throat and gave his high collar a jerk. What

a lean neck the man had: "This business of your husband having to raise five hundred pounds immediately," he said. "It comes at a most unfortunate time."

She tried to swallow and almost choked.

The lawyer's voice continued. "He's written to you about it, of course? You transact the business while he's away, so I assume—"

"Oh yes," she managed to gasp out. "But tell me what he said exactly—to you, I mean."

While he was explaining in his dusty tones, she rose and paced about the room. They will fetch something at Christie's, she thought, staring at the Bow and Chelsea figures on the mantelshelf. How she had admired them as a child! Now their bland complacence would be imprisoned in the glass case of a museum for the mob to gape at. She imagined this dear room stripped of all that made it lovable and lovely. The paper was so faded that there would be staring patches on the walls where pictures had hung, portraits of their ancestors whom now her children would forget.

"But I use the cob for driving produce into Llanon," she heard her own voice saying. "Oh yes. I keep detailed accounts. That pays its way . . We'll advertise the fishing at once then, and the shooting for next autumn... No, I should doubt whether he'll winter here. He was very much knocked about in the war, you know."

Why, oh why, had he not been killed outright? But, if he had, she would never have been mistress of Plâs Einon and mother of its heir. It was now that he ought to die—now, *now,* before he did irreparable harm. She wanted her husband to die. With the whole force and fury of her nature she desired it, as she dug her nails into the palms of her hands in an effort to keep her voice calm. Somehow she managed to give her orders to the family solicitor. Afterwards, she could not recall exactly what she had said, but knew that she had spoken with creditable discretion. When he rose and pressed her hand in his bony fingers, she had held her head high.

"There's been a mortgage on the estate before," he had ventured with a look of sympathy.

She had managed to smile. "Oh yes. We all have ups and downs."

He should not think that her spirit was broken, this man of inferior station who, years ago, if he had dared, would have asked her to marry him. He was said to have thousands. She would have done better to marry him than the suburban governess's son. He was no whit more common; she could not have loved him less. And he had the merit of being much older than herself. He would have died and left her his wealth. In another year or two she might have been sitting in her widow's weeds, smiling to see her cousin Dick squander his fortune. And when he was bankrupt, she would have bought back Plâs Einon for her own—her own.

She watched Mr. Price take his leave. His skin was wrinkled and yellow. They said he had cancer. Widowhood was the only estate fit for a proud and able woman.

She rang the bell and told Powell: "I won't have dinner to-night. I shall lie down here quietly until it's time to go to bed."

But when she was alone she did not rest. Swiftly she went to the door and locked it, took a wax candle from its silver stick and set it on the hob of the old-fashioned fender to melt. What she was about to do was so fantastic that it made her flush and laugh in stealthy excitement like a cruel child planning a forbidden jest. It had been "Martha the wise'oman" who had taught her how to cast a spell. As a little girl she had taken a Christmas pudding to the witch's tumbledown cottage with greenish thatch overhanging its two tiny windows. Martha wore her grey rags of hair loose upon her shoulders and had the flashing eyes of a kestrel. Her features were aquiline, sharp cut like Gwenllian's own. She must have been handsome as a girl. Even in age and squalor, she was of commanding appearance. The servants whispered that her mother had been a gentleman's light o' love, but they never would tell whose—Gwenllian's own great-grandfather's, she had imagined sometimes, prompted by a study of his portrait. The neighbours paid Martha in kind, butter and eggs and milk, to keep her evil eye from them and their cattle. They feared her. But Gwenllian had not been afraid of anything except her father's displeasure. Martha seemed to her to have stepped out of a picture in a fairy-tale book. She laughed and clapped her hands, and Martha had praised her boldness.

"If ever you should have a mortal enemy, my dear," she had said when they were grown friends, "this is how to bring about his death, see?"

Gwenllian took the wax as the witch had done, and twisted it and crushed it in her hands until it had the semblance of a little man. Her pinching fingers gave him a long thin neck and a small head without any chin. They made his chest narrow, his shoulders sloping like a girl's, his hands large and foolishly adangle. Knock knees they fashioned him and a slight body that leant to one side, seeking for a wall to lean up against, she thought. When her puppet of wax was finished, she held him out at arm's length and surveyed him with scorn. "Dick," she said, and, taking an old garnet brooch from her breast, she wrenched off the pin and stuck it through her mannikin's heart.

Now melt, she said within her, melt and die. On the hob she set him, close to the flames and watched his slender little body list yet further to one side. Tears of wax began to trickle down him. You're sorry now, are you, that you made an enemy of me? With a ridiculous pathetic gesture he wilted and sank lower and lower into the pool of grease at his feet. Then he dropped on his knees, and slipped right down into it, and became a dripping candle end. Now you're in your winding sheet, she thought, ready for your coffin. At last he fell away to extinction in the fire and only the pin that had transfixed him remained. She stared at it, sick and fascinated, as at a knife with which she had done murder. Shuddering violently, she seized the poker and scraped both pin and grease off the hob into the consuming flames. Their heat scorched her face as she crouched over the grate. She was burning with shame for this act of folly and peasant witch-craft to which she had stooped, and because he had brought her to it, she hated Dick the more.

The turning of the door-handle made her start up, flushed with guilt.

"Who's there?" she cried out.

Powell's voice answered with its accustomed deference. "The vicar, Ma'am. Shall I say you've too bad a head to see him?"

"No no," exclaimed Gwenllian hurrying to the door. It must not get about the parish that she locked herself into the drawing-room or it would be said she drank.

"Come in, Mr. Evans," she called. "I've been overdoing it and had to take a rest. But I'm never too tired to hear if there's anything I can do for you or your wife."

Smiling obsequiously, he shambled towards her, apologising in his bland Carmarthenshire accents. It was of no importance, no indeed! He ought not to have called after dinner at night. But, really, one did not know when to catch so busy a lady at home and at leisure. There was a saying of Jeremy Taylor's— She lost the thread of his discourse.

My hands smell of blood—of grease, I mean, she thought, rubbing them hard together. Would the old fool never have done and go? At length he came to the point—something towards the sale of work in aid of the Church Lads' Brigade. She tried to smile and wondered whether she had made an awkward grimace. Rubbing her hands still harder, she hurt them, and became aware that they clutched the brooch without a pin. She held it out to the vicar.

"I'm afraid I've no time to spare for making things, and no money either, these days, but will you accept this? Mrs. Roberts always admired it so much. I think she might give you two or three pounds—"

She saw it shining darkly, like a drop of blood, in the palm of his plump white hand. With the pin torn from that brooch she had sought by incantation to murder her own husband. She could never endure to look upon the thing again. The vicar's thanks flowed over her, soft as warmed honey. He was praising her generosity, protesting that she was too good, much too good. She caught at the word good and repeated it in her mind. She was not evil. She was not evil but good. The virtue of her actions must guard her against her secret thought.

Chapter II

SHE MEETS A GHOST

She sat before the mirror, dressing and redressing her hair until it had the neatness of a wig. Two candles burned on either hand, and silver vessels gleamed upon the muslin-draped table. Her big white room was dim as a church at vespers where only one altar is lit. Grave and careful to do all things in order, a priestess ministering to pride, she put on her black velvet gown. It had come out of its lavender-scented bag two or three times every winter since it was bought, five years ago, for the future Lord Llangattoc's coming of age. Last week the dressmaker from Llanon had been fetched in the luggage cart to bring it up to date. But still it did not look quite in the fashion. That was as it should be, Gwenllian told herself. Half the better people at tonight's Hunt Ball would be what Dick called dowdy. Had she the money to waste, she would not make herself look like a milliner's assistant to please him. Plain black enriched the cross of antique emeralds she was hanging about her neck and the long ear-rings hooked through the pierced lobes of her ears. Perhaps, she thought, staring gloomily at their winking reflections, she was wearing them for the last time. They were the only heirlooms left in her jewel case.

For she had sold her own and her mother's brooches—sapphires held with claws of gold to a bar, a flying pheasant and a fox's mask in diamonds. Her grandmother's amethysts, in their ponderous setting, bracelets, necklace and lockets heavy to wear—she had sacrificed them all, first taking out the locks of family hair and burning them, that they might not fall into the hands of strangers. Her great-grandmother's fragile seed pearls were gone, too, her empire tiara and fan-shaped combs of inlaid tortoiseshell. It had torn Gwenllian to part with each of these possessions, but since she had two sons and would never have a daughter, it was better to sell jewellery than land. Money must be raised somehow, for, though she saved, Dick spent.

She might more easily have forgiven him the large debts he incurred when he went abroad "for his health," than his incurable self-indulgence and folly in small matters. Had she not told him, "we can't afford to go to the Hunt Ball this year?" Yet go he would, and take Frances with him.

"If you won't ask your sister to stay for Christmas, I shall," he had blustered.

"Why should we have her again? Once a year is quite enough."

"Because it's a pleasant change to hear someone laughing in this tomb of a place."

"You used to say my sister talked the most arrant nonsense," she answered.

To this he had made no reply, and she had repeated in rising anger what he had said five or six years ago. "You called her London friends 'a lot of queer fish,' and her children 'unlicked cubs,' and her husband ' a highbrow prig ' who wore his hair too long. You were surprised that a man who had been in the Navy—"

"Oh, shut up," Dick had interrupted with the schoolboy rudeness that had lately become his habit. "Frances is a damned good sort. I wish you were more like her."

She had been furious. But better Frances, she had decided, than one of those dancing partners with peroxide curls whom Dick picked up in the South of France; and with an ill grace, she had yielded. Now Frances must needs bring her husband with her and all three of her hungry children, who read the most unsuitable books in the library and put them back in the wrong order.

"As Stanley's come, you'll have to go to the ball with us to make our numbers even," Dick had said with an obvious lack of enthusiasm, and she had answered curtly that he had no need to instruct her in her duties as a hostess.

To make matters worse, Dick had broken the back axle of his car, and a hired taxi must take them twenty miles into the county town. More money would be thrown away. Why had he allowed that accident to happen? Why had he been driving over to the Lewis Vaughans' at all, Gwenllian enquired of her frowning reflection? Since their noisy neighbour had married the prettier of the two Williams girls, Dick was to be seen with them at point-to-point races, at sheep-dog trials, at agricultural shows, at the picnics at which these silly young people squandered their time. What a fool he looked, carrying wraps and baskets for the bride, or keeping her sister amused with the inane prattle that a giggling flapper enjoyed! There was nothing wrong in it, perhaps, but that made it harder to forgive. Gwenllian would have respected him more if violent passion for another woman had made him unfaithful to herself, for, beneath her conventional abhorrence of lax morals, was an unconfessed sympathy with the splendid sinners of romance. But for a petty philanderer, who wasted the deep river of love in babbling, shallow streams of flirtation, she had nothing but scorn. She wondered disdainfully, as she swept downstairs, who would make a fool of Dick this evening—the bride, or her silly sister, or some new girl, empty and vulgar as all the girls were whom the Goldmans brought in their train.

Frances was in the hall, laughing and dragging her husband through the tango. Her gown was patterned in autumn leaves, red, gold and copper. Gwenllian thought it too florid, and her amber beads unsuitable for a full dress occasion. Like a Bacchante she looked, with her unruly black hair, her animated face and lithe movements. How crimson her lips were, how richly tawny her cheeks. Gwenllian did not like to see her sister look so naturally young. She frowned, but had to concede that Frances was handsome to-night.

"Hello," called a happy voice from below, and Frances danced to the foot of the stairs. As she raised her head the lamp light shone on the long curve of her throat, golden with health. "My dear," she cried, her bright eyes according the admiration which Gwenllian had grudged to her, "you look magnificent—like an Empress."

And for an instant Gwenllian perceived that, if she herself had been a happy woman, she might have liked her handsome younger sister. But such bitter insight did not outlast dinner. Frances chattered foolishly, Gwenllian told herself, to account for her own irritation. What bad taste it was to mimic Lady Llangattoc merely because she was a trifle self-important! Throughout the long cold drive that followed Frances continued in irrepressible high spirits, keeping Dick and her husband in perpetual laughter. Stanley was a lean brown man with a tight mouth and very blue eyes. He spoke little except when he was defending his Utopian reforms. Gwenllian dismissed them all under two heads: "pampering criminals and naughty children instead of punishing them as they deserve; and fancying he can stop war by allowing a lot of deceitful foreigners to argue." She never listened to him when he was talking such nonsense, nor did she think much of him at any other time. He was a fool, she considered, to take Frances seriously when she ought to have been laughed at, and to laugh at her, as he was doing tonight, when he should have reproved her lack of dignity.

"My dear goose, you *are* funny," he exclaimed once. And Gwenllian, sitting erect in her comer, as far as possible from Dick, thought contemptuously, Fancy that joke not having grown stale yet! For Frances and Stanley had been married years longer than she and Dick. She grew increasingly bored and annoyed by the nearness of three such fools, laughing, laughing at nothing at all, in the cramped jolting darkness of the taxi. To her the drive seemed unending.

But they ceased, at last, to be flung against one another, and instead of the rutted roads and dark hedgerows, Gwenllian saw the sleek wet pavements of the town. Brightly the shops flashed by in a blur of raindrops on the window-panes. At the entrance to the old coaching inn, a crowd of simple folk waited to see what little they could beneath their neighbours' umbrellas of the gentry with whom they were not privileged to dance. As the Llanon taxi slowed into its place in the queue of motor-cars that were crawling up, one by one, to a muddy strip of red carpet, Dick craned out of the window.

"There's the bride arriving. I say, isn't she holding her skirts high! I shall chaff her about that … By Jove, the Goldmans have brought a dazzler this time! Bet you I get introduced to her before you do, my boy!"

Gwenllian moved to avoid the pressure of his knees against

her own. The stupidity of all he said would have sickened her less, she decided, if she had not always been able to predict it to a word.

"Must I remind you, for your dear Frances's sake, *not* to dance out of our own party all night," she stung at him in a whisper as she alighted.

Inside the lounge, old ladies wearing antiquated capes and fleecy head-shawls were nodding and smiling their way to the foot of the shallow stairs. Others were coming down, showing their bosoms and their diamonds. At their heels, waving laughing signals to friends below, fluttered a bevy of country-bred girls. Their hair and their skirts were cut short, but they had the same starry eyes and radiant, flushed faces that Gwenllian remembered at dances long ago.

"How pretty they all look," Frances exclaimed. "What fun it is!"

But Gwenllian answered not a word, for her throat was tight and her eyes smarted. In painladen silence she went up to the room she remembered so well, with its sagging ceiling and a pierglass that tilted too far forward or swung right back. Another girl was before it now. "Look at the rotten thing!" she cried. "Absurd," was the word Gwenllian had used. There, still, stood the vast mahogany dressing-table with clumsy, twisted legs, and upon it the pin-cushion, big as a baby's pillow, covered in white muslin over pink sateen. A coloured print of "Bubbles " hung on the wall, and a gory battle scene of Lady Butler's, mercifully reproduced in black and white. The former paper of roses and ribbons had been replaced by one of Japanese figures dwarfed by giant wistaria, and a meagre fireplace with ugly green tiles had supplanted the generous one with hobs. Gwenllian did not approve of these changes, any more than she did of Nancy Lloyd's niece, who would never be the belle her aunt was once, and who was actually putting paint on her lips. But there—bless her!—was Betto, with the same very large cap and the three warts with the three hairs on each. Only— alas!—now the hairs were white. She was addressing the mother of a debutante as "Miss Dolly," speaking through the pins she had always held in her mouth. Frances gave her a hug that almost caused the pins to be swallowed, and vowed she was grown prettier than ever.

"Go you on, Miss Frances," she cried, delighted. "You're the same hoyden of a young lady ever you were! Fancy any gentleman asking you to marry him!"

"He didn't, Betto, till I'd made it clear that he'd got to."

"Oh, *duwch!* Isn't the gel a caution," the ancient chambermaid appealed to the company in general.

Newcomers to the district looked surprised, and Gwenllian intervened with an enquiry after Betto's rheumatism, thus making clear her great age and explaining her privileged familiarity.

When they were downstairs again and had found their escort in the press, they pushed their way along a passage that reeked of stale beer, damp whitewash and linoleum. Music came in broken waves above the babble of voices at the ballroom door.

"They're off! Tally ho! Get to it! Get to it!" cried a youth with a face as pink as his coat.

"The Lord Lieutenant isn't here yet," cried an older man, hurrying past. "Stop the band there! Can't possibly begin till he's opened the ball!"

"Oh, I say, what rot," grumbled young Goldman, whose

swarthy glance Gwenllian was careful not to meet. "Are we to have our evening messed up for that old fogey?"

"How too pricelessly formal and Victorian," exclaimed his pretty companion.

And Gwenllian in disgust heard Dick say, "Hello Goldman! You might be a sport and introduce me.

She turned away to join in scattered talk with people of her own kind.

"How d'ye do? Ages since I had the pleasure of meetin' you last!"

"Have a good run the other day?"

"Fourteen brace o' pheasants. Not bad, what?" "… the magistrates have grown too slack to convict."

"Well, *look* what a crew they are on the bench nowadays! Scarcely a gentleman among 'em!"

"Thank you *so* much. I'll ask Mother."

Frances had become the centre of a group of former admirers. How was it, Gwenllian wondered, that, with such Bohemian ways and subversive views, her sister retained the liking of so many quite nice men? She herself was marooned with her brother-in-law. Making no more pretence of enjoying each other's company than good manners required, they danced together. When this duty was performed, they leaned against the wall, exchanging a few civil comments, but both were absorbed in watching, he his wife, and she her husband. It was not love or pride, not even jealousy, that kept her eyes on Dick. To spy upon him with disapproval was her habit. What silly thing was he saying now to make Ena Williams laugh in that blatant way? Why had he attached himself to the Lewis Vaughans the moment they arrived? People would imagine that he was in the bride's tow as usual. Frances disentangled herself from the old friends pressing for dances and returned, radiant, to ask, "Will you dance the next with me, Stanley?"

"Don't I always hang about waiting for orders?" he smiled. "Who were all your adorers?"

"Frances," Gwenllian was prompted to interrupt, "your hair looks as if it might come down. Hadn't you better go up and make yourself presentable?" But the conductor of the band, raised on a palm decorated platform, had flourished his baton. The strife of drum and saxophone was renewed, making Gwenllian wince. She turned her back, not caring to watch her sister closely held in the arms of a ridiculously doting husband. Nor could she endure to see Dick, jigging and grinning and rocking his shoulders to and fro, while his wife stood by without a partner! Had he abandoned even the attempt to behave like a gentleman? She rejoined the crowd of elderly folk by the door and was presently sitting out in the lounge with a lethargic judge.

"I come here to support the Hunt," he informed her. "One must shew up in the ball-room, don't you know, to encourage the young 'uns."

"D'you find they need encouraging these days?" she asked with a bitter laugh.

He looked at her sideways. "You don't much like the present generation? Well, I confess that I shall be glad to get away from them myself for a quiet game of bridge. Will you take a hand?"

She made excuses. Surely she was not come to that yet? And she remembered how she had delighted to waltz all night and had marvelled that any but the infirm could keep to their chairs while dance music was calling. She had never tired of dancing then. At two or three in the morning, when the fiddles played *John Peel* and then *God Save the Queen,* she could have cried with vexation that joy should be so soon ended. How far away, how long ago, seemed those few hours of happiness!

After the judge had left her, she sat alone behind the screen that hid their two chairs, and tried to nerve herself for a return to the ball-room. Dick would have, for appearances' sake, to ask her for at least one dance or two. He danced well, she supposed, in this jerky modern fashion. Like a clockwork toy he looked. But she felt discomfort in yielding herself to so angular a rhythm, and she detested dancing with him. His slightest touch, since Richard's birth, aroused loathing in her. Perhaps, seeing her neglected among the chaperons, a few courteous old men would lead her away and trample on her toes. They would stumble with her round the room where once she had skimmed and darted like a swallow. Still, she could not hide all night. And sighing, she was about to rise, when a black silk skirt rustled against the sheltering screen.

"This will do, dear. No one will overhear us," said a voice she knew.

And another, equally familiar, answered. "Yes, my dear, *do* go on."

The speakers were Doctor Roberts's wife and the sister of Mr. Price the solicitor. They were proud, Gwenllian knew, of being admitted to the Hunt Ball. Afterwards, they would boast to members of the Mothers' Union, whose husbands were in trade, of their intimate acquaintance with the misdoings of their betters. Gwenllian gathered much useful knowledge of local affairs from Mrs. Doctor Roberts. But sometimes, she suspected, the lady withheld information for fear of giving offence. To Miss Price, the friend of her bosom, she might talk more openly, and, with a scornful grimace, Gwenllian stayed to eavesdrop.

"It's gone beyond a joke," she heard the soft Pembrokeshire voice cooing. "Of course the Doctor never breathes a word to me. You've no idea the *discretion* I have to put up with from that man!" Miss Price made clicking sounds of sympathy, and Gwenllian, in her place of hiding, smiled.

"But he's truly vexed," the Doctor's wife went on, "I know from his looks whenever he's called there, to see her marriage such an *utter* failure."

"What could you expect?" demanded Miss Price with self-righteous gusto. "I never could have made *myself a* laughing-stock, marrying a man young enough to be my son."

Gwenllian stiffened.

"Of course it was a sad mistake. But he needn't run after his neighbour's wife so scandalously. All the servants at the Lewis Vaughans are talking."

"His neighbour's *wife,*" exclaimed Miss Price. "I heard it was the unmarried one with whom he was behaving so badly. Miss Powell the Schools was saying she felt it her duty to write Mrs. Williams a letter about her daughter—an anonymous letter, of course."

"It's *both* of them, if you must know, dear," said Mrs. Roberts, more than ever resembling a wood-pigeon in the gentleness of her tone. "It's truly shocking. And when that over-trusting husband, young Vaughan, finds out—"

Miss Price drew in her breath as though she were sucking some juicy fruit.

"They say he has a violent temper, once it's roused," murmured Mrs. Roberts.

"What a frightful scandal there's bound to be then!"

"Yes indeed. Poor, poor Gwenllian! How I pity her!"

"So do I, though, of course, she's only herself to blame. My brother says that husband of hers will soon have squandered every penny of the money she married him for. The estate's already mortgaged as heavily as ever it was under the old Squire."

"You don't say so!"

"Yes, but I was to keep it an absolute secret."

"Things like that are bound to come out, my dear. Poor Gwenllian, with all her virtues, was always much too stuck up. I'm afraid the whole country will soon see her pride have a fall." Gwenllian started up with the mad intention of flinging down the screen on top of the two gossips. But she controlled her fury, and sat down again until the crowd of laughing couples coming past after another dance enabled her to slip away undetected. She drifted through the red plush drawing-room and gazed up the stairs. Everywhere young men and maidens were sitting two by two, looking at one another with laughter or love in their glances.

"You *know* I haven't another thought in the world," someone whispered from behind a bank of flowers as she passed by. Her own sweetheart had once said the same fond foolish thing to her. "But you," he had added, "think only of your position as mistress of your father's house." *"*I don't! I don't!" she had protested. *"*I'm always thinking of you." And yet she had let him go. Aimless now and alone, she walked down a passage leading to the garden. Here once she had been led, all eagerness, her finger tips in a shy flutter on his sleeve. A curtain hung across the entrance. She drew it aside, and in the half darkness saw a tall youth stooping to kiss a girl. His encircling arm was black against the pallor of her dress. She was turned away, her little head and slim bare shoulders drooped from him as though she were afraid. But as Gwenllian retreated, she saw the girl turn round and, with a sudden gesture of passionate response, fling her arms round her lover's neck and strain upward to the lips that sought her own. It might have been herself! How fast her heart beat with disquieting recollections! No longer caring where she went, she let herself be swept by the returning tide of dancers back into the ball-room.

Supporters of the Hunt no longer impeded the way. There lingered only such mammas as surveyed their daughters for an excuse to interfere, and a few bald men who watched the dancing that they might complain how ungraceful it was grown. The amiable old men were gone to enjoy themselves at the supper- or the card-table. Gwenllian listened to the talk of those ill-natured elders who chose not to let youth alone. Their discontent accorded with her own.

"The banging of this infernal nigger music sets my teeth on edge."

"Walkin' up and down! Did you ever see anything so ridiculous? There's nothing in it!"

" No, by Jove! In our day we danced. I had to change my collar three times in an evening."

"Don't you think he holds his partner unnecessarily close?"

"Oh my dear, they all do now."

"Well, I think it ought to be stopped. It's really quite disgusting."

"One would not have *dreamed* of receiving them before the war."

"That's never your youngest? Dear me, how sadly time flies!"

"… got herself talked about with old Pelham's heir."

"They tried to hush it up."

. four, plain unmarriageable daughters."

"…drummed out of his regiment…"

Clack, clack, clack went their spiteful tongues. Some of them were people of whom she was accustomed to approve. To-night she hated them, everyone. They would be clacking about her affairs soon, blaming her, pitying her, dragging her pride, her cherished domestic privacy through the mud of their mean gossip, as those two common women had already dared to do. She, whose morals had been stricter than any of theirs, would come off no better with them than an adulteress. They wouldn't spare the pride they had once envied. But she'd face them all out. Over their wagging grey heads she stared, smiling a smile of steel, while the young couples swirled past her, smiling because they were happy.

After a while she noticed the broad shoulders and head of a tall man, standing with his back to her. His hair was as dark as her own and refused to be sleeked down. The glimpse she had of his firm profile set her dreaming of the young man she had loved so long ago. His hair, too, had been defiant. But it had been thicker, more glossy than this stranger's. She began to take an interest in him, forgetting her anger with the rest of the world. Who was he? Why did he stand aloof from the dancers, gazing at them with an intent sadness that had been communicated to her even by the fragmentary glimpse that she had had of his face? It was not her custom to shew curiosity about a man whom she did not know, and she surprised herself by edging through the crowd to make a closer inspection of this one. Look at him more nearly, she must, she knew not why. Many old acquaintances tried to detain her with their shew of affability, but she evaded them all. Lady Llangattoc was signalling from her chair against the wall, but Gwenllian was purposefully blind. At last she was divided from the stranger only by an osprey plume that whisked to and fro in an Edwardian head-dress. She slipped past the obstruction and stood close behind him. He turned round at once as if he had felt her presence. He had the large square jaw that she admired. Perhaps he was fifty years of age. But she found him very handsome, far handsomer than any younger man in the room. A spasm of recognition contracted his mouth.

"Hello," he exclaimed.

She stared at him, frozen in surprise.

"How d'you do?" he said, and in a very low tone, he added, "Bitty."

No-one had called her that for—it must be twenty years! And suddenly she felt a flutter and jump of her heart, startling, exciting, of promise, as full of wonder as the earliest movement of a first child within the womb. She held out her hand. He took it, and she looked down at their clasped hands as from a very long way off. It was not often that hers was made by comparison to seem so small. There were little black hairs on the back of his great hand. She did not remember them, nor the veins standing out, raised and blue. It was aged, but it felt the same—very strong, warm, enclosing! How that tormenting new music thumped and clattered! The room seemed to be rocking with the dancers.

She was shaken by its vibration. Never in her life had she fainted. I mustn't faint, she told herself. I can't faint! I won't faint.

"Isn't it hot?" she heard a voice saying that had once been

her own. It had ceased to be under her control. It made a surging sound like that of the sea in a big shell. There was a shell on the nursery mantelpiece. She used to hold it to her ear. He had kissed her for the first time in the old nursery at home. She had been arranging a vase of red dahlias, and the flowers had dropped through her fingers to the floor. So *that* was why she had grown red dahlias ever since! She had forgotten the reason—but not the kiss. Did any woman ever forget the first kiss of her first love? It was that, not any later experience, which deflowered her.

"Supposing we find somewhere to sit down," she heard his voice suggest

"Yes. By a window, if you don't mind."

"Take my arm."

Once again she laid her hand on that sleeve which sent so vibrant a tremor through her finger tips. "Thank you," she murmured. "These crushes always make me feel rather breathless."

"Terrible mob," he said, staring straight in front of him with set face.

"Yes," she agreed, because she must needs say something. "But the band is good, don't you think? They keep such excellent time."

She had loathed the beat, beat, beat, as of tom-toms, arousing savages to an obscene orgy. It was not fit that white men and women of breeding should dance to such music. Thank heaven it had stopped! Why did it echo still in her leaping pulses?

He did not lead her in the wake of the laughing talkative stream that flowed from the ball-room in search of secluded sitting-out places, but took her to the window embrasure farthest from the dowagers and the band. He found her a chair and she dropped down on to it, her knees weak, as though she had been running until she was exhausted. He flung open a window and the icy air flowed in over her naked arms and neck.

Once they had gone swimming together in the river below her home. It was very early on a June morning before even the country folk were astir to wonder at such "goings on." She remembered the quivering white mist in the valleys, and the hill-tops appearing like islands of gold. How sweet the flowering may trees and the lilac had been! How the dew-drenched grass had sparkled, and the birds twittered! He and she had seemed to be the only pair of lovers in a new world—a world miraculously beautiful, created by a kindly God for their delight. They had taken hands and run down through the shrubbery together, startling a heron from the pool where he was fishing and two otters at play upon the bank. The plunge into cold water had been invigorating and had set her more than ever aglow.

But through the long day afterwards, when he was gone, she had been dull, so dull!

She gazed across the polished spaces of the floor from which the dancing feet were departed and thought how empty, how drear, had been the days and weeks that had dragged out into years, since she drove him away disappointed. She had grasped at the shadow of Plâs Einon and let go the substance of her happiness. Now her happiness was returned as a spectre to torment her. And with a strange terror, as if she were conversing with a ghost, she began to ask him why he was here and what he had been doing since they parted. Their talk seemed remote and thin as that of two souls in purgatory. Yet her spoken questions and his answers were plain enough. It was what they left unsaid that made their silences so hard to bear. He was staying with the Lloyds of Dolforgan, he told her. They had often urged him to revisit the district but, somehow, he had never cared to do so. Gwenllian longed, at that, to cry out in an agony of repentance. Instead, she forced herself to go on plying him with conventional enquiries. Yes. He had become a Brigadier-General during the war; had seen enough service to last his lifetime; had unexpectedly inherited a property, and retired, "to make a garden," he said, "and replant some of the million trees that were cut down."

"On your estate in Norfolk?" she asked.

And he answered, looking at her mournfully, "Oh, not there, only. I have an odd nightmare—quite often—trees, like the long avenues in Flanders after heavy shell fire, broken off, cut short, mutilated. Can't quite explain why it should be so horrible to remember things like that. But it is."

She shivered and answered, "Yes, I know."

For a long while neither of them spoke again. At last he said: "I don't care much for the flat country. Sometimes I've half a mind to sell out and come back to Wales."

Then we might have married after all, she mused, without my having to give up my own country for more than a few years, or the way of life to which I clung. She felt like one standing upon the scaffold with the noose about her neck, to whom the chaplain should say, "Let us contemplate the joyful years that would have stretched before you, had you but been more wise."

The music struck up and another dance began. After a while a stout, elaborately preserved woman came up, escorted by her last partner. Her painted lips wore a hard smile.

"*Here* you are!" she cried with a shrew's flourish of joviality. "So like a husband to forget his duty to dance with his wife!"

He did not stop to introduce her to Gwenllian, but slid away, looking as dazed and miserable as she was feeling. She stared after him from her cold embrasure, until someone—she scarcely knew who—stood over her claiming the promised dance she had forgotten.

"I've lost my programme," she said, vaguely, holding it in her hands. "I seem to have lost everything."

Later in the evening, the ghost of her sweetheart came back to her. "Will you dance this with me?" She looked up at him, trembling, hoping, she dared not think for what. "I've asked for one of Joyce's old waltzes. D'you remember?"

Could she ever forget? For the thousandth time she remembered her coming-out dance—her white dress, her stiffening dread of tearing its many frills— and how, meeting him, she had discovered that she could reverse, and had lost her nervousness and been happy and proud, giving not another thought to anything, not even to her dropping hairpins.

The lilting, sensuous music began. Soon elderly sentimentalists were looking in from the card-room to nod and beat time to the gay pathos of an old tune. But in January of the year 1926 few young couples could dance an old-fashioned waltz. Those accustomed to walk their way through a "hesitation," knew not what to make of this faster, more exciting melody. So Gwenllian and her lover sped unhindered, like swift skaters upon ice. No man had ever waltzed, she believed, as he did, making of his body and of hers instruments on which the music played, until they were one with it, one with each other, no longer a man and a woman dancing in time to a tune, but the creations of a sweetly, a passionately vibrating song—a love song—the Song of Songs! She forgot her age and her sorrows and the years that the locust had eaten, forgot that she was an unhappy wife, an over-anxious mother, the care-worn mistress of a household burdened with debt and threatened with dissolution. She thought no more of her endangered future than of her embittered past. There was an end to the long war between her unsatisfied woman's body and her dominating mascu- line spirit. She loved. She danced. It was enough. She had no wish to rule or lead. There was no will left in her but to abandon her will to his. Wherever he moved, she followed, as easily as one who, in a dream possesses the power of flight. Never had they danced with so delicious a rhythm, even when he and she were boy and girl, supple, full of vigour, idyl- lically in love. For then she had been virgin in spirit and in flesh. Now she knew with what fiery, joyous self-surrender she could have given herself to the man she had refused, and, in her passionate thought, a shadow fell across her motherhood. They were not his children she had borne. Therefore, they had polluted her. Never again, she thought for one wild moment, would she be able to feel their little fond- ling hands without a shudder of disgust. But she was in his arms: nothing mattered that had been or that might be.

Why had the music of their bridal ceased? Why was she standing, dizzy and forlorn? Oh God, she thought, could I not have died while I was dancing?

It was torment unendurable to be awakened to the life she must henceforth lead. She had dreamed she was a happy girl again, dressed in white as for her wedding. But staring down now at her gown she saw that it was black, and it reminded her that she was growing old. Elderly neighbours began to buzz round her like stinging flies.

"Capital! Never saw a better performance in my life!"

"I say, Gwenllian, you and your partner ought to go in for exhibition dancing!"

"Who is he?"

"A ghost," she answered, and saw her questioner's mouth drop open in astonishment.

As arbitrarily as they had begun, they ceased to pester her and stood upright and rigid. She supposed that the band must be playing *God save the King*. But what she heard was only a noise like thunder. When it was over, she looked up, imploring him with her gaze to stay.

"I must go."

"Why?"

"My wife's waiting." And he added in a dull, expressionless tone, "We shan't ever meet again, I'm afraid."

She could not bear it. "Oh no! Why not?" she gasped. "You promised—you said, I mean, something about returning to Wales?"

"That's only what I dream of." He spoke heavily as before. "My wife's rooted to Norfolk."

In desperation she asked what she must not ask. "Are you very fond of her?"

"We have children," he answered.

"Yes. So have I."

Side by side they stood in a leaden silence. They were no longer a pair of lovers to whom no other people in the world were of importance. They were the father and the mother of a family, members of the Established Church and of the landed gentry, staunch upholders of sound old-fashioned morality, believers in the finality of marriage.

Slowly she laid her hand in his. She thought he was going to speak, for his lips moved.

"Good-bye then," was all he said, at last.

"Good—" she began, and could say no more.

When she had watched him go towards his wife, she went into the hall, because people seemed to be going that way. I suppose I must go home, she reflected, staring about her, bemused, and perceiving a flutter of leave-taking. Parents were trying to shepherd their charges away; young people to prolong their noisy farewells. Amid the cheerful herd, shaking hands and kissing, the laughter, the running up and down stairs, Gwenllian felt sick and stunned. She sat down abruptly on the nearest chair. To steady her sight, that was become blurred, she fixed her eyes on the first man she saw before her. He was insignificant, not worth a glance, but he would serve her turn. His chest was flat, his slender shoulders sloped, and his mouth was too soft and small for a man's mouth. There was scarcely any colour in his face and his little moustache and eyebrows were pale as straw. He had blue eyes of the light shade she disliked. They were at present bloodshot. He's been drinking too much champagne, she told herself. He looks the sort of poor weak thing who'd drink. Suddenly he returned her stare and scowled; and she knew him.

Chapter III

HE RECEIVES A WARNING

Within Plâs Einon it was cool. As Dick passed through the large airy rooms, he heard the winged flutter of curtains and saw the tall flowers in their vases gently sway, but when he went out beneath the portico, it was as though he had entered a hot-house. The lawns were steaming—scented with white jasmine and roses, like a bath, he thought. A cloud of midges danced above the carriage sweep, always in motion, for ever in the same place. Bees droned from blossom to blossom. But the birds were strangely hushed. Why was the garden so silent, he wondered, missing something but not knowing what it was he missed. Only the rippling of the river, hidden by the beech trees' midsummer foliage, came up from the dingle.

He stood blinking at the rich colours of the herbaceous border. The flowers had pretty names: larkspur and London-pride, sweet-william and snapdragon, peony, pansy, poppy, love-in-a-mist and golden-rod! It was a very beautiful place. Why didn't he enjoy his ownership? Was it his fault? His brows began to wrinkle in puppyish perplexity. Could they have been mistaken, all those fellows in his regiment who believed that to own a fine house and an estate must make a man content?

I don't take much pleasure in all this, Dick thought, scowling at the empty lawns. Gwen would say that that was because he hadn't been bom to it; and, though he scarcely liked to admit it to himself, he was envious of the city clerks who lived in comfortable obscurity among their own class. He'd like to have more money than they had and he didn't want to sit in an office all day, but he wanted everything else of theirs—their girls, their motorbikes, their boat on the river with a gramophone—and he'd like working in the back garden on Saturdays. Get your coat off, work a bit, come in for tea; perhaps a game of bridge afterwards. Better than giving orders and making speeches. He imagined at the tea-table under a pink-shaded lamp a young wife whom he could banter. There'd be jokes between them; they'd chatter in bed in the dark. And when he was working in the garden she'd trip after him in high- heeled shoes. He saw her shoes very clearly. Gwen would call them bad style. Still, they were what he liked on a pretty girl's feet.

He was extremely sorry for himself. There was no-one here in whom he could confide, explaining that really he had very simple tastes and was quite easy to get on with if he was taken the right way. He would like to tell the truth about himself; but he never had—no, not to anyone, not to his mother— it sounded so damned silly. You couldn't confess to a love of high-heeled shoes worn out of doors with diamond buckles and little straps criss-cross over the instep. Or was it sillier to go on pretending? He didn't know. He had slept ill, and was in a mood, this sultry July morning, to question all the things he habitually accepted. That came of listening to Frances. Her annual visit disturbed him as much as it irritated Gwen. Frances upset everything.

Look at her at this moment, lolling in a deck chair, supple, enviably at ease, with a litter of books at her feet! Dick scowled at the untidy back of her head. Her hair was magnificent. But why must it always seem to be on the point of tumbling down? This rubbish she had taken to reviewing for the Lord only knew what sort of papers had given her more *notions* than ever. To Dick there was but one kind of notion; the sort that people were better without. Luckily, the things Frances said were not intended to be taken seriously; at any rate, he supposed not. But he found it hard to remember that some folk played with ideas as he had been taught to play with balls, and he wished that Frances would take up golf instead. Then he could motor her daily to the neighbouring links. Pleasant, that would be. For, in spite of her highbrow folly, she was a companionable woman—smooth and warm, with a dash to her. She understood so many things that a decent fellow had to leave unsaid, and, unlike her sister, she had not the mind of an old maid. He wanted to interrupt her odious reading, but was withheld by fear that she might laugh at his clothes.

This bright blue jacket and plus-fours, this scarlet tie and stockings increased his self-consciousness. And the worst of it was that he didn't want to go otter hunting any more than she did. But, of course, he had been too civil to say so. The day she had told the Master what she thought of his pastime, Dick and his wife had been united for fully ten minutes by their feelings of disapproval.

"Frances has shocking manners!"

"I quite agree with you, my dear! And what rot she talked!"

Yet Dick had memories of a good day's sport that left him ill at ease. When the little wet head bobbed up for the last time, he had seen terror in the hunted eyes and had felt a sharp twinge of kinship. Could the creature be suffering as he had suffered when the wail of a shell sounded above the angry popping of machine guns? Nonsense, he had told himself. Otters hadn't a human imagination. But then—why those eyes? He had been sickened by the raging of the hounds, and even more by the yelling of men and women who surrounded the pool, cutting off their victim's retreat, upstream or down. So big a pack, so large a crowd of people armed with poles … but he had forced himself to join them. They had told him that otters showed no mercy to salmon. That had been a relief.

Looking now at Frances, he decided that he would make the most of that argument to her. Strange that, while disagreeing with her opinions, he had come to crave for her approval! Grasping his pole, he walked across to her.

"Change your mind?" he hailed.

Frances let a volume of essays on economics drop through her fingers, and stretched her long arms above her head. He liked to watch her movements, graceful and unconcerned as those of a wild animal.

"What a grind it is having to think on such a sultry day," she yawned.

"Chuck it then, for once!"

She shook her head, and he tried again. "It's an awfully pretty sight, all this colour reflected in the water." He made a wry face at his clothes. "And the country's looking its best."

She nodded. "I know. I used to love the setting."

"You're such an outdoor sort, really," he went on. "I can't understand what made you chuck every form of sport."

"Decadence, I dare say," she answered, smiling up at him. "Why do you hate killing things? Grandfather didn't mind."

"Nor do I," Dick lied valiantly. "Not when it's a case of vermin or game. They've got to be kept down, you know. If you're so squeamish," he added, "you needn't stay for the kill."

How oppressive the heat and the stillness were! When he had spoken, he noticed that she was pale, and as he watched her, she grew so much paler that he feared she was going to faint.

"I say," he exclaimed, "has the weather knocked you up?"

She did not reply, but began to gaze at him as though she saw something tragic in his gaudily- clad figure. The sudden gravity of her look startled him.

"Are you all right? I say, are you all right?"

"Yes," she answered almost in a whisper.

"Then what are you staring at me for, as if you'd seen a ghost?" He tried to laugh away a pang of fear.

"I was thinking of what you'd just said." Her tone was that of one in a trance.

"What did I say? Only that you needn't stay for the kill."

The word had filled her with an unaccountable foreboding. It had drawn her mind out into regions where nothing was known but all things were secretly and profoundly certain. She shivered and sat up.

"Did you know, Dick," she said, "that some of us Einon-Thomases are cursed with second-sight?" And she added, in a tone almost of entreaty: "I wish you hated all this!"

"All what? Otter hunting and so on?"

"This place—all of it. The whole way of life here."

"What's wrong? It's comfortable, isn't it?" he asked, at once defensive, his gaze moving over the garden he admired so much and enjoyed so little. "Why should I hate it?"

There was no warning that she could make him understand, but she said:

"If things go on as they are, Dick, something dreadful will happen here."

He opened his eyes wide, alarmed by her earnestness. "There's thunder about," he said with a wriggle of discomfort. "It's got on your nerves."

And he continued to stare at her, fascinated by the pallor of her face, until he heard his wife's voice cry out: "Dick, I'm waiting!"

He turned, startled, and saw her coming towards him out of the hall's deep shadow. Dread touched him—a dread that was changed, as he looked her over, into a mood of frustrate and rebellious anger. Her short skirt and jacket were of the crude blue and her tie of the yet cruder scarlet prescribed for the killing of otters. Against these strident colours and the white of her masculine shirt, her skin looked faded and old. The collar she was wearing intensified her resemblance to those sporting spinsters of whom he had made fun in his boyhood. How could he have married such a woman, he asked himself in a sudden spasm of distaste. "What a beastly ugly kit that is," he exclaimed.

Her eyebrows went up. "D'you think so? Then why d'you wear it yourself?"

He tried to pass off the clash of their antagonism with a laugh. "You insisted on it."

"My dear Dick, you're not a child. Though," she added looking him up and down with disdain, "you so often behave like one."

"Oh, well," he said, still trying to appear unconcerned. "When in Rome, do as the Romans— eh, Frances?"

"*I* don't, unless I happen to like their ways," answered his sister-in-law.

"Oh," said Gwenllian, "it's no good your appealing against me to her. Frances never thinks or acts as other people do. You'd lose your reputation for originality if you did, wouldn't you, dear?" There was malice in the elder sister's smile, and Dick hated her for it. Frances might be eccentric; but she was a good sort. He'd be damned if that old cat should sneer at her!

"I've changed my mind," he blurted out. "I'm going to stay and keep Frances company."

He saw the detested black eyebrows raised once more and he turned his back on his wife.

"Indeed," he heard her say. She was waiting there, silently, behind him. He felt her overpowering presence. In a flurry he added, "It's too damned hot to go chasing up and down the country today."

"I never heard you complain of the heat before. You are generally grumbling about the cold," said the voice at his shoulder.

"Well, it *is* hot! Can't I ever say what I like without your jumping down my throat?" he almost shouted.

Frances intervened. "Children! Children! What a thing to quarrel about! For goodness sake let him stay if he wants to!"

Dick turned round in time to see Gwenllian throw her sister a glance of icy resentment. "By all means," she said, "if you have made him your convert. What excuse shall I give Colonel Howells—that Dick is busy reading Socialist economics?"

"Why the devil should you offer any excuse?" Dick broke out.

"They're on our water," Gwenllian replied, scrutinising a distant tree above his head.

"They're there to please themselves, aren't they?" he retorted, and he longed to shout at her, "Can't you even look at me, you stuck-up prig?"

"You promised to be there," she said, without lowering her glance.

"I've changed my mind, I tell you."

"I see. So I shall have to keep your obligations for you." And she added: "Perhaps I'd better say you were detained by estate business."

He felt the flame of a blush run up his spine and burn his face. *Damn* her, taunting him with his ineptitude as a landlord and in front of her sister too!

"I'm afraid I only ordered a light luncheon for one," she resumed, acidly polite, now that she had the satisfaction of seeing him turn red.

"I prefer bread and cheese," he muttered, and scowled after her as she turned her back upon him and walked away.

Frances had sunk down again into her deck-chair.

"Bread and cheese and kisses," he heard her murmur. He glanced at her with suspicion to see whether she was mocking him, but she seemed lapsed in a state of dreamy exhaustion. That queer turn she had, he thought, has left her fagged out. Damned uncanny, it was. He fetched a chair and flopped into it beside her to enjoy a quiet sulk. Filling a pipe, he brooded over his misfortunes. These odious wrangles with Gwen were becoming more frequent. They made him angrier while they lasted; their passing left him more shaken and sore. A life of continence was enough to sour any man who hadn't chosen to be a monk. Yet, God knew, he had no desire ever again to be her lover! As for taking a mistress, that seemed to him as foreign as the eating of frogs. Once when he had remarked to Frank, "that sort of thing's not quite English, what?" Frank had jeered, "you mean that it's not respectable middle-class." What Dick had meant in his heart was that it would have shocked his mother.

There were furtive things a fellow didn't want to do, unless he was driven to them. But it might come to that. You couldn't *look* at a girl in this dreary district, without all the old tabbies getting on your track. Damned unfair when you'd done no wrong, but only wished you dared. And sitting hunched beneath his stately colonnade, scowling at the gay flowers in his garden, Dick wondered why everything seemed to go against him in spite of the honesty of his intentions.

Presently he saw the nursery procession making its careful way over the gravel. "*Mind,* darling," he heard Nannie admonish. She was leading his wife's heir by the hand. Her stout person was tightly encased in a grey coat that looked superfluous on so hot a day. Dick thought with discomfort of the thick corsets and petticoats she so obviously wore. The nursery-maid, who walked behind her, slowly pushing a glossy pram, was a meagre imitation of her elder, grey with black points, and closely girthed. The girl's face was shiny with perspiration, yet on her hands, as on Nannie's, were white cotton gloves, and on her feet stockings of black wool. Gwen *would* insist on making the poor devils uncomfortable, Dick thought, and the children too. No use his trying to interfere on behalf of the little blighters! Illtyd was so utterly her own. And if he tried to give Richard his share of attention, she grew furious with jealousy on her favourite's behalf. They wouldn't have much of a life with a mother who coddled one, snubbed the other, and would leave neither alone. What had been the use, anyway, of bringing more people into a world he couldn't make head or tail of himself? But there they were. He had begotten them, though he hadn't much wanted to, and it filled him with contradictory irritation that Gwen should behave as though she owed them to none but the Holy Ghost.

White clouds, piled up in rounded blobs like whipped cream, were beginning to cover the hard blue sky. But still the sunshine gilded Plâs Einon garden with an intense, metallic light. The green of the lawns was grown vivid as the covering of a billiard table. The motionless trees appeared no longer to be living things, but painted scenery against the backcloth of a stage. Theatrical, that's what it looks, Dick suddenly said to himself. Like the setting on an empty stage for a play that's about to begin. And it'll be a tragedy according to Frances.

Out of the stifling silence she said: "Dick, in all the six years we've known each other, we've never told the truth."

"Oh, I say," he protested.

"You know quite well what I mean. About your marriage."

"Don't," he muttered hastily. "I can't possibly discuss it—with you of all people." But he knew that it was in her he longed to confide.

"My dear," she said, "why don't you and Gwenllian separate?"

"Oh," he declared, shocked that Gwen's sister should suggest such a thing, "it hasn't become unbearable—not yet."

"Why go on until it does?"

"Oh, I don't know," he answered vaguely. "There are the kids to be thought of."

"D'you think children benefit so much by seeing their father and mother always at loggerheads?"

"People expect a married couple to stick it out for the sake of their kids," he sighed.

Frances sat up and flashed her bright eyes on him. There were golden lights in their darkness. They seemed to burn with an impatient flame. "For heaven's sake, try to think this matter out for yourself," she cried. "How much do you mean to your children, or they to you?"

"Well, I couldn't bear to hurt the little beggars," he answered, trying to evade the issue. "I don't even like to see Gwen as strict as she is."

"That's only your universal attitude of passive goodwill," she told him. "How much do you and your children mean to one another *positively*?"

Her searching eyes compelled candour.

"Nothing," he muttered, and hung his head.

"Don't imagine I'm blaming you, my dear," she said, laying one of her hands on his. "It's simply that you're not a born parent. You've always funked power and responsibility, haven't you?"

"Yes," he answered, less humiliated than relieved to be telling the truth at last.

"Then leave it all to Gwenllian who revels in it," she urged. "Go away from here at once, and find a job among the sort of people with whom you're most at ease. You'd be popular in some sets, my dear. But you'll never go down here."

"I know that," he admitted.

"And to be liked means such a lot to you," she went on vehemently. "I hate to see you being starved of what you need."

Then he confessed his real objection to a separation.

"I'd be in danger of starving, literally, if we tried to run two establishments, Gwen and I. And you must agree it would be inhuman to part her from all this."

"Of course," said Frances. "She'd have to stay on here. It belongs to her, in a sense."

"That's all very fine," he grumbled, "but with present

taxation and the boys to educate, how much d'you suppose there'd be left over for me to live on? Gwen never stops nagging if I take a month or two abroad in the winter."

"I know, I know," Frances exclaimed. "But poverty couldn't be as damnable as living with someone who hates you."

"I've tasted poverty before," he declared, his small mouth grown stubborn under its trim moustache. "I'd clear out soon enough, if I could afford to live comfortably in my own quiet way. But there wouldn't be enough, I tell you."

"Then set to and earn it," she flashed at him.

"What earthly chance has a fellow of my age, brought up in the Service? The best I could hope to pick up would be a billet abroad in some vile climate. You seem to forget how I was knocked about in the war. My health would never stand it." And he fought with a foolish inclination to cry. "Besides," he added, after a gloomy silence, "it isn't as though I should ever be free to marry again and have another shot at being happy."

"Gwenllian might be induced to divorce you."

Dick wearily shook his head. "I don't think so. She'd say it looked so bad."

The clouds, which had by now blotted out all the blue of the sky, were no longer creamy. Some were of a lowering grey, others were toadstool yellow. One last gleam of sun fell upon the hillside that rose above the tree-tops of the dingle. Dick saw the whitewashed buildings of his farms, shining like pearls against their green setting, and he recalled the day on which he had first beheld his property. It had brought him none of the joy for which he looked. But since for Gwen and her heir's sake he must not sell it, he'd be hanged if he didn't at least wring what pride and comfort there was to be had out of the damned place! Frances was one of these unworldly fools who cared only for people and ideas. She hadn't the sense to understand that a fellow couldn't inherit a magnificent old country house, an estate, a position in the best county society, and then go back, of his own free will, to being a penniless suburban nobody. It might be jolly if he could. But it couldn't be done.

The sky became a leaden lid closing down upon him. All sunlight was gone, and colour faded from the landscape. Over the hill opposite he saw a veil of rain descending and with its approach the sultry air grew chill and he shivered. A roll of thunder, reminding him of distant gun-fire, made him start.

"It's coming," he said. "Better take shelter."

Frances did not reply. She gave a long sigh and began to gather up her books.

A cold shaft of rain struck him. "Come on in," he cried, obstinate against this mad woman who wanted to part him from his money. Obstinate against her, angry with her for having troubled him, and yet, as she stood for an instant with the edge of a book forced upward into the curve of her breast, suddenly desiring to kiss her. He hesitated; perhaps, if he asked her, she might in her present mood, consent; and he lightened the weight on one of his feet as though he had the courage to take a pace towards her.

"Well, Dick," she said, "what's the matter?"

"I thought," he began. "That is, I felt that—"

A blinding dazzle of lightning interrupted him. "Look," he said, "let me carry the books," and, though a clap of thunder had killed his words, he took the books almost roughly, and began to run for shelter, finding in this an excuse for putting his hand into hers.

Chapter IV

SHE DOES HER DUTY

Gwenllian crouched over the hearth in his bedroom. Her elbows dug into her knees. She felt the hard pressure of her jaw-bone thrust between clenched fists. The heat and the jigging light of the fire made her wince. But she moved only to turn Dick's night clothes, that were hung upon a towel rail; and, when he fought for breath, to rise and bend over the sick man on the bed. Deftly she eased his body, propping it with pillows. He acknowledged these services with a gasp of thanks. Yet she saw that he shrank from her touch; and in angry contempt she thought: The fool's afraid of me! Back to her chair she would go then and sit as before, shoulders hunched, muscles taut, tired beyond the longing for rest. Hours passed. There was no sound but of Dick's distressed breathing, the unconcerned, gossiping voices of the fire, and the ticking of the clock. But, all the while, over the pale walls and ceiling, shadows were dancing; and to Gwenllian, the stillness was peopled with ghosts.

This was the bridal chamber of her race. Man and woman, betrothed in the interests of property, had lain beneath that canopy night after night through the years, until one or other, pitied by time, was put away, alone at last, in a yet straighter box. Cowering over the grate, Gwenllian pictured those proud, chaste women, her forebears, enduring such moments of rumpled shame as she could not forget. Never would she pardon Dick for what she had made him do. "The *animal*," she muttered, "to be tricked by his lust!"

The fire seemed to have become fiercer. Rapidly she passed trembling hands over her face. Her hot thoughts ran on. On that night last winter, when she had danced again with the man she had once loved in virginal innocence, she, too, had learned desire. Asleep, she had dreamed warm, troubling dreams; and, waking, been restless. Curiosity, that crept and pried, had tainted her former cold compassion for young women that erred. Often of late, she had insinuated: "Tell me just how it happened? You need not be afraid to speak quite openly. You see, I'm married," and had at once been suspicious of her own motive in making these enquiries. She found that she craved more and more detail of reply, and hating this obscene eagerness in herself, laid the blame for it on her marriage, which had awakened her to passions it could not satisfy. Dick's shadow darkened her soul, corrupting even her deeds of mercy. Yet he himself was so small a thing, lying alone on that big hateful bed!

When the fire burned cheerful and steady, there came to her memories of childhood. Then the sense of her duty towards him was uppermost. The shaded lamp, the airing garments, the hushed warmth of the room, these were as they had been in the beginning. Forty years ago in the nursery overhead, Nanny had bidden her say her prayers. No matter how the day's injustices and thwarted cravings for self-assertion had driven her to fury, she must beg a blessing on her relations. Often she had flung away from the firm hands tucking her in.

"I don't *want* God to bless Howel! He started it, and when I hit back, Mother sent me out of the room. I *hate* him! I *hate* Mother!"

"Now Miss Gwennie, you're talking like a bad wicked girl. Never let me hear you say such shocking things no more. Haven't I taught you to love all your relations?"

"I *can't*, Nanny!"

"But you *must*. You must *make* yourself. Now get on with Gentle Jesus meek and mild… Well? Have the naughty cross thoughts put the nice pretty hymn out of your head? That comes of hating those it's your duty to love. 'Look upon a little child. Pity my simplicity. Suffer me to come to Thee.' Not so fast! 'Tisn't reverent."

As she recalled the unconscious irony of Nanny's parting benediction, which no preceding rages, tears or chastisements ever altered—"Good night my little lamb. Go to sleep at once like a good girl, and you'll have sweet dreams "—Gwenllian's tight lips relaxed into a smile. Of Nanny's peasant piety she could now make light. But she could not thus dismiss the grand words of the Book of Common Prayer. Unlike Frances, she had never disturbed her faith. There had been no doubt in her mind of the doctrine contained in the marriage service when she stood before the altar rails with Dick. Yet, how could she be bound to honour a fool who brought discredit upon herself and her house? Frances would say that promises, which could not be kept, might without blame be broken. But Gwenllian scorned to be as her sister was. She would continue to do her duty by the man she had married. Perhaps the end was nearer than she dared to hope. …Trapped by this thought, she flushed with guilt, assuring herself again and again that she was not evil but good, *good*. Then with a shudder she remembered the night on which she had modelled her husband in wax and melted him to death. She must have been mad then. Was she losing her reason again now? She had a vision of herself laying a wreath upon his coffin, and the woman in the vision smiled, drawing a widow's long black veil across her mouth that none should see her rejoice. In imagination, Gwenllian tasted the veil upon her lips.

Something dark slid over the rug at her feet. There was no movement of running. It passed as smooth as a shadow and as soundless. She started up, clutching at her throat to stifle a scream. A moment later, the familiar scuttering behind the wainscot told her that it was but a mouse. She was twisted by a fit of silent, hysterical laughter, and, in the midst of it was checked, stricken by a new fear, hearing a new sound. This was no fancy, bred of solitude, but a footfall! Quivering, she listened, and heard it again. Someone was coming slowly upstairs. The boards creaked beneath a heavy tread. And, with a shock that stayed her breath and made her heart leap, she exclaimed: "It's Father I ... Because I've failed ...I can't bear it! I can't!" But this mocking spectre drew steadily nearer. Always, she had struggled to escape his derision. Because she was female and disinherited, she had struggled in vain. But she had sworn to convince him, in the end, that her brain, at least, was not contemptible and girlish. Had she failed in this also? Would he stand with his feet wide apart, as he used to do, and laugh at her?

Gwenllian's head turned this way and that, like the head of a wild cat in a snare, until her eyes fell upon the sick man she had been keeping alive. On him it would be easy to avenge herself.

The white china knob shook. She seized the back of a chair with both hands to keep herself from screaming. With a choking sensation she saw the door begin to open. The crack widened. The Doctor entered on tiptoe.

"Hello," he whispered, "I'm afraid I startled you. I made 'em give me the side door key, you know."

She was unable to utter a word.

"You look pretty white," she heard him say.

She dropped down on to the chair at which she had been clutching. "Just a little tired, perhaps."

"I don't wonder," his voice droned over her head. "I ought to have insisted on wiring for a nurse the moment he was taken ill. You're not fit to deal with a pneumonia case just after having the children with whooping-cough. But thank goodness, one will be here in the morning. And I've a good mind to send for another."

"You mustn't," she heard herself protest from force of habit. "We can't afford it."

He went over to the bed, grumbling, below his breath, about false economy.

"You ought to get some good nights' sleep."

"I shall sleep all day as soon as nurse arrives." She spoke mechanically, sitting, inert, exhausted, with hands hanging limp at her sides.

She heard the Doctor ask: "Have those linseed poultices relieved him?"

She had been given to murderous and abominable thoughts. The devil must have slipped them into her mind when she was too tired to resist. She must make amends: and, dragging herself to her feet, she crept to the bedside, and showed her carefully kept chart, and answered the Doctor's questions with the precision of a trained nurse. "Herpes," she heard herself whisper, and "rusty sputum. …Yes, his respiration was sixty again… The pain in his back seems to trouble him and that nasty short, dry cough keeps on disturbing his sleep."

"The crisis won't be for another five days," the Doctor said. "We'll have to look out for his heart then. It isn't up to much, as you know. I shall have injections of strychnine ready for the nurse to give at a moment's notice. He'll have to be watched as a cat watches a mouse, mind—day and night— and his pulse taken constantly... Now look here, my dear girl, you'd much better let me send for a night nurse, as well, before you crock up."

She shook her head.

"If you're so obstinate about saving a few pounds, I shall insist—"

She clutched at his arm. "It's not the money, only," she protested in an urgent whisper, "it's— oh, how can I tell you? I blame myself so! Please, *please* let me do something for him now that I can be of service."

The big steadying hand of the Doctor descended on her shoulder. "Blame yourself!" he exclaimed. "Stuff and nonsense!"

"But I do," she insisted, her eyes filling with tears, so that the Doctor loomed over her, blurred in the firelight, like a shaggy giant. "You see, he doesn't love me." But she did not speak the rest of her thought, "and I hate him."

"Is that any reason," said the Doctor, gripping her shoulder very hard, "why you should wear yourself out nursing him?"

"Yes," she answered, in a low, strained tone.

"Have it your own way," he grumbled.

Presently she was left in the bridal chamber where she and Dick had lain but never loved. She stood on guard beside the bed she would never share again, and stared down at the cyanosed face she loathed.

Chapter V

SHE SETS THEM BOTH FREE

BETWEEN tall trees bordering the drive, she had followed a ribbon of pallor through the dark of a clouded night; but within the circle of yews was a final blackness. She stretched out her hands, groping with her fingers, turning herself round and round. Now I can talk aloud, she thought. Mad people do.

She held her breath and listened. There was no stir of the air, nor drip of rain. Such an emptiness of all sound was strange in a country whose life was in the lisp of waters, the rustle of wind, and she seemed to have left earth behind. "I am released," she whispered, hugging herself tight with folded arms.

She crouched near to the earth and played upon it with her fingers as though she were playing a dance. She was free. He was dying who had served his turn. She had given her strength to maintain the hated burden of his life; but God was merciful. The man was dying. She rocked to and fro, clutching her knees and laughing. She had done her duty, and was to be rewarded. She was exalted above the fatigue of her body. A delicious giddiness lapped against her mind.

There came to her memory the close of a day's hunting at her father's heels. He had taken her into an inn and given her a tumblerful of hot rum and milk. His friends had stood round her, asking why she was solemn and silent. They had laughed at her. She had been a little girl then, but she bad known already that she must keep guarded silence when ever she felt her self-control slipping. That knowledge had served her well since. Now, once more, she was floating on a warm, gently rocking tide. Here she might yield to it.

She had been so long without profound and continuous sleep that the palms of her hands and the soles of her feet ached. There were tremors in all her limbs, and she began to ask herself—as if she were imagining a holiday after a long period of tension and labour—whether her nerve would go after her husband's death. She could afford a breakdown then. She imagined herself tearing things to shreds, hearing the rip of linen. Tomorrow, perhaps, she said.

Not until yesterday, had she dared count on release. Until the crisis was over, fever had lent a flush to his face, brightening his eyes and giving to his struggles for breath an urgent, agonised vitality. Day and night he had been tossing, hot as an engine that was running too fast. The speed of his pulse and respiration had given him the air of living more intensely than a normal man. "He's putting up a better fight than I thought he could," the Doctor had declared, and she had said within her: He'll survive. He'll live on for ever. Now he was cool and white and damp as a lily on a grave. No deceptive spot of colour disguised the clay of his cheeks. The eyes were lustreless in their sockets. The limp hands on the counterpane were bones with waxen skin wrinkled over them. Yesterday, Dr. Roberts had examined his patient's heart and been silent. An hour later the nurse had come unexpectedly to Gwenllian's room, saying that she had taken it upon herself to send for the Doctor.

"But he will be here tonight as usual," Gwenllian had said. "What made you think it necessary?"

The woman's thin lips tightened into minute creases. "I didn't like to be responsible," she had answered.

And Gwenllian had dared to hope. She had visited Dick at once, and stared into his face. Hope had grown to certainty. Mad with joy, she had fled from the house that she might not betray her secret, and when the Doctor drove up to the house, she had remained in hiding. Now, alone in blackness, she twisted her hands together, unlocked them, and with her fingers played upon the ground. Suddenly, from a long way off, she heard a throbbing sound, and, starting up, exclaimed, "the Doctor's car!" To escape from the encircling yews was not easy. She lost her way, and a bough struck her face. She was breathless and angry when at last she reached the drive and stumbled into the glare of headlights. Blinking and dazed, she stood in the ditch.

The car passed her, slowed down, and came to a standstill a few yards ahead, leaving her in a darkness lit only by the red eye of a tail-lamp. "Drive on to the lodge and wait there," she heard the Doctor say, and his big stooping figure loomed towards her. He's sent the driver out of earshot because he's going to tell me, she said to herself, and she clenched her fists and waited, her body tingling.

The Doctor's face, peering down into hers, was a pale rectangle, the big chin thrust forward.

"Whatever were you doing among those trees?"

"A breath of air."

"It's infernally dark "

"I can see in the dark, like a 'witch's fowl,' " she told him.

"Wish I could," he grumbled. "Can't make your face out now a foot away."

She was glad of that. "You've seen him?" she asked.

"Yes. I've seen him." There was a pause. Somewhere in the night's black stillness a fox barked. Instantly, the dogs at a farm far up the valley began to clamour. They want to kill, Gwenllian thought, and she said aloud: "Have you nothing to tell me?" The question choked her and she put a hand to her neck where a pulse was beating like a quick angry drum.

"Yes, I think I've something to tell you."

There was another silence.

"Nurse was afraid—" she prompted, and began to bite her fingers, unable to finish the sentence.

"I know. I know," the Doctor replied. "His heart needs every care. You're to give him half an ounce of champagne in milk, as before, every hour, whenever he's awake. Keep on feeling his pulse. Don't on any account let him sit up. Don't prop him up at all. Keep him flat on his back. Feed him out of a feeding cup. And watch his pulse. Have a kettle ready to dissolve one of the strychnine tablets I gave you. And, in case of collapse, be sure to lose no time in giving an injection."

"I know all that by heart already," she cried. "I shan't bungle it."

A hand grasped her shoulder. "My dear girl, I haven't been a medico for close on fifty years without knowing a born nurse when I see her. I couldn't have saved your husband's life, and all Harley Street couldn't have saved it, what's more. It's good nursing takes this trick. So don't imagine I've any misgivings about your carrying out orders. It's you who have saved him."

"Saved him?" she said. "Have I done that?"

"I think I can say as much. I believe he's safe now. Until yesterday, I don't mind confessing to you, my dear, I feared you'd lose him. But now, though he's as weak as a kitten, I'm confident he'll pull through."

It seemed that the darkness had weight. She put her hands to her head, trying to lift the cruel pressure. She must not faint. To keep herself up, she clutched at the Doctor's arm.

He patted her gripping fingers. "You're to be congratulated. You were right all through. Aren't you pretty pleased with yourself?"

She gave a small dry sob, which he interpreted in his own fashion.

"Yes. So I should think!"

Holding each other's hands they stood for a long while, close together.

"Are you all right?" he asked at length. "A bit overwrought, eh?"

"Just a bit."

"Are you fit to take your turn to-night?"

"I'm equal to anything now."

"Good girl! But it won't be easy."

"No," she muttered, "I don't suppose it will." How did one kill a man? Men had as many lives as cats. How much easier to kill herself! She would not fear to take her own life, though that, too, was a sin. But her life was of value. His was not. She must live for the sake of Plâs Einon and its heirs.

She found herself in the hall, staring at the weapons that gleamed upon the walls. Swords and daggers and spears, and little sly stilettos: all had been made and used for killing men. But climbing the stairs, she went into the sick room, treading soft, as a good nurse should.

"How is he?" she whispered.

The nurse rose, rustling, from her low chair by the fireside. What a silly dress, thought Gwenllian. I do the job far better than she, without all that starch. She began to put on her old dressing gown and padded slippers.

"Better, Doctor seemed to think," the nurse told her. "He said I'd been unduly anxious. One never knows."

"You were perfectly right to send for him."

"Yes," said the nurse with her brisk professional smile. "I'm glad for your sake, Mrs. Einon-Thomas, that I did. How relieved you must be! Doctor is quite sure tonight that your husband will recover."

"Quite sure?" Gwenllian repeated. "Did he use those very words?"

"'Positive,' I think was his expression," the nurse answered, more brightly than ever. "He's so pleased with the way things are going, he won't call again till noon tomorrow."

"Thank you," said Gwenllian. "You go off to bed and have a good night."

"I wish you were going to, Mrs. Einon-Thomas." Gwenllian heard herself utter a queer noise that might have been a laugh, and became aware of the nurse's pale eyes fixed critically upon her.

"You'll forgive my saying so, Mrs. Einon-Thomas," said the pruned, genteel voice, "but you do look bad! You ought to send for another nurse. Really you ought. It never does for relatives to nurse a case like this. They get worked up. It's that wears you out, I always say."

"Yes," Gwenllian agreed, "it's emotion that wears one out." She sank into the nearest chair. "We'll talk of it tomorrow, nurse."

"I'm glad to hear you say so, I'm sure. Have you everything you want?"

"Thank you. Everything."

"I'll say good night, then."

"Good night."

When she was left alone, Gwenllian buried her face in her hands. Rage, grief and despair, too heavy to find ease in tears, weighed her down. After a long while a groan escaped her. Why had she borne heirs to this man? In this mood of desolation, she felt no love for her own children. Her heart was a cell without light.

A faint voice asked for water. The word was repeated, but she did not move. Leave me alone, she thought. Leave me alone now. But at last she rose and took a feeding-cup to the sick man. I ought to be giving him champagne and milk, she told herself as she watched the feeble effort of his bloodless lips to suck. And suddenly, she knew not why, she slid her arms behind his thin shoulders, and, lifting him until he was almost upright, propped him with pillows. There were not enough on the bed to support him. She snatched the cushions from a settee and put these also behind his back. His listless eyes opened a little in surprise.

"Ought I—?" he tried to ask.

"You'll be more comfortable like that," she told him with decision, and turned away.

"Thank you," she heard him murmur. His thanks cut her. What was she about, disobeying the Doctor's orders? Had she done it on purpose? Could she go through with what she had begun? She paced about the room squeezing her hands together and staring at her white knuckles. She glanced at the clock on the mantelpiece. Five minutes past two. When next she looked, it was a quarter past. Many hours of waiting seemed to have intervened. From the hall below, came the chiming of the half-hour. Was that all? Would dawn never break? Her patient stirred. She stood afar off and observed his struggle for speech.

"I feel," he managed to gasp, "I feel— so—"

She stood over him, watching intently. "Queer," was the word he tried to say. He had been pale before. Now his pallor was tinged with a blueish hue, and his lips were grey. The thinness of his face was accentuated; and his nostrils were pinched in. Though she listened for his breathing, she could not hear it. His eyes were closed. His head had sunk forward and drooped a little to one side. He gave a long sigh. "Lie down," he whispered. But she did not take away the pillows.

"I'm going to give you an injection," she said into his ear.

"Yes," he breathed out with another sigh. "Yes, please."

She went to the table where a clean white towel covered the apparatus of the sickroom. With deliberate movements, she folded the towel and laid it aside, measured out two doses of champagne and milk and drank them. A shudder ran through her limbs. The drink left a sour taste in her mouth. For a moment she stood irresolute, staring at the bed. My father slept in it. He died in it, she told herself, and taking up a little glass tube, carefully removed from it a tablet which, in the cup of her left hand, she carried to the fire. She gripped the poker with her right hand and beat a hollow place among the flames. Into this she dropped the tablet and, with a sudden darting gesture, ground it to pieces and covered it with live coals. She was trembling violently when she returned to the bedside with a syringe full of plain water, but steadied herself to make a quick, neat incision into her patient's arm. He flinched but did not open his eyes.

With her head turned away from him, she restored everything to its place. Ten minutes to three. She heaped more fuel upon the already blazing fire; then, with her dressing-gown close about her shoulders, crept on tiptoe from the room.

In the upstairs study that she used as an estate office, everything was in its usual precise order. She could lay her hand in the dark upon candle and matches. In a moment, a tiny spearhead of light quivered within the shelter of her curved palm. When it was pointing steadily upwards, she raised it towards the scowling face of her father. She feared him no longer; she had transcended him. Would you, a man, have dared as much? she asked silently. Then with an abrupt twist of her shoulders, final and contemptuous, she turned her back upon him.

She extinguished the candle and stole back to the bedroom. The body on her marriage bed had listed over: the eyelids were fallen a little apart. Gwenllian pulled away the pillows, and without touching it, let the corpse flop backwards. It stared with half open eyes at the pleated crimson canopy on which she, too, had gazed from below. She made as if to touch the wrist, but her fingers would not accept the contact. There's no need, anyhow, she told herself, and went out to awaken the nurse.

EPILOGUE

Chapter I

FRANCES IS ENLIGHTENED

Frances flung wide her bedroom window and leaned out. Beneath her palm's pressure, the stone felt kindly warm. Tendrils of ivy, glistening wet, stirred about the sill; and, further off, tiny new beech leaves danced to the breeze. Day and night, the west wind had drawn swathes of white mist and grey squalls of rain over the branches of the trees; but a week of wet weather was little to pay for such a morning as this. Was ever Eden so enchanting in its freshness as her home in May?

Repressed here in childhood, she had fled from Plâs Einon in her rebellious youth, but on this quiet Sunday morning its cloistral loveliness enthralled her. Almost, she could have wished to live and die within its green horizon. Here was no smudge of factory smoke, no jostle of crowds, no anger of speed. To the east, she followed the silver loops of the river towards its peaty source; to the west, through a wooded valley, it moved seaward in a graceful curve. On the opposite hillside, to the south, the farmhouses were white as hawthorn flower and beside each homestead an orchard was pink with apple-blossom. Every tree in the landscape was unfurling at its own pace, for spring here had as many shades of green as autumn of yellow. She was tired of the rattle of towns, and would have liked to spend the morning among the song of birds and the ripple of water, idly and good humouredly envious of her sister's life.

It was a mood, no more. She was not envious of Gwenllian nor did she regret her own choice of life. She had married for love and for love's sake only had borne children. For fifteen years she had lent money she could ill spare and had listened, perhaps too patiently, to all who came to her with their loves or their disappointments, their ambitions, failures, desires. If she had had Gwenllian's wisdom, conserving her vitality for her own ends, she would have warded them off. But to ward them off, to cling to what was hers, was contrary to her nature. A fool, perhaps, by her sister's standards, but not an unhappy one. Certainly, she thought with a smile, it's too late to change. After this interlude in the stately quiet of Plâs Einon she must return to book-reviewing and washing-up and hire-purchase furniture and eager, ruthless children; not to property, not to security; not to hoarding—for she had nothing to hoard. Well, she had made her choice long ago, and would make it again on the same terms.

But how happy Gwenllian ought to be, she reflected. Gwenllian loves possessions and now everything here is hers, as if she were an only son; and Frances, remembering that she had always believed her sister to have a character of iron, was surprised by the change in her. She had become more pious, less self-sufficient. She, who never begged, had begged for company at church, and Frances had heard in her voice something forlorn and troubled and very urgent. Even on weekdays, hearing the bells of Cwmnant, she would look up. sometimes with a strange glance of entreaty. "Will you come, too? We shall be in time, perhaps, if we make haste." The neighbourhood was beginning to speak of her as of a saint; and Frances, remembering the tea-parties to which she had been taken during the past week, smiled, half in derision, half in wonder.

Mrs. Roberts had led her into the warm dankness of her conservatory.

"We all know how wrong it is to speak ill of the departed," she had begun as soon as the other ladies were gone out of earshot to admire the maidenhair fern. "But to you, dear Frances, I can confess none of us considered your poor brother-in-law *worthy* of his *splendid* wife. I wouldn't for the world suggest that his death—so young, poor thing!—was a merciful release. That would be shocking. Still ..."

"It might be true, like so many shocking things," Frances had retorted, thinking of the worried, puppy-look on Dick's face.

Mrs. Roberts had had no answer ready.

"How naughty you are," she had exclaimed, taking refuge in archness. "But I did say to my husband, after that tragic night, 'God *does* know what's best for all parties—sometimes.' You know, dear, he was sent for—the Doctor, I mean—at half-past three in the morning. And he found the patient dead, stone dead, and your poor, *poor* sister quite distracted with grief. Really *beside* herself, as though she hadn't made every effort to save his life! The Doctor says he has never seen such devotion as hers. But it happens sometimes, he says, in spite of the best nursing in the world, that a patient's strength gives out at the very moment when he seems to be recovering nicely. If the injection Gwenllian gave your poor brother-in-law couldn't save him, nothing could. 'It's mere morbidity for you to blame yourself,' the Doctor has repeatedly told your dear sister. But really, Frances, the Doctor admires your sister so much," Mrs. Roberts had concluded with a simper, "that he makes me quite jealous. And he's not the only man in the district to say how truly good she is. She *is* goodness itself, of course. But I always say, 'oh, you *men*! If she didn't look so handsome in her widow's garb—' But there!"

And Mrs. Evans had waited for Frances in the church porch. "I'm so relieved to see you here," she had whispered. "You may be able to improve your dear sister's health and spirits. If ever a wife wore herself out for her husband, she did. The servants were all talking about it in the village. My husband hears everything when he goes on his parochial rounds. They say she wouldn't let a soul do a thing for him but herself. And just fancy her being quite alone when he passed away! Any other woman would have left him to summon help, I'm sure. But she wouldn't desert his bedside even to ring a bell. Wonderful, isn't she? The vicar and I did pity and admire her so. I only hope her husband appreciated her great goodness—at the last." And Mrs. Evans had let fall a sigh full of reproach. "But," she had added brightly, "we mustn't say a word against those who have left all their errors and follies behind."

Recalling these and kindred speeches, Frances turned away from the sunlit landscape, and with a grimace dragged on her church-going hat. Poor, inoffensive Dick! Adverse criticism could no longer make him wince. But was it conceivable that Gwenllian genuinely missed him, as the neighbours imagined? An unexplained shadow darkened her pride of ownership. That much was plain. But its cause? Had she not all she desired, who loved to be mistress of this house, to command its servants, to train its heirs?

"I'm thankful to say, I'm able to live within my means now," she had told Frances last night. "It isn't easy. But I take a pride in keeping this place as it should be kept, and for less than any one else could do it." A slight emphasis on the word "now " had been the nearest approach to any mention of Dick that Frances had heard his widow make. His name was never spoken. Something has happened to Gwenllian, Frances thought, that none of us will ever understand.

She went down the shallow stairs that had been built for dignity and ease. Gwenllian was waiting in the hall. One of her black-gloved hands held a prayer book, and the other the child she was training to be head of the house.

"I've wound twenty-five clocks while you were dressing," she said in a tone of reproof; and Frances knew from her glance that to herself she added: "And you aren't tidy, even now." But there were many tart speeches from which Gwenllian now-a-days refrained. She contented herself with urging: "We must hurry, or we shan't be settled in our pew before the five minute bell begins. It sets such a bad example to scramble in at the last moment... Illtyd, have you your sixpence quite safe?"

The little boy looked up. A faint, bewildered anxiety was the normal expression of his pale face. But, knowing that he had the right answer this time, he ventured a small smile. "Yes, Mother. Nannie washed it, so as it shouldn't leave a mark on my gloves."

They were white, and fitted him so well that his tiny fingers were stiffened by them. His sailor suit was snowy as his mother's bed-linen, a credit to the gardener's wife who was the family laundress. Frances, sorry for a child whose mother loved him so little for his own sake, smiled to think how astonished the neighbours would be by her pity. Gwenllian was considered a faultless parent.

"That's right," she was saying. "Now you may run along

ahead of us. But you're to keep to the middle of the drive. You are not to chase birds or pick flowers or jump about and get hot, remember. Mother will be very cross if you disobey her."

"Yes, Mother," he murmured, hanging his head, and sedately they set forth.

The fluttering young leaves threw a delicate pattern of light and shade over the child's white suit, but Gwenllian's habit was too sombre to receive it. On week days she trudged about her estate in a short black skirt, greenish with exposure. But every Sunday, she put on her weeds of state. The dress became her well with its mournful folds and its lines of white at neck and wrist. Her incisive features were given an added severity by a close-fitting bonnet, made to resemble a nun's head-dress by the long veil falling from it over her shoulders. She seemed a tragic figure as she passed up the aisle of the village church, holding her little orphaned boy by the hand.

In wonder, Frances watched her kneeling, her attitude a prayer. Long after others were seated, she stayed upon her knees with head bowed low over clasped hands. Her finely chiselled fingers were interlaced. Upon one of them gleamed a wedding ring, her only ornament. If she had been a Catholic, one would have supposed that she was interceding for the soul of her beloved dead. Or did she pray that she might soon rejoin him? Yet she had commanded and bitterly despised him. His death alone could not have transformed her. But this posture of sorrow was no pose. The woman kneeling there, her tragic dark eyes gazing up now at the cross upon the altar, was deeply suffering. Frances stared, and marvelled more and more, until the clatter of hob-nailed boots on tesselated pavement disturbed her. A group of farm labourers was entering together in a last minute rush. A whiff of hair pomade and peppermint floated up to the Plâs Einon pew in its front rank below the pulpit. There was a creaking of leather as the lads jostled one another at the back of the church. The ancient sexton turned round to glare at them.

A muffled Amen came from the Vestry. The organ quavered into sound, though scarcely into music, under the anxious fingers of Mrs. Evans. Everyone stood up and sat down again. Only Gwenllian sank upon her knees. The vicar looked complacently round his congregation, smoothed down his surplice with plump short-fingered hands, and in a creamy Carmarthenshire voice began to recite.

"When the wicked man turneth away from his wickedness that he hath committed, and doeth that which is lawful and right, he shall save his soul alive."

A spasm of eagerness contracted Gwenllian's pale face. Frances saw her flinch at the words, "acknowledge and confess …" What made her conscience so sore? Why did she pour such a passion of entreaty into her murmured recital of the General Confession? "We have erred, and strayed from thy ways like lost sheep. We have followed too much the devices and desires of our own hearts. We have offended against thy holy law. We have left undone those things which we ought to have done; and we have done those things which we ought not to have done; and there is no health in us."

Frances looked round the church. Women, from behind their hands, or beneath the brims of their hats, were examining Mrs. Roberts's new toque. Old men, already half asleep, muttered the words they had learned by rote long ago. A little boy slid a marble out of his trouser pocket and showed it privily to his fellow. A shy quick glance was exchanged between a youth and a maiden who shared the same book, though others were within reach. The sexton blew his nose and wiped his spectacles, and looked about him irritably, disapproving of those who were sucking lozenges by stealth. But Gwenllian was pouring her soul into every word of contrition that she uttered. Now her lips were moving in silence, following the form of the Priest's Absolution: "And that the rest of our life hereafter may be pure and holy." She seemed to be whispering that phrase again and again to herself.

The lulling mustiness of the church reminded Frances of the loft at Plâs Einon where fruit was stored and sometimes rotted. She saw the motes of dust drift down a shaft of sunlight. She listened to the soothing chants to which the psalms were droned and the stately cadence of words so old that their meaning had been worn away like the lettering on the stone slab before her eyes. A new generation of boys' faces bloomed, pink and round as ripe apples, in the choir stalls; but they were indistinguishable from those she had known as a girl. Her crusading ancestor lay, still as ever, in the self-same spot, his crossed feet at rest upon his faithful dog.

"As it was in the beginning, is now and ever shall be, world without end. Amen." Among the congregation she saw no new faces; only familiar ones grown more resigned; only features that had been childish, set fast now in a parent's likeness. Some, also, were missing. And above the Plâs Einon pew hovered the figure of death with a scythe in his hands. Upon the tablet commemorating Owain ap Einon, who departed this life in the year of grace sixteen hundred and twenty-one, the sculptor had lavished all the gruesome conceits of his age. Time's hour-glass, the writhing worm and the grinning skull of corruption, were carved at each of its four corners. Frances as a child had been afraid to look upon it except when the sun shone on her from the lancet window across the nave, for she had been told that if sunlight fell upon a woman at her prayers it presaged a special blessing.

The only new thing in the ancient church was a memorial on the wall above Gwenllian's head. Frances, looking up, read Dick's name, his regiment, the dates of his birth and of his succession to Plâs Einon, and below them the odd claim that Gwenllian had included in his epitaph:

Who, having served throughout the Great War, died, in indirect consequence of that Service, February 13, 1926. "DULCE ET DECORUM EST PRO PATRIA MORI"

It was a blemish here, this crude brazen tablet, Frances thought, turning her eyes away. How gently grave and sheltering were these grey stone walls that had stood through the centuries! How lovely, after all, was the shrine of those traditions against which she had rebelled! Church and home: she said the words to herself, lulled by their sound. Had not Gwenllian, perhaps, been wise to stay in the quiet valley of her birth, accepting as sufficient the external beauty of her ancestors' way of life? Must not that existence be fair which wore so gracious a face? In the midst of her musing, she heard the vicar pronouncing the Ten Commandments. His benevo- lent tone implied that they were a formula and no more; it was unnecessary to speak to his flock of the less polite transgressions.

"Honour thy father and thy mother," he purred, "that thy days may be long in the land which the Lord thy God giveth thee."

"Lord have mercy upon us and incline our hearts to keep

this law," mumbled the people. The clear voice of the lady of the manor led them.

"Thou shalt do no murder," the vicar said. His rosy fat face almost smiled an apology.

Gwenllian's response was not audible. An arrow of sunlight struck across the place where she knelt, but did not touch her. The brass tablet above her was kindled by the flash. The capital letters of the inscription gleamed with a brilliant, liquid red. Gwenllian's eyes became fixed on them in a look of extreme horror; her cheeks turned pale and her mouth sagged. Before clasped hands could hide it, Frances had seen her face and had read it.

Beyond need of proof or hope of refutation, she perceived the truth. She knew now what it was that she had dreaded when she urged Dick to escape from his inheritance: and, rising from the place that had become intolerable to her, she fled out of the church.

Chapter II

FRANCES LOOKS ON HER FORMER HOME

In the churchyard, her knees felt weak as melting wax; but she managed to run, so great was her haste to be gone. From the grey headstones and the dark rampart of yew trees she broke away, and began to hurry, she did not know whither, along the empty village street. Queer Lloyd, the Anabaptist, who tended neither church nor chapel, came out of his cottage door and tried to stay her with speech. She could not grasp its meaning, and shook her head and fled from him. She climbed over the nearest hedge to avoid further encounter. Thoms pricked her legs and tore her clothes. Uphill she ran, through long wet grass that sucked at her skirt and clogged her feet. Soon the cold moisture soaked through her shoes, and her breath came in sobs. Her eyes were fixed upon the highest point she could see, a round lump on the shoulder of the hill she was ascending. From there she would be able to look down, perhaps with calm, for she would be far from the horror that had gripped her in church, far as the larks that filled the blue sky above her head with song. In that high place she might be able to think. But thinking would do no good. Murder had been done, and nothing could undo it. No-one but herself would know, but she would not forget.

At last she came to the tumulus and climbed its steep side. When she reached the top, she started back, seeing a man at her feet. He was lying on his stomach in the hollow made by the digging of a treasure seeker. Seeing a woman's skirt almost over him, he raised himself on his elbow and looked up with a grin. She encountered the bright glance of black, birdlike eyes. His expression changed at once to dismay.

"*Duwch,*" he exclaimed, leaping up. "Well, indeed now, if it isn't Miss Frances! I wasn't looking to see you here, Ma'am, partic'lar not on a Sunday morning."

He began to dart sidelong glances right and left, as though he expected another to appear. It crossed her mind that he was there to court, and her presence was a check on his pleasing anticipations. She ought to be gone at once, but was too shaken to move.

When he had shuffled from foot to foot and waited for her to go, he asked: "May I make so bold as to ask how long you are staying this time at the Plâs?" With a jerk of his thumb, he indicated the grey chimneys and roof of the big house below them.

"I'm leaving today," she said on a sudden impulse. "There's a mail train on Sundays. I could catch it at Llanon if I were to walk there now, couldn't I?" That was what she must do. She could not go back. She would never go back. Never.

Aware of the countryman's furtive regard, she asked at random. "Have you ever known anyone who could foretell coming events, Jones?"

He grinned. "I've heard a deal o' talk among the old folk about such."

"You don't believe in it yourself, though?"

He shifted his gaze and shrugged, evidently made uneasy by so direct a question. "Well, indeed now, what are you thinking yourself o' such things, Ma'am? They are reckoned a bit old fashioned like, aren't they, now-a-days?"

"I am believed in my family to have second sight," she told him.

"You don't say! Could you spot the winner of a horse-race, now?"

She did not answer, but presently she said: "Would you take a message for me to the Plâs in about half-an-hour?"

"Anything to pleasure one o' your family, Ma'am," he assured her. "Isn't it the most highly respected in the district?"

"My sister will be home from church by then," Frances continued with a frown. "Will you please explain to her that I've a feeling I simply *must* return at once to my own home? Say I will write to her."

He repeated the message, darting inquisitive looks at her and seeming to relish the mystery. "Is that right, Ma'am?"

"That's right." She would write to Gwenllian, saying only that she had nothing to fear. Gwenllian would understand. They would never meet again.

"But hadn't I better be fetching a car from the Plâs to drive you to the station," he suggested. "'Tis a terrible long step for a lady."

"I prefer to go on my own feet," she told him. Gwenllian and I shall never meet again, she was thinking. I shall never come to beautiful, devouring Plâs Einon again.

He pocketed her half-crown, and in return began to pay her Celtic compliments, that started with her well-preserved appearance, and ended with the magnitude of her sister's possessions.

"This old tump be a grand place to see her estate from," he said, rubbing his hands together in satisfaction. "Unrolled like a map, just as it is below us, woods, and mansion, and farms and all. You couldn't have a prettier property, now could you,

Ma'am, not if you were to search the earth over for 'en? Ah, Miss Gwenllian, she did ought to be a happy lady."

Frances was gazing down upon the patchwork of little fields. She was trying to discover the trees in the park she used to climb, and the river's silver shallows across which she had waded. The scent of sap and woodland moisture came up to her and her eyes filled with tears. The curve of the valley with oak and beech and feathery mountain-ash, blurred into a shapeless smudge of green. Only the ring of ancient yews by the lodge remained darkly distinguishable through her tears.

"Good-bye," she murmured.

"Good day to you, Ma'am," said her companion in a cheerful tone. But discovering that she had not spoken to him, and that she was silently weeping, he tactfully turned away and began to whistle a mournful hymn tune. "Ah," he said, at last, "I mind the day when first I shewed this fine view to the poor Captain. 'All o' this is yours, Sir,' I was telling him. Indeed, Ma'am, I felt as grand as Satan hisself must have done, shewing the Lord all the kingdoms o' the earth. And if *I* was a proud man that day, Ma'am, what must the Captain have been?" Without answering, she smiled and held out her hand. He shook it with hearty pleasure. After all, queer lady though she might be, she was an Einon-Thomas of Plâs Einon. As she turned away, he became eager to detain her.

"Some do say one thing and some another," he began, as though settling down to prolonged conversation. "Perhaps you could be telling me what this place where we are standing rightly is?"

With her eyes upon Plâs Einon, she answered that it had been a place of burial.

Welsh Women's Classics

Series Editor: *Jane Aaron*

Formerly known as the *Honno Classics* Series, now renamed and relaunched for Honno's 25th Anniversary in 2012.

This series, published by Honno Press, brings back into print neglected and virtually forgotten literary texts by Welsh women from the past.

Each of the titles published includes an introduction setting the text in its historical context and suggesting ways of approaching and understanding the work from the viewpoint of women's experience today. The editor's aim is to select works which are not only of literary merit but which remain readable and appealing to a contemporary audience. An additional aim for the series is to provide materials for students of Welsh writing in English, who have until recently remained largely ignorant of the contribution of women writers to the Welsh literary tradition simply because their works have been unavailable.

The many and various portrayals of Welsh female identity found in these authors' books bear witness to the complex processes that have gone into the shaping of the Welsh women of today. Perusing these portrayals from the past will help us to understand our own situations better, as well as providing, in a variety of different genres – novels, short stories, poetry, autobiography and prose pieces – a fresh and fascinating store of good reading matter.

> "*[It is] difficult to imagine a Welsh literary landscape*
> *without the Honno Classics series [...]*
> *it remains an energising and vibrant feminist imprint.*"
> (Kirsti Bohata, *New Welsh Review*)

> "*[The Honno Classics series is] possibly the Press'*
> *most important achievement, helping to combat*
> *the absence of women's literature in the Welsh canon.*"
> (*Mslexia*)

Titles published in this series:

Jane Aaron, ed.	*A View across the Valley: Short Stories by Women from Wales 1850-1950*
Jane Aaron and Ursula Masson, eds,	*The Very Salt of Life: Welsh Women's Political Writings from Chartism to Suffrage*
Elizabeth Andrews,	*A Woman's Work is Never Done* (1957), with an introduction by Ursula Masson
Amy Dillwyn,	*The Rebecca Rioter* (1880), with an introduction by Katie Gramich
	A Burglary (1883), with an introduction by Alison Favre
	Jill (1884), with an introduction by Kirsti Bohata
Dorothy Edwards,	*Winter Sonata* (1928), with an introduction by Claire Flay
Margiad Evans,	*The Wooden Doctor* (1933), with an introduction by Sue Asbee
Menna Gallie,	*Strike for a Kingdom* (1959), with an introduction by Angela John
	The Small Mine (1962), with an introduction by Jane Aaron
	Travels with a Duchess (1968), with an introduction by Angela John
	You're Welcome to Ulster (1970), with an introduction by Angela John and Claire Connolly
Katie Gramich and Catherine Brennan, eds,	*Welsh Women's Poetry 1460-2001*
Eiluned Lewis,	*Dew on the Grass* (1934), with an introduction by Katie Gramich
	The Captain's Wife (1943), with an introduction by Katie Gramich
Allen Raine,	*A Welsh Witch* (1902), with an introduction by Jane Aaron
	Queen of the Rushes (1906), with an introduction by Katie Gramich
Bertha Thomas,	*Stranger within the Gates* (1912), with an introduction by Kirsti Bohata
Lily Tobias,	*Eunice Fleet* (1933), with an introduction by Jasmine Donahaye
Hilda Vaughan,	*Here Are Lovers* (1926), with an introduction by Diana Wallace
	Iron and Gold (1948), with an introduction by Jane Aaron
Jane Williams,	*Betsy Cadwaladyr: A Balaclava Nurse* (1857), with an introduction by Deirdre Beddoe

Clasuron Honno

Honno also publish an equivalent series, *Clasuron Honno*, in Welsh, also recently re-launched with a new look:

Published with the support of the Welsh Books Council

ABOUT HONNO

Honno Welsh Women's Press was set up in 1986 by a group of women who felt strongly that women in Wales needed wider opportunities to see their writing in print and to become involved in the publishing process. Our aim is to develop the writing talents of women in Wales, give them new and exciting opportunities to see their work published and often to give them their first 'break' as a writer. Honno is registered as a community co-operative. Any profit that Honno makes is invested in the publishing programme. Women from Wales and around the world have expressed their support for Honno. Each supporter has a vote at the Annual General Meeting. For more information and to buy our publications, please write to Honno at the address below, or visit our website: www.honno.co.uk

Honno, 14 Creative Units, Aberystwyth Arts Centre
Aberystwyth, Ceredigion SY23 3GL

Honno Friends

We are very grateful for the support of the Honno Friends:
Jane Aaron, Annette Ecuyere, Audrey Jones, Gwyneth
Tyson Roberts, Beryl Roberts, Jenny Sabine.

For more information on how you can become a Honno
Friend, see: http://www.honno.co.uk/friends.php